REBOT

Justin Taylor

PANTHEON BOOKS   NEW YORK

LIBRARY OF CONGRESS CATALOGING-IN-PUBLICATION DATA
Name: Taylor, Justin, [date] author.
Title: Reboot : a novel / Justin Taylor.
Description: First edition. | New York : Pantheon Books, 2024.
Identifiers: LCCN 2023033448 (print) | LCCN 2023033449 (ebook) |
ISBN 9780553387629 (hardcover) | ISBN 9780553387636 (ebook)
Subjects: LCGFT: Satirical literature. | Humorous fiction. | Novels.
Classification: PS3620.A9466 R43 2024 (print) |
PS3620.A9466 (ebook) | DDC 813/.6—dc23
LC record available at https://lccn.loc.gov/2023033448
LC ebook record available at https://lccn.loc.gov/2023033449

www.pantheonbooks.com

Jacket design and illustration by Philip Pascuzzo

Printed in the United States of America
First Edition
2 4 6 8 9 7 5 3 1

To Dr. Terry Harpold

&

To ST

A false alarm on the night bell once answered—
it cannot be made good, not ever.

—FRANZ KAFKA, "A COUNTRY DOCTOR"

I looked again; I was not there.

—CYRUS TEED, *THE ILLUMINATION OF KORESH:
MARVELOUS EXPERIENCES OF THE GREAT ALCHEMIST
THIRTY YEARS AGO, AT UTICA, NEW YORK*

CONTENTS

COLD OPEN

Logging off for the last time, and shouldn't it feel like something? Maybe it does. It feels like dry, aching eyes. Bright screens in dark rooms, room really. Just one room. Room and screen, singular, because there have been many over the dreary years, but they have narrowed to these. This screen and this room. This screen and this room are what he leaves behind.

Okay, two screens if you count the phone.

Three if you include the handheld gaming console.

He doesn't count the console.

Hasn't owned a TV in years. He streams what he needs, which is nothing now.

Two screens, one room. That's funny. Like that old video, the horrendous OG meme. Did we use that word yet? He was a kid. Dad saw the clip before he did, blue light in the other room, door ajar, wouldn't show it to him. What are you laughing at? Get the hell out of here. Learn to knock. It didn't matter. He found it on his own soon enough. He looked and looked and looked for more and found it. If you were into origin myths—he isn't—you might find one here. The look on Dad's face in screen light, the barked command to leave . . . A primal scene, perhaps. The formal Freudian derangement. But isn't that supposed to be, you know, Mom and Dad . . .

Can it be the primal scene if what he saw was Dad in front of the computer, alone?

Because every earlier generation caught the parents in the act. The old two-backed beast (Is that Shakespeare? Is that literally in fucking Shakespeare? LOL.) but this was different. Advent of a new modality, or it felt that way at the time. Glitch in the matrix. And Dad wasn't doing anything. Zipped up, he was just disgusted. Disgusted and enraptured and caught by his son. In the act of watching. It wasn't the image on the screen so much as the screen itself. Blue light burning in the dark of Dad's office. After he moved out, his own bedroom became Mom's sewing room. Later (not that much later) he had to move back home: a failure, flameout, incel in everything but name and, yeah, okay, maybe, on certain boards, he even goes by that name, too. Went by. Dad's retired, doesn't need an office. Mom still sews, of course, but never mind. You see the point? That room with the blue light, the site of the primal scene, that's this room. The one where he's been living. The one he's leaving now.

The computer sighs itself to silence. Goodbye, user. Good night, cooling fan. Good night, screen. The phone vibrates once and then goes black. He leaves the phone on the bedside table, then thinks better, puts it under the pillow like a tooth. If Mom pops in to check and sees it there, turned off and him gone, she'll know. He doesn't know exactly what she'll know, but she'll know something. Anything. Not worth it. He fixes the pillows. He makes the bed because if he doesn't, she will, and if she does . . .

How many times have we seen this scene before? IRL and on-screen, like there's any difference. It's so cliché, so portentous, so—easy. Lone loser with a gun prowling the anonymous American night. As gimmicks go, it's cheap, and only barely justifiable at this late date in the history of narrative, the decline of prestige television. One justification is that the guy and his gun are a pretext, a point of entry, for a story about something else. But isn't even that move a little hackneyed now? You can't do it without self-awareness. The gestures contains its own ironized wink.

So be it, he thinks. *Wink.*

The pistol heavy in the pocket of his jacket. It's a warm night, but not as bad as the last few days. The big storm broke the heat wave, but it's still too muggy for this jacket. He knows that he sticks out, but also that nobody is watching. He has three old MetroCards in his jeans pocket. Will one of them have fare? He's been using hands-free payment for months now, but of course he would need his phone for that. Or a credit card. He doesn't have one of those.

The second MetroCard has seventeen dollars on it. Miracle. He swipes through the turnstile. Fourteen and something left. Whatever the numbers on the readout read. There's a guy playing guitar on the platform, finishing up the Eagles' "Take It Easy" (he thinks of the Lebowski joke—who wouldn't?) and then plinking over into Green Day's "Good Riddance (Time of Your Life)," sappy classic heavily ironized by circumstance, like something that the Jew Coen brothers might put on the soundtrack in a scene like this one in a movie about a guy like him. Not that anyone would make a movie about a guy like him. Except maybe someone will now. Loner loser gone to glory, "embrace infamy," like Ron Watkins used to say. Not the Jew Coens, this isn't for them. But someone could do a reboot of *Natural Born Killers* about him, that'd be cool, except he isn't interested in mass death, still less in spectacle. Spectacle is inevitable but subsidiary. He doesn't want to be on big screens and chyrons, breaking news updates, push notifications. We interrupt this program. Or he does want that stuff, but not badly. He could take it or leave it. Or rather, takes it as a given. He wants to be on threads and channels, message boards, DMs. He wants to be on small screens, blue light burning out of scratched-glass faces, devices held in damp hands of men breathing heavily alone in darkened rooms.

Also, his violence is not random. He knows who he wants to kill and why.

It feels like a retro gesture, this having a target. To break with the venerable 2010s tradition of ideologically motivated mass death.

He has his ideologies, sure, but they've got nothing to do with this. This is more about affiliation. Fandom. What it means to be part of something.

Mark David Chapman has a posse.

Or what it would have been like if he did.

Maybe the singer on the platform is playing "Time of Your Life" as a gag. The gag being that he's doing it so straight-faced. The joke being that this isn't a joke at all. Anyway, the train's here. He considers flipping the MetroCard into the open guitar case, pockets it instead. He'd rather see it wasted than put to use.

A father and daughter huddled around a Speak & Spell. Slumped-over office drones, or maybe they're in retail. Guys in beige suits and women in sheer tights, kitten heels. Some fat-titted bitch in a Barnard T-shirt and plaid skirt. Cosplaying schoolgirl porn, maybe actual slut. The pistol in his pocket. What he'd say on the message board about a photo of her versus the way he casts his eyes down to the floor of the subway car rather than meet her not entirely unwelcoming gaze. Some girls don't mind being noticed. Truth to tell, that scares him more. He's not bad-looking, not that much older than she is, probably. Maybe they've read some of the same books. He's pretty well-read, though these days he does—did—most of his reading online, which he knows isn't the same, but it's not necessarily worse, right, and maybe in some ways it's better. An emergent modality, the scrolling, direct access to content and a blessed absence of gatekeepers, middlemen, censors—but maybe that's true of her, too, this bitch crossing and uncrossing her legs, fine blond hairs on her bare knees like in *Lolita*.

See? He reads.

She exits at 116th, walks right by him. The wash of her scent as she scrolls past, his eyes still on the floor, tracing patterns in the red-and-black mottle like you'd look for animal shapes in the clouds. Still sort of weird to be riding on here without a mask.

The train fills up as it trundles south. Mostly he is bored. No phone means no posting, no podcasts. Also, no music, though he stopped listening to music awhile back, which was when he really realized how fucked he was, not that he did anything about it. His life was just some train he was riding, might as well have been this one, and now it is. He stays standing even though there are seats open. Standing is something to do.

It's unbearable, this reality. This being and standing, unmediated, screenless, nothing to do but feel your toes sweat in your socks and listen to yourself think. The whole point of the internet is to never be alone. This is especially important if you are, like he is, always alone. Parents don't count. Job, when he had a job, didn't count.

Nothing counts.

Times Square Forty-Second Street. The flood of disembarking tourists, workers, people trying to transfer. The counter-throng of boarders pressing in at the edges of the doors. Down the platform, up the stairs, elbow to elbow, breath on necks. Some people still have masks on. They'll never take them off. Some people never get over shit; they can't move on. Someone is going to say that about him when this is over, he knows it. That he was fixated, that he was stuck in the past. It isn't true. Here he is in forward motion, taking determined, irreversible steps. No backtracking. Cool metal in warm pocket. No pussing out (as Dad would have said, as he often said). No manifesto, or not one of his own. It'll all be obvious after. Wholly legible. Fatties with rubbed-raw dicks will post on trad forums to sanctify his name. God-tier, they'll say. We stan a true king.

He's not trying to make a mark. He's trying to erase one. He's only trolling a fandom. It's a venerable tradition, his by right, the only inheritance to which he feels heir. If there were a way to pull this off without leaving his bedroom, without logging off, he would have. He might have. On the other hand, fuck these people and fuck himself, too. *Fuck my life,* he thinks giddily. It feels so good to say the words. Fuck this fandom and fuck their dreams. He's only sorry that he'll be too dead to see how hard they're being dunked on.

GamerGate due for a reboot.

He watched the HBO Q doc, and the other one. Seemed

sad, more than anything. How you can blow up the whole world and still just be this bored loser living in a small room, checking your feeds.

North to Forty-Seventh Street, then over to Ninth Ave. Too early, still. Go to the water first. Walk to the river and back.

City streets are boring. Tourists are boring. New York is boring. Life, friends, is boring.

Learn to knock.

Wind on the water. Joggers on the path. Weight on one side of the jacket. Long light to cross back over the West Side Highway. Music coming from bars. The military stillness of the bank kiosks. Pigeons group and scatter. Someone screaming about something, somewhere not far off, maybe a few floors up. Fresh pizza, a slamming door. He's no longer bummed out that this feels like nothing. Only simps crave significance. LOLZ are better. The thing to understand is that meaning itself is a cultural hyperstition. He had to look that word up the first time he saw it in a post. What it means is, like, the reverse of a superstition, i.e., something a lot of people believe even though it isn't true. But then—he loves this—the thing that isn't true becomes true once enough people believe in it. That's what meaning means to him. The truth is a false flag operation. Reality is an inside job.

He's hot, tired, getting hungry, running late. But not too late, he's pretty sure. He walks a little faster. Not too much faster. Not an all-out run.

Take it easy. Have the time of your life. Is it time for some game theory? A flick to free the safety. Closing hot fingers around trigger and grip. The normies will find deep meaning where there is none. Meaning is their addiction, their weakness, their libtard fantasy. He's going out on top, that's all. On a high note, like George Costanza or Jeffrey Epstein. That's funny. Too bad he can't post it. Hand coming out of pocket as he steps into the circle of light. Mostly he's looking forward to never again being bored.

PART 1
EVENING
ALL DAY
LONG

(Portland & Los Angeles)

There were fires in the gorge outside of Portland and there were fires in the hills in LA. From the plane as we departed PDX I had seen the river of smoke flowing above the actual river and now, as we made our initial approach to LAX, I saw a slightly different version of the same thing over again: whole hills were missing, or their topmost reaches peeked out like islands from this other smoke. The flight attendant, a narrow-featured man with a soul patch, noticed my noticing this.

He said, "It's not as bad as it looks." A breath. "Or it is but it isn't, I mean it feels normal at this point, doesn't it?"

I nodded.

"Still better than lockdown," he continued.

"Yes," I said. "My business was closed nearly a year."

"Were you shooting a movie?"

"I own a bar. A restaurant, really. A bar and restaurant."

"In LA?"

"In Portland."

"Oh."

He asked if I wanted another drink before we landed. I said no.

Thank you, but no.

I was trying this new thing where I only drank in moderation. I know what that must sound like, and I admit that this wasn't the first time that I was trying it, but hear me out. I wasn't one of those people who couldn't walk past a bar without ducking inside, or who counted down the minutes until the liquor store opened. I was never a morning or a maintenance drunk. I was capable of keeping bottles in the house, and sometimes when people offered me drinks I said no, No, thank you, not tonight. Saying no was simple, at least to the first round. My problem was—or rather, it had been—that once I said yes I wanted yes to last forever. Once I started, I didn't stop.

So I quit cold turkey. A few fits and starts there: one step forward, two back, you know how it goes. Two back, or three or four. Whatever. Then I tried AA, which went better, seemed to be working, but lockdown put an end to the meetings, and the Zoom version didn't do it for me, so there were a couple of bigger slips. Then I went rogue. I started watching cognitive-behavioral therapy videos on YouTube, treacly self-help and smug "one weird trick"–type life hacks promoted by self-licensed life coaches. But you know what? It worked. I hated it, but it worked. Maybe it worked because I hated it. Night after night I let myself in to my locked-down bar and sat there and streamed videos and built willpower, discipline, self-awareness, self-control. *Control, control,* I would repeat to myself, sometimes aloud and sometimes just in my head, as a little grounding mantra, almost a prayer. I taught myself—or the internet taught me—to catch the bad thought before it hatches, patch the egg back up. Bad birds stay unborn.

Now I can have a glass of wine with dinner, two beers at a ball game—not that I go to ball games, but if I did. I can even have liquor if I want, though I usually don't, though for whatever reason, I did today. I'd ordered a Woodford when I took my seat, and when the flight attendant came by an hour later to ask if I wanted another, I'd said yes without thinking, and he poured it before I could retract what I'd said. I suppose I could have let it sit untouched. I had that power now. Instead I drank it slowly and reminded myself that two was my self-imposed daily limit and that I would be fine as long as I refused a third drink. As you've seen for yourself, this is exactly what I did.

A lot of bad nights began with bourbon, but all the worst ones ended with gin. Something about the juniper, I suppose, or maybe it's the quinine in the tonic. (I'm kidding; there was no tonic.) I'd be out on the town, or at home, enjoying some run-of-the-mill debauchery, and I'd get this kind of psychic prickle, like the first twinge of a hard-on crossed with the feeling of walking alone at night and knowing you're being watched. The feeling would plant its flag in me. Palm sweat and salivation. I'd wake up in a strange bed or a wrecked car. (Strange cars and wrecked beds were not unheard of, either.) One time I came to on a small yacht full of workers from the main office of the network that used to broadcast the TV show I had used to star on: secretaries, assistants, payroll, a couple of janitors. *Why did they invite me to the company picnic?* I wondered. *And why did I accept?* They explained to me, delicately, that I had chartered and provisioned this ship and invited all of them aboard.

Gin is my final boss, the Big Bad of a game I've almost beaten. Oblivion tastes like cucumbers. But all that was a long, long time ago. As ancient as my so-called fame.

The flight attendant returned with my would-be third bottle of Woodford and a fresh plastic cup full of ice. "I know you said no," he said, "but then I thought—this is *David freaking Crader!* How am I not gonna hook him up?"

I understood that he thought he was impressing me; he may have believed he was being kind. There was murder in his heart, though he did not know it. He wanted a story to tell his friends later, or perhaps he hoped to embed himself in a memory of mine, small and gleaming like a sliver of glass. I asked him not to pour it. I said thank you but no, I'm really serious, I can't. Abruptly, he got it; apologized. I said I appreciated the gesture all the same. He asked if he could take a selfie with me, and I said sure.

"I'd be there," he said, seeming to mean the fan convention

where I was headed, "if I didn't have this shift." He was kneeling in the aisle now, scrunching his shoulder into mine. I could smell his Old Spice, beads of forehead sweat, and I knew that he would have liked to throw an arm around me but wasn't sure if he should. If I had accepted the drink he would have done it, but he didn't want to risk a second offense before he got his pic.

"When does your day end?" I asked.

"Eleven tonight," he said. "In Dallas."

The pilot called for seat belts.

"Better hurry," I said. "We don't want to get in trouble." He snapped the picture.

"It's an honor," he said. "I grew up on you." Then he hurried off to finish the preparations for landing, and I noticed that he'd left the Woodford on my tray. I pocketed it. *You will still be unopened tomorrow,* I told the little bottle. *I am the man I think I am, and I know how to mean what I say.*

This was my first time flying in a while. I'd taken this gig less for the money (though I wanted the money) than for the excuse to get on a plane. I'd weathered quarantine largely alone and entirely sober, aforementioned slips notwithstanding. During lockdown I sometimes had strange, immersive dreams that felt more real than reality while I was in them and were difficult to shake upon waking, perhaps since the actual locked-down day was something of a strange dream itself. The idea for a *Rev Beach* reboot had come to me in one of these.

In the dream, me and Corey Burch were standing on a beach; there were all these flashbulbs firing off, but I couldn't see any cameras. As near as I could tell we were entirely alone, the lone and level sands stretching out in both directions and the resort hotels looking oddly desolate, unoccupied but more than that, sort of—deflated? Defeated. Used-up, somehow, like in Stephen King's *The Langoliers*. Do you remember this one? I've never read the book, but I've seen the miniseries that Tom Holland made for ABC in the mid-nineties with Dean Stockwell and Bronson Pinchot. It's the one where the LAX to BOS red-eye flies through a rip in the fabric of time so when the plane lands in Boston they're stuck in yesterday, where everything tastes stale, matches don't strike, colors are faded, and so on. A used-up world awaiting consignment to oblivion, a place no living thing belongs. That's where me and Corey were, in the dream, in a used-up place where the only sign of life was these disembodied flashbulb flashes bursting in the storm-warning sky. I couldn't tell which coast we were on, East or West, i.e., Florida or California, and if it was—as I suspected—Florida, whether we were on the East or West coast of that epic accursed peninsula. There was no sun in the sky with which to orient us. All I knew was that I stood with my back to the water and Corey stood with his back to the resorts. We were talking to each other, but I couldn't understand what we were saying. It was like the Parseltongue parts of the Harry Potter movies except without the subtitles. It sounded a little like Hebrew, but I don't know Hebrew any more than I know Harry Potter snake language, so whatever intelligence we were sharing remained wholly unintelligible to me. To him, too, perhaps, though that made no sense insofar as "he" was only an element of my dream, which was precisely what I was having a hard time keeping in mind. So I listened to him, and I listened to myself, and I couldn't parse a word that passed between us. And the ghost bulbs kept flashing, and then I woke up.

I woke up wanting, for the first time in a very long time, to talk to Corey. To see his face. Instead of trying to track down his contact info, I texted Grace Travis, our old costar and my first ex-wife, to tell her that we should reboot *Rev Beach* for the upcoming twentieth anniversary of its premiere. She did not answer me. I made coffee, shook the dream, white-knuckled through the rest of lockdown alone save for CBT YouTube, CBD soda, and scheduled visits with my son.

There had been a time when I was a frequent flier. For the first season of *Rev Beach,* we faked Florida. But the breakout second and disastrous (unfinished) third seasons were shot on location in and around a gulf town south of Tampa called Guiding Star. There was plenty of back-and-forth in those days between TPA and LAX or JFK. Talk shows, fashion shoots. Just going to go. To get out, to get seen. Back to Portland for Christmas, maybe. Vegas for a weekend. Sundance, Cannes. Flying became second nature, and flying first class of course made it much easier to get settled, tune out, run lines, nod off. Whatever. I know I say that a lot: whatever. It's a tic but also honest, which is why I won't let my ghostwriter edit it out.

That's a joke about celebrity memoirs, if you were wondering. But it's also true.

My point is only this: for a long time *whatever* was the way it was.

These days I rarely have reason to fly, and it's not nearly as much fun when you're paying your own way. My medallion status is long since lapsed. But there is still something special about flying, the mystic terror of takeoff, how the city pixelates and grids itself as you pull away from earth, and then the glorious disappearing into banks of cloud. In the old days the flight was just the long delay between me and wherever I was headed, whatever I thought I had coming when I arrived. These days I find pleasure in the experience itself, all the little rituals and subroutines of the security line and the coffee kiosk and the meal service, of scrolling through the seatback screen for the perfect movie to not quite pay attention to, or digging around in your bag for the book or magazine you brought from home or perhaps bought at the newsstand just before or after the coffee, the gambler's thrill of thumbing to the first page and hoping that your former self's decision will satisfy the present self who is stuck with what seemed like a safe bet against boredom when you chose it yesterday or this morning.

I love to switch my phone into airplane mode. I never buy Wi-Fi. It's a wonderful feeling, and vanishingly rare, to be utterly unreachable for a set stretch of hours, not that anyone needs anything from me so badly, but it's nice to know that they wouldn't get it even if they did. It's nice too to gift yourself a brief hiatus from all the scrolling, clicking, and skimming that defines our distracted days.

A world of muffled noise and muted color, personal space that speaks in inches, bland food served cool. It's an apt time for reflection. Retrospection, I guess you'd say. On a long enough flight you could screen the whole movie of your life, director's cut and all the bonus features. But the Portland–LA flight was barely two hours, and I wasn't looking to root around in the archives of my memory palace. I was mulling and brooding, yes, but not over ancient history. It was the events of the previous day that demanded my attention, that refused to let themselves be Langoliered. I reclined my seat, set my gaze window-ward, pressed the play button in my mind.

The polar bear moped in his luxe enclosure. There was a white concrete hill to remind him of ice floes, a blue pool for diving, toys strewn about the ample grounds. The polar bear ignored all this. He lazed in his patch of shade, to the deep chagrin of my six-year-old son.

This was yesterday, visitation day, mine and his. The fires had started that morning but still seemed modest, containable. That's what the city had said, was saying, which was why we'd decided to go ahead with our planned trip to the zoo.

"What's he waiting for?" Henry asked.

There was a strained quality in his voice that I prayed wasn't a prelude to tears. *Look at the bright side,* I thought. *Nobody's wearing a mask. They say the fires are under control. The sky is normal. Normality is making a comeback. You are a father making good use of his visitation. You are making memories and spending quality time.*

To my son I said, "It's the middle of the afternoon, Hank, he's probably tired. Animals rest to save energy for when they need to hunt." Hank was a nickname only I was allowed to use. It was a special thing we had, maybe the only one. *Give it time,* I thought. *He's young yet.* To my son I said, "Give it time."

"Doesn't he know we're here?" he said. "We paid to see him. Our tickets were eighteen dollars each."

"Yours was only half that much, actually," I said.

"That's still twenty-seven dollars," he said, and though this whole line of thinking alarmed me, I took the opportunity to praise his math skills before attempting to redirect.

"Let's go to the aviary," I said. "I bet the birds are up to something. We can check back here in a while."

He consented to this, but even as we walked away, the polar bear weighed on his mind.

"He doesn't have to hunt," Hank said, plaintive and almost sympathetic. Almost. "Doesn't he know it's different here and that's not what his life is anymore?"

We got to the aviary, and he dashed off, chasing the flashes of color that darted among the trees, while I actively avoided reading too much meaning—any meaning—into what he had just said. From the mouths of babes, et cetera. Instead I mulled my upcoming trip to Los Angeles, i.e., the trip I was currently embarking upon, which was giving me occasion to revisit what had happened yesterday. So with apologies for going *Looper* on you, today's problem was yesterday in more or less the same sense that yesterday's problem had been today.

This is my tell-all memoir, and I'll tell it all how I want.

Today I was headed to LA for a fan convention. Though it had been the better part of a decade since I'd last appeared on-screen, and longer than that since I'd appeared in anything worth seeing, and though I no longer thought of myself in any sense as "an actor," and only nominally as "a celebrity," I still did occasional voice work: cartoons, video games, sometimes an audiobook. The work was easy, and while I didn't exactly need the money, it didn't hurt to have. Of late, as you probably already know, I had been the voice of Shibboleth Gold: titular antiheroic, superheroic, charismatic solipsist-protagonist of a popular roguelike video game, single-handedly written and coded by my friend Sam Kirchner, who himself had a vestigial connection to *Rev Beach*.

Sorry for the word salad there. And what are the odds that "roguelike" is the only word that you need me to define? Per Wikipedia (where I first learned it, after—but not long after—signing the contract to take the job) "roguelikes" are a subcategory of the role-playing game (that's RPG) genre. Their defining characteristic is a dungeon crawl through procedurally generated levels, which is to say that the game randomly creates its map every time you sit down to play it, so it's always kind of the same but it's never exactly the same, because it's always reimagining itself. And also that every time you die you have to start over from the beginning. If you've ever played *Dead Cells, The Binding of Isaac,* or *Hades,* then you know what I'm talking about. And if you haven't, well, don't sweat it. Let's just move on.

Shibboleth Gold was a surprise hit, hastily ported for home consoles and supported with a hasty expansion pack that was extremely well-received. Beaucoup awards and downloads, scads of fan art and sequel clamor. Fans understood the game's end scene—the one on the mountain—to be a depiction of Scartaris, the (fictional) Icelandic peak on the (real) Snaefellsnes peninsula, where the journey to the center of the earth in *Journey to the Center of the Earth* begins. As a result of all this, *Shibboleth Gold 2: Caverns Measureless to Man,* aka *CM2M,* was hotly anticipated and long awaited. At this point, overdue.

I didn't know anything about game development. I read the lines Sam sent me at a studio in Portland, every imaginable branch for every branching-tree conversation that Shibboleth would have with various NPCs (that's nonplayer characters, like Corey in my dream) that he would encounter in the vast world Sam built for Shibboleth to maraud through. Sometimes I knew what my dialogue meant, and sometimes—again, as in the dream—I didn't. It didn't matter. I did my lines when he asked me and cashed the checks when they came. There was loose talk about a film adaptation, but that wouldn't have much to do with me unless they went full CGI. I was the voice of Shibboleth Gold, but I didn't look anything like him. And anyway, I had no interest—at closer to forty than thirty years old—in trying to reboot my film career by launching a fantasy-action franchise.

I loved being Shibboleth Gold. He required only occasional labor on my part, but he paid out regular dividends. I didn't get recognized on the street for being him. He'd kept me afloat through the year my restaurant had been closed. And now he got me invites to fan conventions, where I took home a few grand for a day spent signing autographs and posing for photos and being told how great I was. I wasn't in huge demand, but with *Rev Beach* streaming again, and *CM2M* supposedly looming, I was getting more invitations than usual. Was I making a comeback? Having a moment? Maybe! Money, at least, was reestablishing itself as a minor concern, a back-burner issue, which was how I liked it: on the back burner. A big pot of money simmering on a stove and me not worried about it at all.

Was there some way to explain this to my overanxious son?

I watched Hank run around the aviary, happy that he was happy, that whatever was bugging him about the money and the bear was no longer at the forefront of his mind. It crossed my mind that maybe he was enjoying the break from me. One of the hardest things to get used to about visitation day is that while the adult's tendency is to maximize attention and quality time, the child is not accustomed to six to eight hours of ceaseless engagement. The child wants to build with blocks, stream cartoons on Dad's phone. The child does not want to have a long conversation about the status of the relationship, its goals and challenges, the importance of communication. The child wants to catch a parrot but can't do it. The child says the petting zoo is "for babies" but that if you want to go there he'd accept a dollar to buy a handful of pellets to feed the goat. And can you please take a picture of him petting the rabbit? Now can you text it to Mom?

Mostly what the child wants is to have his anxieties drowned out by the white noise of normality, which is impossible, since the situation is anything but normal. Visitation day is a perpetual first date. You do what you can to simulate normality within the framework of the aberration that is your time with the child, because that is what the child requires. It's what he wants. The only other way to make your presence felt would be if you could force that fucking polar bear to get off his ass.

"Did you see me?" Hank asked, flushed and bright-eyed, back from his jaunt.

"I did," I said. "You were fast."

"Can we check on the bear now?"

"What about the monkeys?"

"But you said! It's not fair."

"Hank, I'm not saying no to you. It's your choice. I'm saying, think about your options. You want to see the bear the most, but you also want to see the monkeys. The monkeys are probably awake right now. They might be playing. But it's your decision where we go next."

He crinkled his brow and frowned: the great deliberator. I loved him. But I also saw enough of myself in him to know that he was going to choose the bear.

And so it was back to the bear we were headed when I spotted the ice cream vendor. Figuring this for an easy victory (and a hedged bet against imminent ursine disappointment), I suggested we stop for a treat. At first Hank seemed very excited.

"Anything you want," I said, and his eyes got big. I had that swell of Good Dad pride. Then I realized he wasn't looking at the flavors but the prices.

"We can't afford this," he said, his voice barely above a whisper.

"Of course we can!" I said.

"I really don't think so."

"Hank," I said, willing into my voice a calm that I did not feel. "I promise you, it's okay. I have plenty of money. And anyway, money isn't a kid concern. That's for grown-ups to worry about. If one of us says it's okay, it is." I saw that he wanted to believe me, but also that he didn't—not fully. And why would he? Who was I to him? Some guy who showed up on the weekend to drag him out of the house for a few hours of mandatory fun. His mom and his grandmother were the ones he lived with, saw struggling. They were the ones whose hushed conversations he had surely overheard.

"Hey," said the ice cream man. "You fellas want something? Because—" He gestured with his silver scoop to the line that had formed behind us.

"Fudge sundae," I said. "Two scoops of vanilla and two spoons, please. Thank you." I turned to Hank. "How about it, slugger? We can share one. That's thrifty, right?"

He grinned up at me, apparently satisfied.

"Can one of the scoops be Oreo?" he asked. I relayed this to the ice cream man, who opened the cold case. The sundae cost seven bucks. I handed him a ten, and he gave me three back. I stuck it all in his tip jar.

"Thanks," I said. "For bearing with us."

"Pleasure's mine."

We sat on a bench by the tiger paddock. There were two of them, and they were curled together. I hoped this constituted an exciting animal activity for Hank to witness, even though they—like the polar bear—were sleeping. But it was a moot point because Hank, thankfully, was focused on the sundae. I held the biodegradable plastic bowl between us, taking one bite for every two of his. I wanted to make sure he got enough, that he had his share of fun. For a few minutes we were both so occupied by the ice cream that we didn't speak at all. When we were finished, he had hot fudge all over his mouth. I fished a Wet-Nap packet from my pocket (who says I don't know the dad tricks?) and he was patient while I wiped him clean. He looked up at me, sanitized face agleam, suddenly solemn again.

"Three dollars was too big of a tip, Dad," he said.

"You're right," I said, defeated. "But that man took good care of us. Anyway, forget about that. How about let's go see if your bear woke up?"

My phone buzzed but I ignored it.

"If he isn't up, we should ask for a refund."

"That's not how it works," I said.

"Then that's not fair."

"I think it is," I said. "Our tickets didn't buy us a promise. They bought us a chance."

But the bear was awake now, thankfully. He paced the perimeter of his luxe enclosure. He dove into his diving pool, sending water splashing everywhere. He swam a few laps, then heaved up onto the bank and shook himself dry.

Hank was enthralled. It was everything he'd wanted. My heart soared for him. At the same time, I knew, this was my moment to steal a glance down at my phone. So I did, and there was Grace.

"Read this," she'd texted. "Pains me to say but you might have been right about something."

Below this gratuitous dig, a link, Bitly'd for mystery, which I had to admit was a nice touch. I looked up to check that Hank was still in deep communion with the polar bear. I looked back down. I clicked.

People Are Tweeting: Will the *Rev Beach* reboot happen? Will it suck? How much do I need to pretend to care?

BY MOLLY WEBSTER

Tags: People Are Tweeting, explainers, takes, aughtstolgia, David Crader, Shayne Glade, Grace Travis, Ty Travis, Corey Burch, TV, reboots

We all remember *Rev Beach* (2003–2005)—or do we? A year ago you would have almost certainly said, "No, Molly, I don't, tell me more," or else, "Yes, Molly, I do, because I am about to drop off the far edge of the coveted eighteen to thirty-nine advertising demo, just like these ex-teens whose hotness circa 2004 played an outsize role in my burgeoning sexuality."

But that, as I said, was last year. Today, a lot of what I'm about to say could probably go without saying, but ya girl is attempting to Do Journalism here, so bear with me a minute while I recap the last, oh, twenty years.

Rev Beach was a short-lived teen dramedy that launched Shayne Glade's career and almost ruined Grace Travis's. Pitched as *Dawson's Creek* meets *Buffy the Vampire Slayer*, *Rev Beach* premiered the same year that both those shows went off the air. *The OC*—another beach-town soap, albeit one without ghosts and mermen—also premiered that year, and ended up eating *RB*'s lunch. Like *The OC, RB* is named for where it's set: the Gulf Coast beach town known officially as Reveille Beach, but referred to as Revenant Beach by those who know of its supernatural underbelly—what, in the Buffy-verse, would be referred to as a Hellmouth, except *Rev Beach* didn't have access to that IP, so the place is just crawling with monsters for no particular reason, other than Florida itself, which is reason enough.

   Rev Beach debuted with a half season, a trial balloon launched in May of '03 to fill the void left by the *Dawson's* finale and *Smallville* being off for the summer. (Fill the void *emotionally,* I mean; obviously we all remember that the WB itself was airing Mark Burnett's *Boarding House: North Shore,* which dared to ask the question, *What if some surfers lived in a house?*) *Rev Beach* was widely panned, but enough teenagers preferred the fake beach in Florida to the real beach in Hawaii to justify ordering a full second season, which was a huge hit largely thanks to the rapidly rising stardom of Shayne Glade. When Glade left at the end of season 2 in order to devote his full attention to being an indie film darling and sex god, the show reverted to critical damnation and popular neglect.

   Except among a sliver of hard-core fans (aka the Revheads) who happened to all be hyperactively online at a time when that meant something more than "alive and awake." On the fifth anniversary of the show's premiere, in 2008, a fan campaign for then-candidate Obama to make the "uncancellation" of *Rev Beach* his first executive order went minorly viral on then-still-newish Tumblr. This seems to have anticipated a lot of things about our current cultural moment, where it is as if every show runner in Hollywood took exactly one Intro to Philosophy course sophomore year of college, wherein they heard about (but did not read) Nietzsche's concept of eternal recurrence, which now that I've typed it out seems like it's not an "as if" but what actually occurred and will occur again (cf. *Battlestar Galactica*). *RB* might have been memory-holed forever. But instead it popped up on streaming during lockdown, part of some overall content backfill deal, and the algorithm got a hard-on for it, and people—you ridiculous people, you clicked.

You streamed.

You binged.

And, most important, you memed.

Rev Beach has proven a meme reservoir the likes of which we haven't seen since *SpongeBob* or *Marriage Story*.

The most popular meme spun from the show is the one of the half-vampire Cole Jansen, played by Shayne Glade, weeping tears of blood. In the scene, Cole is spying on his girlfriend, Misty Green (Grace Travis), as she walks down the path to the haunted beach with his brother, Will Jansen (David Crader). At the end of the episode, Cole will learn that they went to the haunted beach to communicate with the spirit of Misty's father, because she is trying to solve his murder. They didn't tell Cole, only because they didn't want to worry him the night before his big football game. But in the meantime, he assumes Misty is cheating on him with his bro.

Cole is standing under a streetlight, wearing black jeans and a red T-shirt, on which the words "REV BEACH MARINERS" are printed in blue. The tears of blood, one line down each cheek, are approximately the same red as the shirt and are so straight they must have been drawn with a ruler. In some versions of the meme, all but Cole's face are cropped out of the frame, to create something similar to "Dawson's ugly cry." But the most common version shows the whole frame, with the words on Cole's T-shirt switched out for something else. Two days ago, someone replaced the name of the football team simply with "me" and then added a second caption to the halo around the streetlight he is standing under: "my anxiety." This is, of course, just the latest iteration of an old—at this point, practically historic—meme, and yesterday someone else posted the same meme but with the labels swapped, which I think is even funnier, and so did the internet, and so, apparently, did Shayne Glade himself. He RT'd the image with the needlessly cryptic caption "hearty lolz"—which sent fans into such a frenzy that I was invited to write this on a twelve-hour turnaround.

Glade, as I said, quit *Rev Beach* at the end of season 2 (which, incidentally, is the show's only full season, since both seasons 1 and 3 were truncated) and he has taken great pains to separate himself from its goofy, troubled legacy. The apparent softening of this position has led fans to speculate about and/or openly call for some sort of reunion or reboot. The twentieth anniversary of the show's premiere is barely eighteen months away. So if anything is going to happen, production needs to kick into gear soon, or at least while Shayne Glade is in the mood. *RB* fans—crassly, I admit, though at the same time, spot the lie—also cite persistent rumors of David Crader's drug and alcohol abuse as a reason to move swiftly. Crader, for his part, hasn't had a meltdown in a couple of years. He lives in Portland, Oregon, and is largely retired from public life, though he does some voice acting for a video game that, unfortunately, I can't tell you anything about because I am an adult woman who has had sex before. He's appearing at a fan convention in LA this weekend if you want to put up twenty bucks to get in his signing line and use your seven seconds of face time to ask him what the hell is going on.

Grace Travis is the daughter of Ty Travis, the show's creator. Her uneven performance on *Rev Beach* earned the pair persistent comparison to Aaron and Tori Spelling. Ty Travis's refusal to replace her is understood to have been a major factor in Shayne Glade's decision to quit.

Corey Burch, who you might remember played Warren Hunt, aka the Designated Fat Kid™, was killed off in the season 3 premiere, a move apparently intended to inaugurate an edgier, darker turn, but mostly served to further cripple the show, now missing both its biggest star and its comic relief. Burch has had, by some measures, a hard road. He never landed another significant role after *Rev Beach,* and after failing to launch a singing career, an energy drink, a reality series, and a Trump-era stint as a #Resistancelib (which, hey, who among us?), made a heel turn to Q-pilled anti-vax activist, which actually gained him a bit of traction and so, in a twist of fate so random it could only have been anticipated by the *Saved by the Bell* reboot making Zack Morris the governor of California, he's now running a long-shot campaign for mayor of Guiding Star, the South Florida Gulf Coast town where *Rev Beach* was filmed and so—presumably— where it would (will?) be shooting if (when?) it reboots. Which is why it's worth remembering that all of Burch's old costars hate his fucking guts because of what he wrote about them in his self-published memoir, *The Coreyections,* which seems to not be a pun on the word "erection" but rather on the title of the Jonathan Franzen novel whose Noah Baumbach–directed adaptation HBO passed on in 2012.

What was I saying?

Oh yeah, *Rev Beach*. After Burch was fired and Glade quit, Ty Travis attempted to rebuild the show around his daughter and David Crader. To explain Cole's absence, the writers said he was away at boarding school on a football scholarship. This plot point left fans hoping that Glade might return to the series, with some speculating that he hadn't really quit at all, and the whole thing was an attempt to drum up headlines and set the stage for a "surprise" midseason return to juice ratings. In fact, the boarding school/football thing had been plagiarized from *Dawson's Creek,* who had come up with it in 2000 to explain the absence of Henry Parker, played by Michael Pitt, who had guest-starred on the show for most of its third season but refused the offer of a permanent spot in the cast.

The third season of *Rev Beach* focuses on a romance between Misty and Will, a divisive move that frustrated that faction of the fanbase who had come to the show for its ghouls and ghosts rather than for its relationship drama. In fact, there was quite a bit of supernatural content in these episodes. A succession of guest stars, including Buffy veteran Michelle Trachtenberg and Michael Pitt himself, appeared as otherworldly antagonists introduced and then dispatched within the space of an episode.

This juxtaposition of season-long story arcs with a "Monster of the Week" approach had been pioneered by *The X-Files* and further developed by (again) *Buffy,* but *Rev Beach* never found its footing with the formula (though neither did *The X-Files;* do not @ me) and the show continued to hemorrhage viewer share. Those fans who remained, however, became intensely evangelical, as though they felt themselves to be a persecuted minority. They wanted to be martyred for loving this bad network drama that nobody cared about, as though the sheer force of their overinvestment could make it into something better than it was. (Again: Do. Not. @.) When the show was canceled midway through its third season, it seemed as though LiveJournal itself might jump off a bridge. The lack of a proper finale was especially galling to fans, though now this incompleteness is understood as a sort of advantage, since any reboot of *Rev Beach* would be less bound by its own lore than other shows that finished their runs back in the day when endings were endings, and half-vampires were half-vampires.

Grace Travis and David Crader were briefly married (2005–2007), a dubious romance echoing that of their on-screen personae. Some have argued that it was a Stockholm syndrome–like response to the fanaticism of the fanbase, whose unhinged love must have registered as welcome refuge from the constant media abuse they were enduring during the period.

Of their marriage and its dissolution, Grace Travis has said, simply, "We loved each other, but we were too young." Corey Burch, in his self-published memoir, claimed that she plagiarized this line from Rachel Miner, who said the same thing about her marriage to Macaulay Culkin (1998–2002), but it is this reporter's sense that it was probably just true in both cases.

So why are we talking about this now? Well, the first thing I already told you: Shayne Glade RT'ing his own meme. That plus the fact that *Rev Beach* was one of the surprise hits of the lockdown era, plus the imminent (ish) anniversary of the premiere. Take all of this together, and the long-longed-for reboot suddenly seems—maybe for the first time—possible, even probable, not to say a great idea.

Weirdly (or perhaps inevitably) this revival of interest has already occasioned its own backlash, with some OG *RB* fans attacking new converts in online spaces, and others arguing that the show should not be rebooted because they don't want to see nearly twenty years' worth of fanfic and headcanon supplanted by new "canonical" material with which their own work would then have to reckon.

This seems really fucked to me, and of course my mentions are now forever cursed, but sometimes a girl's just gotta stand up and face her reply guys, because if the show actually does get rebooted, these creeps are going to pitch a holy internet fit. On a scale of lady-*Ghostbusters* to #Snydercut, all I can tell you is that it's going to be bad. Grace Travis, if you're listening: the time to delete your nudez from the cloud is NOW.

Which brings me to the last reason this reboot might actually happen. Ty Travis, as you probably know, is dead. The rights to *Rev Beach* belong to Grace. She's the one who negotiated the streaming deal, and she has always said that she would welcome the chance to "see what Misty and the gang are up to these days," which is a hell of a way of putting it, but okay, sure.

What is Shayne Glade thinking? What does any of this mean? I have no idea, and I don't have time to speculate because this piece is now two thousand words long, and I'm getting paid eighty bucks for it, so your intrepid lady journalist has to go change into comfortable shoes and a top that shows her tits off because my shift tending bar in Gowanus starts in an hour, and that—not this—is how I pay the rent, not to mention the interest on my student loans. Anyway, I sure do hope these rich people get marginally richer by feeding us steaming heaps of nostalgia for our own adolescence, or for theirs, or for whatever, while the fucking world burns. If there's any breaking news on the *Rev Beach* front, I'll be sure to let you know. But in the meantime, please retweet my article. If this hits fifty thousand clicks I get another eighty bucks.

I watched my son watch the polar bear, who was now sitting on his haunches like an enormous house cat, his back to us, staring at the sky, which had developed an unusual orange tinge. The sun was reduced to a dull red corona, a vague hint of itself barely visible through an occlusive cloud layer backlit by what it hid. This could have been the fires, or it could have just been a regular overcast Portland day, but I smelled burnt toast on the breeze and found myself reaching into my pocket for a face mask that was not there.

I tried to put the fires out of my mind.

I texted Grace back: "That was a lot."

"So you'll be in town tomorrow," she replied.

"For the convention, yeah."

"Make some time?"

"Flight back at eight. Not even bringing a change of clothes."

She did not reply to this.

She was waiting me out.

We both knew she was going to win, and then she won.

"I'm done at FanCon at five," I typed. "So there's time if you can meet me."

"I'll have someone pick you up," she replied. "And don't worry, you'll make your flight."

"Looking forward to it!" I wrote, regretting the exclamation point as soon as I sent the text. I put my phone away, eyed the sky.

"Hey, Hank," I called. "You about ready, bud?"

Hank bid the bear goodbye and we made our way back to the parking lot. My phone buzzed once while I was driving, but I didn't check it until we parked back at home—my son's home, that is.

Surprise and delight, also some apprehension, when I cut the car's engine and unbuckled my seat belt.

"You're coming in?"

"Only for a minute."

He seemed pleased by this but took care to scramble to the door ahead of me. He had recently been entrusted with his own key to the house and wanted to show me that he could unlock the door. It was also likely that he wanted to get in there far enough ahead of me to warn his mom. He had no memories of us living together but had seen enough movies to harbor certain impossible hopes.

In the hallway I stole a glance at my phone.

Grace had graced my "Looking forward to it!" with a tap-back thumbs-up.

Amber received me coolly in the kitchen. She had a red sauce simmering, water for pasta heating up. She had her hair in a medium bob, the longest I'd seen it since she cut off her dreads, and was wearing Target's answer to Eileen Fisher. A highlight reel of unseemly scenes from our past flashed in my mind's eye. When I met her she was unbanked and unshaven, a fire dancer and shoplifter extraordinaire. Where had that girl gone? But of course I knew the answer to that question: she had sacrificed that girl to save herself, herself and Henry. New Amber had slit Old Amber's throat without a second thought. Or, to put it less gruesomely, in having our child she'd also birthed a new version of herself: a reboot, let's say. We'd both rebooted for him, only my show had gotten canceled while hers had not.

I had had second thoughts, hesitations. Not about having Hank but about the brave new me. Still, I got clean with her—and stayed clean, mostly. I mean there were some hangovers, sure, but Schedule I was foresworn altogether, and certainly there was nothing like the blessed bender that had first brought us into each other's lives. Our son was blessing enough, at least for a while. Sober, we were better people and better parents, but it turned out that we bored each other silly. For the first year, we were so blissed out on parenthood that we hardly noticed how little we had in common. The second year was a mixture of big fights over small things and long stretches of decorous silence, which were somehow worse. Like the polar bear in his luxe enclosure, I might have just curled up and moped about it, but Amber wasn't going to live that way. One weekend I went away to a fan convention and when I got home there was a note. She'd taken Hank and moved in with her mother, to her childhood home, in the kitchen doorway of which I now stood, watching her cook, wishing she'd invite me to stay for dinner and knowing that there wasn't a snowball's chance in hell. Unless it was Dante's hell, which culminates in a frozen wasteland at the center of the earth. A snowball could thrive there. But smart money said that Amber's fantasies of me in Gehenna featured fire and pitchforks, not ice and icy tears.

"Do you need something?" she asked. "Are you going to miss next week's visit or something?"

"I'm going to LA tomorrow," I said, "but just for the day. I wouldn't miss a visit, I wanted to talk to you about Hank. He seems a little stressed."

"I see," she said. She faced away from me, surveying her gas range and stirring her sauce with determination, giving herself the privacy to make any facial expression she might want to make in reaction to whatever I was about to say. "What was the issue, exactly?"

"Money," I said. "I practically had to beg him to let me buy us ice cream, and then he wanted to argue about how much I tipped."

"Shit," she said, turning toward me, her lower lip between her teeth. I could see in her eyes the debate with herself over whether to say what she was thinking. I watched her decide to say it. "He must have heard us talking. Things are tight."

This, I did not doubt. And I knew that by "us" she meant her and Nancy, her mother. This house had been purchased many years ago for what surely, these days, seemed like a song but had, at the time, been barely within Nancy's reach. But she'd bought it and hung on to it and owned it outright. Now that Portland was a hot market, selling the house could easily set up Nancy for the rest of her days: little apartment somewhere, maybe assisted living later on; whatever she needed. Only instead she was living with her grown daughter and young grandson, providing free childcare and delaying the inevitable for as long as she could stand to do it. One reason money was tight was that my divorce lawyer had made mincemeat of Amber's. At the time this had felt like a victory; now it was part of the weight of guilt I carried. But Amber was a proud woman and while she would, on occasion, let me provide this or that for my son beyond what the law required, she never asked me for anything. When I made unsolicited offers of assistance she rarely accepted, and always took as little as she could.

"Can I help?" I asked.

"I don't know," she said. "Can you?"

This might have been an allusion to our divorce settlement or it might have been a more generic spite. Then her gaze softened, her whole stance did, or maybe she was simply slumping her shoulders. It was a fine line between conciliation and despair, and I knew better than to assume that because she was softening it meant she was softening toward me.

I thought about my own mother, also still working, and my father, so many years gone, and I was about to say—something, I don't know what, when Amber said, "Look, it's nothing. He wants some game system. It's out of the question right now, and I told him that. I said maybe for his birthday."

"That's not until next March."

"Heartening to know you know."

"Hey," I said. "That only happened once."

Then neither of us said anything for a minute. And I do mean that. People say that all the time, "nobody said anything for a minute," when really it was just a few seconds. That's not what happened here. If you don't believe me, take your phone out of your pocket (I'll wait) and click open the timer and set it for a minute and then just stare at it while the numbers crawl by, and think about my second ex-wife standing in the kitchen of the house she grew up in, and me standing in that kitchen's doorway, thinking about how we had ended up here, my eyes on the tile and hers on the sauce, while a full minute's worth of silence gathered between us, and we each wondered who was going to break first, and we both knew it was going to be her because unlike me she actually had to get on with her evening.

"I'm sorry I said that," she said, turning toward me again.

"No, you're not," I said. "But it's fine, really. Just, I don't know, let me know if I can help. Not with the game thing, that's whatever, your call, I mean he can have one, I'll get it, if you want me to, it doesn't have to be this whole big thing with the birthday, but if there's other stuff you need, like if there's an issue, just, you know, tell me, because I don't want to push and I know you hate asking even more than me offering, but I guess what I'm trying to say is, you know, here I am, I mean, I'm here."

"Go say goodbye to your son," she said. "And then send him in for supper, please."

"Sure thing," I said. "And thanks for talking."

She might have nodded in acknowledgment, but I couldn't be certain; she had turned away from me and back to the pot on the stove.

Hank's room had been Amber's room when she was a girl. It was still painted the same pale peach color she'd grown up with, had the same beat-up hardwood floors. A new bed; her same old dresser. When he turned four, he got really into outer space, so there were glow-in-the-dark star stickers on the ceiling, a rocket ship–themed border on the walls. Hank was playing with some action figures that I'd brought him: a Shibboleth Gold with posable arms and a couple of tentacle-faced monsters for Shib to fight. The game was rated sixteen-and-up for violence and some swearing, but the product tie-ins were all ages. Go figure. Hank had never played *SG*. I'm not sure he knew what it was, or that he knew that the figure in his hand had anything to do with me. One day, I thought, or rather hoped and prayed, it would be something cool that he could tell his friends. They would all get obsessed with *SG2:CM2M* and he'd get to have a swell of pride in his voice when he told them, "That's my dad!"

I told Hank I'd had a very fun day with him and that I hoped he had had fun, too. I promised ice cream again next time, maybe the science museum. I took out my wallet.

"Things are going to be okay," I said. "Don't worry about money. Money's not a kid concern. Mommy and Daddy and Grandma Nancy have got it handled." I opened the wallet. After giving the ten to the ice cream man, all I had now was a rumpled single and a bank-crisp hundred. Too late to go back, I thought, and anyway I wanted him to know I meant what I'd said. Since the buck wasn't enough to make this point, I forked over the Benjamin, told him to take good care of it.

"Keep it safe," I said. "Call it a down payment on that game you want, okay?"

"What's a down payment?"

"It's like you pay for part of it so they know you're good for the whole thing. Like for a house."

"Did Mom make a down payment on this house?"

"No, but Grandma Nancy did a long time ago, and that's why it's hers now."

"Mom doesn't own the house?"

"No, Grandma does."

"But what if Grandma wants us to leave? Where would we go?"

"Grandma doesn't want you to leave. Why would you say that?"

"Because what if we're too expensive?"

"You aren't, I promise. And if you ever did have to leave here—which you don't—you can always come live with me."

"And Mom, too?"

"You'll have to ask Mom about that. But actually, don't ask Mom about that. Seriously, please don't. Listen, it's dinnertime and I have to go. Take this money and put it in your piggy bank, and when I come back next week we can talk about it some more. Okay?"

"Okay."

He hugged me. I held him tight until he squirmed. I let him go, and we walked down the hall together, until he turned toward the kitchen and I turned toward the front door.

I drove home to my own luxe enclosure above the fog line, where I had a short and utilitarian exchange with a sentient digital speaker with a woman's voice and name. In a dulcet but not quite come-hither tone she advised me about the weather in Los Angeles. I had not solicited this. She'd observed—if that's the word—the upcoming flight on my calendar, and so inferred that this was news I could use. The forecast, she said, was for smoke.

"Thank you," I said by idiot reflex.

"You're welcome," she said warmly.

"Good night," I said.

"Good night, David."

She never turned all the way off unless you unplugged her, but at my bidding good night she put herself into sleep mode. The apartment now felt empty in a new way. I thought about listening to some music, but it felt rude to wake her so soon after putting her to bed.

I was still hungry, the dinner hour past and the sugar from the ice cream long since spent. I could have ordered in, but that would have required, again, awakening the speaker. I decided to take a walk instead. I would get a late dinner at my bar.

The bar itself was a reboot. The original Wing and Prayer had opened in the early seventies in what had once upon a time been a VFW post. It was a true dive, windowless, dollar drafts through gunked-up lines. It was a place where sad men could chain-smoke and play video poker starting at 10:00 a.m. In the nineties it was colonized by hipsters, a shift that the regulars barely acknowledged, which was what the hipsters liked. Despite the small margins, the place made money, which the original owner was very bad at handling. Wing and Prayer, as a business, was true to its name. In the early aughts, while I was on TV, the original owner sold it to a local kid who'd been coming there his whole life. He sat first at the knee of his father—who had been one of the sad men—and later showed up on his own, flashing a fake ID that was laughed at before being accepted anyway. Eventually he came of age and came to work there. His name was Ken Paulson, and, unlike his boss, he saw the way Portland was changing. He thought he could cash in without selling out, or at least without selling out all the way.

There was much consternation when he took over, though he promised no changes beyond a slight expansion of the food menu, which itself only existed because the liquor commission now required it. He put in a griddle and a fryer. When the price of a draft went up to two bucks, there were nearly riots. It was 2006, Ken said; what did people want from him? Plus, he pointed out, he'd gotten the tap lines cleaned for the first time in a generation. The old heads said they missed that gunk terroir.

By this point Wing and Prayer was practically a time capsule. People loved to hate it but they also just plain loved it. Then, right before the great recession, when the future still looked peachy, the owner of the property hit Wing and Prayer with a rent hike that served as a de facto eviction notice. Ken owned the business but not the building, which was to be torn down because the land it sat on was worth more than it was. An apartment tower, one of the first of the steel-and-glass monstrosities, rose up swiftly in its place, though it stood mostly empty through the lean years that followed. It's not empty now. At street level there's an eyeglasses store and a bank kiosk where Wing and Prayer used to be.

I read an article about the loss of the space back while Ken was still rallying to save it. I was in LA at the time but feeling increasingly homesick, so I was often clicking around the websites of the Portland alt weeklies. I reached out to Ken, and with my help he was able to relocate. We bought an old shuttered Chinese restaurant a mere twelve blocks south of the original location. Staying in the neighborhood was a huge victory, given that said neighborhood was no longer the scummy paradise that had birthed and nurtured Wing and Prayer. The neighborhood was gentrified and granola'd now, utterly Subaru'd, but there were enough young dads in hoodies to support a place that reminded them (albeit in limited doses) of what this part of town had been like before they'd swept in and made it safe and clean.

The new Wing and Prayer was bigger, even spacious. A little spacious. I mean, it had windows and a kitchen, though we kept the menu small. You could get a veggie burger now, or actual vegetables; four different premium cheeses in the grilled cheese. Pool table and a couple of pinball machines in lieu of video poker, and, of course, no more smoking, which the city outlawed in all bars in 2009. But we didn't get chic. You'd never mistake us for a coworking space. There was bad tattoo art on the walls, heavy metal on the juke. The newbies loved us because we hearkened to a Portland they'd only ever read about.

The old-timers hated everything we'd done. They felt we'd become a theme park version of ourselves. My involvement ("celebrity backer") did not mitigate their rage, never mind that I was another native son, that Ken and I would have gone to high school together if I hadn't spent my high school years in Los Angeles and Florida, pretending to be in high school while actually studying with a set tutor, and not particularly often or hard. But the people who directed the most vociferous hatred toward the rebooted Wing and Prayer were our most loyal customers. Their anger was a badge of belonging, a secret handshake, a pedigree, a point of pride. A theme park was preferable to a bank kiosk and an eyeglasses store.

The hipster dads drank rye on the rocks while their kids abused our pinball tables. (We were all ages until 7:00 p.m. We even had crayons!) They reminisced about the good old days when they were poor and everything was shitty, then they slapped down a platinum Amex when it was time to settle up. They rarely had a third drink, never a fourth one. They were curious about the seasonal cider on the rotating tap and the biodynamic pinot we were trying out as the house red. They loved the fontina-and-Bosc-pear grilled cheese with a hint of truffle oil. So did I.

And what about the old alcoholics, the sad men like Ken's dad? Nobody cared what they thought about all this, which was nothing. They didn't think anything, and they didn't drink anywhere. They were dead.

I bought Ken's share of Wing and Prayer a few months into the pandemic. He needed the liquidity, and I didn't. It was sad and necessary. I still don't know if I bailed him out or fucked him over. I'd ask him, but we don't talk much anymore.

I sat at my bar and sipped a soda water (lime wedge and two splashes of cardamom bitters) and ate my Bosc-and-fontina grilled cheese and thought about seeing Grace the next day. She was, I knew, probably not in a great headspace. She remarried not long after we broke up, and this marriage had, a few months before lockdown, come to an abrupt and ugly end. I don't need to tell you about Grace's breakup because I'm sure you all saw the supermarket tabloid headlines like I did. Saw the tweets and late-night opening-monologue jokes. That *SNL* sketch. So you know all about Zane Michael Price getting caught canoodling with Adalena McAllister, his costar in a since-canceled series set in some galactic hinterland of the MCU. I remember (as I'm sure you do) the leaked photo of their spandex costumes draped over the back of the couch in the trailer, the blinds of which had been left open, suggesting that either one of their assistants had betrayed them or else that this was their own way of announcing their love to the world. Good as a press release. Maybe better, in that nobody had to write it up or send an email blast. They locked down together on Martha's Vineyard and are in Estonia now, working on some Terrence Malick thing I'm sure Shayne Glade thinks he should have starred in. Maybe they'll make their way down to Africa after, hoard some orphans, launch a travel show.

Point is, Grace was single again. Single and, I should say, somewhat newly orphaned herself. Ty died not long after her marriage imploded, and I would have liked to have been there for the funeral, but I was on dish duty in a halfway house when they buried him, and though a kindly caseworker offered me furlough, I didn't take it. I had seen that episode of *BoJack Horseman* where he gets the weekend off to go to Princess Carolyn's wedding, and even though a wedding was obviously not a funeral, and even though he was being furloughed from prison for (don't worry, no spoilers) something far worse than the low-rent basic-bitch self-destruction I'd engaged in, and even though he was a talking horse whose past was an eighties sitcom rather than an early aughts teen drama, still I could never get through that last scene on the roof with Diane (okay, I guess that is kind of a spoiler, sorry) without completely losing it, and I didn't want to make Grace's loss about my bullshit, or even about ours, so that's why I skipped the funeral of the father of the only woman who ever really loved me, all of which I assumed she was aware of, and which I suspected had something to do with why she wanted to see me now.

I swigged my soda, eyed the gin behind the bar. When you own your own, nobody can stop you. I had to stand up to myself. I stood.

I left without saying goodbye to my bartender, which was rude but within my purview as the owner. I left my sandwich unfinished. Not because I had lost my appetite, but because it was time to go and I knew it. Wasn't that, in a way, the big thing that white-knuckle CBT had taught me—to know when it was time to go?

So that was yesterday. Today I'd gotten up and driven through the smoky Portland morning, a dawn that smelled less like burnt toast than bonfire. A dawn that looked like a sunset. I worried about the flight being delayed, but the sentient speaker, when she woke me up, had said she didn't foresee any problems. She was right. We took off on time and I saw the fires from the sky, the plumes and islands, all that stuff I said before. Took my picture with the flight attendant, had an appropriate number of drinks. (This last claim is debatable given the time of day, but never mind). Did not fall through a hole in the fabric of space-time. That would come later, maybe, when I saw Grace.

The plane landed, and I disembarked. No luggage line since I'd brought only a carry-on. I was met by a car service that the fan convention had sent to ferry me to the convention center. I sat in the comfortable back seat of the luxurious black car.

It was eleven o'clock in the morning, and we were a small fig-
ment of the freeway's dream of a vast and perfect stillness. I
was drinking chilled water from a compostable plastic bottle,
made of corn according to its glossy label printed (it said) with
soy inks. A few hundred people had prepaid twenty bucks a
pop for the chance to stand beside me for twelve seconds, pose
for a photo, and walk away with an autograph. (I know Molly
said seven, but sometimes I make small talk.) I had Purell and
zinc pills in my bag, plus hand lotion and Advil for afterward.

I couldn't see the fires from the road, but the air was thick
with particulate ash and I had noticed the driver hitting the
wipers every few minutes; a single pump to clear the wind-
shield, no water, which would have turned the ash to mud. It
would be better, he said, when traffic got moving. I told him
I wasn't worried, that I was sure he'd get me there with time
to spare, and he said, "You know it, boss," in a tone foreclos-
ing any notion of repartee. We let a silence settle: AC and
engine, my fingers drumming on my kneecap, the coyote cries
of car horns all around us, all those Beamers and Porsches
desperate—more desperate than we were—to get to wherever
they were headed.

I looked out the window and considered the quality of the
light. It was the middle of the day, but the world still had that
magic-hour glow, the same glow it had had that morning in
Portland, which at the time I had attributed to the morning
itself—sunrise light, I'd thought. Now I was seeing the same
thing again, several hours later and a thousand miles south.
It was the fires that had produced this daylong evening, this
continuity of doom.

I ignored the little lump of the Woodford in my pocket,

zoned out a while, might have dozed. In my dream the freeway was awake and the black car was moving. I didn't stir until we stopped again. I blinked and beheld the convention center, a hollow monolith, a measureless cavern, its outer grounds teeming with costumed attendees. Four people walked by dressed in Shibboleth Gold costumes of varying verisimilitude. They were laughing together over something one of them had said. A pack of Shibboleths. Or a flock or a murder or a school.

"Can you take me around the back?" I asked the driver, slumping in my seat a little.

He shrugged, shifted into reverse.

I signed and posed and smiled and shook hands and the hours went by in a blur of brief encounters with women dressed up as sexy elves and men dressed up as me.

Well, not me, but Shib, in his trademark black leather duster and matching cowboy hat. Under said duster he wore (they wore? "I" wore?) a gray long-sleeved T-shirt with three buttons at the neck, all undone, exposing a swath of chest hair only partially obscured by Shib's trademark gold kerchief, which matched his trademark leather gloves and golden glowing eyes, from which, when abetted by certain power-ups, he could blast golden laser beams that flash-fried the tentacle-faced men who aimed to thwart him. The eyes stumped the average cosplayer. Serious heads sprang for custom contact lenses. Also, I know I keep saying "trademark" sarcastically, but these things were all actually copyrighted. That said, it was notable to me (and to no small portion of our fanbase) that

Shibboleth Gold looked an awful lot like a palette-swapped Roland Deschain, aka Gunslinger of the Stephen King Dark Tower novels. And moreover, that the *SG* franchise—which trafficked in the same bootleg mash-up of noir, western, and fantasy as the DT books did—had been scripted first as DT fan fiction and only later revised into (nominal) originality when Sam failed to secure the IP. The more successful the game got, the more it found itself haunted by the specter of its imitative origin. This was, I suspected, another reason why *CM2M* was delayed like a prophesied apocalypse. Sam knew enough to know that this was our chance to break the surly bonds of fandom and stake our own claim in the western-noir-fantasy genre that King had more or less invented but could hardly claim a monopoly on, since he'd invented it by mashing up Tolkien and Sergio Leone, with a patina of that Robert Browning poem that was itself a retelling of that old French poem. King was always as much postmodernist as poptimist, so we had to assume that he'd have a good sense of humor about what *SG* was up to, if and when he found out about it. His lawyers on the other hand might be less inclined to embrace the death of the author and the theory of cultural memes. So *CM2M* was going long on Hollow Earth theory and doubling down on what it had borrowed from Lovecraft (for instance, the tentacle-faced men) whose work had been in the public domain for generations, and ripped off so many times by so many people (King included) that most of what he'd made up was taken at this point for genuine folklore, old weird Americana, like a life-size cow sculpted from butter or the Grateful Dead.

Shibboleth Gold had noir aesthetics, but it was no detective story. As Shibboleth, you button-mashed your way past hordes of bad guys on the procedurally generated backstreets of what wasn't exactly Chicago. If you made it through the alleys to fight the boss of the city's biggest street gang, and if you beat him, he collapsed into a puddle of purple goo that drained into an open sewer grate that you too could climb into, thence to the procedurally generated sewer system and a new set of enemies—the tentacle men—at which point Gold got his hands on a flamethrower and the aesthetics shifted fully to sci-fi/fantasy. If you made it through the sewers, you found the subterranean caves. Here I would say "and so on," but the caves were the final level of the original game, almost incidental really, the next logical step after the streets and the sewers.

People loved the caves. Fans stanned. The caves spawned ten times as much headcanon as the other two biomes combined. Sam decided to lean into what was working. In the expansion pack (aka *SG 1.5*) Shib is revealed to be half-tentacular himself and therefore capable of breathing underwater, a crucial skill since significant swaths of the ex pack take place in an underground ocean. If you fight your way to the bottom of this sea and defeat the very Cthulhu-ish Lord of the Deep, you get sucked into a whirlpool that drags you through a cataract, at which point Shibboleth blacks out, though indeed the screen goes white, not black, when this occurs. He awakens, impossibly, on a snowy mountain peak presumed to be Verne's Scartaris, and it is on this cliffhanger that the game concludes.

A few things about this. First, *SG 1.5* is clearly ripping off— or, in the parlance of our time, paying homage to, or better yet, rebooting—not just Verne but also Poe. Why? Because nobody reads Poe's only novel, *The Narrative of Arthur Gordon Pym of*

Nantucket, from which Sam had borrowed the cataract, not to mention the giant penguins and the briefly glimpsed angelic figure in the spumes of cataract mist. These elements were, as far as most of our fans were concerned, original to *SG.* Maybe a few thought the penguins were in homage to Lovecraft's *At the Mountains of Madness,* which we were happy to let them believe, because we thought they were, too. We only learned later that Lovecraft had stolen them from Poe, who stole huge swaths of Pym from one Jeremiah Reynolds, an all-but-forgotten nineteenth-century oddball who stole his theory of the hollow earth from his one-time lecture-circuit partner, John Cleves Symmes Jr., and who (Reynolds, not Symmes) is one of American literature's great unacknowledged legislators insofar as his travel writing was ripped off by both Poe and Melville, the latter of whom read Reynolds's account of an albino whale off the coast of Chile and thought, *Hey, I can do something with this.* Which is more or less what Sam Kirchner thought when he read "Kubla Khan" and "MS. Found in a Bottle" in an English class he took to fulfill a core-curriculum requirement during his freshman year at Princeton, where he went on to study computer science and digital narrative.

Sam Kirchner is a nice Jewish boy from New Jersey who briefly, as a teenager, flirted with an acting career, which never got further than a recurring part as an extra on season 2 of *Rev Beach.* His was one of the many out-of-focus faces in the background of classroom and diner scenes. "Rhubarb, rhubarb, peas and carrots." We hung out on set a bit and I always liked him, but then he left the industry, went to college, started designing games. We happened to run into each other years later, at a release party for a different game I'd done some voice work on. That game, which had a massive budget and epic rollout and disappeared without a trace, was this big open-world thing. They'd built a digital continent, basically, and ginned up five hundred hours' worth of reasons to keep players running back and forth across it, looking for various magical artifacts, hunting dragons, and chatting up— this again—sexy elves.

I was pretty far gone when he found me on the back deck of the McMansion where the party was being held. I did not recognize him right away. He reminded me of who he was and offered me a cigarette. I remember being surprised that he had one.

"You don't look like a smoker," I slurred.

"I'm not," he said. "But I want to pitch you on something, and I figure if I give you this, courtesy dictates you stand here as long as it's lit."

"I don't smoke," I said. "But I like your style." In fact I did smoke then, sort of. What I mean by that is I was a casual smoker, and what I mean by that is I smoked when I drank, which was all the time. So what I mean is I lied to Sam Kirchner. I was a smoker, and I wanted a smoke. I think he saw all that.

I took the cigarette from him, pulled out my own light, hit the wheel. Flame kissed paper.

"You're on the clock," I said.

He sketched out his idea for a claustrophobic, punishingly addictive, endlessly repetitive but also infinitely variable game. I dug the descent into the underworld, the tentacle men, all of it. And by "dug" I mean I didn't care one way or the other, or see how it had anything to do with me. Then he asked me to be the voice of Shibboleth Gold, and I said no. Absolutely not. No way.

"But why? You just said it sounds cool."

"Yeah, but I don't work for cool, and the eagerness in your voice plus the fact that you've got sophisticated aesthetic ideas tells me that you can't possibly afford to pay me my regular rate."

"I can't pay you anything."

"Even better."

"But I'll give you a share of the franchise. What do you want—ten percent?"

"Fifteen. But I'm not going to do it. Because the shares don't exist, and there is no franchise."

"Yet."

"And why do you want so badly for it to be me?"

"Because the game is all about digging back into your own history, trying to right these cosmic wrongs."

"I thought it was about fish monster mobsters in Chicago?"

"It's about a lot of things. Having the connection to *Rev Beach* adds an extra layer of meaning. Easter egg for the superfans. And it means something to me personally."

"The superfans?" I said, incredulous. "Actually, never mind that, say more about the personal thing."

"Well, it was being on the set of the show and being around all of you that set me on my path. My true path."

"Because you realized you'd never be as good as us?" My cigarette was burning low, and I could hear myself getting mean. I was ready for another drink.

"No," he said. "That wasn't what I meant at all. It was because all the rest of them seemed so comfortable, so happy to be doing what they were doing, and you, well, you didn't. I always thought that deep down you really hated being on-screen, having to show yourself off that way. Maybe that was a projection on my part, but it's what I felt, and I identified totally with that feeling. I realized that I didn't want to get to where you were. So when they offered me a speaking part, I said no. Not staying in Florida was the best thing I ever did."

"That's a pretty common sentiment," I said. "Anyway, thanks for the pitch, but I think we're out of time."

"Listen, will you at least think about it? Take my card?"

And I had meant to throw that card away as soon as he was out of sight, but as soon as he was out of sight, I went in search of a fresh cocktail, and then another, and then the rest of that night was a blur, and when I woke up the next morning, there the card was on the dresser next to (thank God) my wallet, keys, and phone.

I don't know what moved me, but a few days later I called him. I took the percentage, did the voice, learned a whole lot about the history of Hollow Earth theory, laid the Easter eggs that the superfans later sat on until they hatched—or whatever the operative metaphor would be here. And a lucky thing, too, because after the world shut down and I bought out my bar's co-owner, things got tighter than I was used to. *Rev Beach* streams didn't pay like cable rerun residuals in days of yore. *Shibboleth Gold* had been my ark through what otherwise might have been a washout year. I mean it was a washout, an apocalypse, in a lot of ways for a lot of people. Just not for me.

·   ·   ·

Some goon in my signing line was wearing a homemade shirt. It was a drawing of the young C. Thomas Howell, circa *The Outsiders*, with tentacles coming out of his face. Underneath the image it said *Stay (((Gold)))*. This was a meme from one of our most dedicated Reddit threads, to the effect that Shibboleth Gold was Jewish, which was plausible insofar as his creator was, but also raised the prospect of antisemitism, since Lovecraft was a rabid antisemite and so were the MAGA chuds who originated the brackets-around-names thing, though Sam insisted that this label had been reclaimed, apparently, by Jews in the media who started adding it to their Twitter handles. (And yes, LOL, "Jews in the media" itself feels like an antisemitic thing to say, though it is literally true, and I'm half Jewish myself, so who's gonna tell me I can't?)

Maybe the guy wearing the shirt meant it sarcastically, or ironically, I'm honestly not sure which is the right word to use here, or if the latter, what exactly was being ironized by the shirt. It was all part of the ever-elusive, ever-shifting, all-pervasive irony of social media itself, and this was one big reason why I didn't use any of those services. The last thing I wanted was a platform. The second-to-last thing I wanted was to appear in a photograph with a person wearing that T-shirt. It would be death by ten thousand RTs.

My handler stood off to the side; I waved him over, pointed out the guy. "Tell Ponyboy Squidface to zip up his hoodie or get out of my signing line," I said.

The handler nodded, frowned, walked over. I wanted to watch, in part to make sure things didn't escalate and in part for the perverse pleasure—so long forgotten, so quickly recalled—of making a guy like the handler into the instrument of my will. Of giving orders and having them followed. This world—the world of the fan con—was one where I could get just about anything I wanted. That knowledge felt good. But I didn't watch the conversation unfold, because the one thing I couldn't do was hold up the signing line. The fans kept coming. Someone switched out my Sharpie at some point. Did Ponyboy Squidface zip his hoodie or did they boot him? I couldn't tell you. You'd have to check his Instagram, see if there's a picture of us posted there.

The *Shibboleth Gold* fans knew what they wanted, which was more *Shibboleth Gold*. The *Rev Beach* fandom, having been around a lot longer, was less cohesive. It had had decades to evolve and change, to build up its own history and lore, complete with origin myths (the failed Tumblr petition), a medieval period (the early unmodded message boards), and a sense that it was now in the full flush of modernity (streaming and meme-ing). The question was how to face the future. Whether to embrace it, and more to the point, which future it was they were fighting for. The fandom had fractured into factions. The first and biggest cohort were the enthusiasts, who were eager to see their long-held hope of a reboot realized. Then there were the small but vocal convergencers, by and large younger than the enthusiasts, at least some of whom had come to *Shibboleth Gold* first and *Rev Beach* second. Since both pieces of IP involved me and Sam, and because the convergencers had been foie gras'd on Marvel movies since birth, they saw no reason why the game and the show shouldn't become part of the same expanded universe. Indeed, a copious and ever-growing body of fan fiction fleshed out the potential of such a crossover. It seemed to involve a lot of Grace having sex with tentacle men, and me having sex with Shayne. The latter scenario didn't even require an expanded universe to imagine, as some enthusiasts were quick to point out. Some of them had been shipping me and Shayne for twenty years.

Safe to say that I wasn't the biggest fan of our convergencer fans, but they weren't the ones I worried about. Frankly, I liked the idea that there were people out there for whom the thought of me having sex was a subject worthy of five or ten or forty thousand words of sustained imagination. Never mind who they imagined me having it with. I didn't want to read it, and it was weird knowing it was out there, but I was happy to take it as the compliment that I assumed it mostly was. I knew their undying lust for my on-screen teenage self was what paid my fan convention fee. What else were they going to do with my signed headshots, with the half-second memory of how my hand had felt in theirs?

So no, the pervs weren't my main worry.

My worry were the Revheaded Strangers.

They were a tiny group, maybe ten or twelve people tops, or they had been before the reboot rumors. Now they had new-found visibility and, I suspected, swelling ranks. They tested the limit of my live-and-let-live philosophy.

The Revheaded Strangers dated back to the show's original run. They were OG fans. One of the founders had coauthored the Tumblr petition, and three others were counted among its first five signatories. They'd been enthusiasts back then, their devotion pure and unsurpassed. They wrote tons of fanfic, most of it blessedly free of imagery inspired by hentai. It was the *Rev Beach* universe itself that interested them: the vampires, the haunted beach, the don't-call-it-a-hellmouth Hellmouth, and so on. They took this stuff and ran with it, like August Derleth with Lovecraft's Cthulhu mythos or Stephen King doing George Romero karaoke by writing that novel where cell phones turn everyone into zombies and then dedicating it to George Romero. We, the actors, were the least interesting part of the whole equation, as far as this apostate order was concerned. Over time, the Revheaded Strangers came to see the show itself as vestigial. They regarded it roughly the same way that the early Christians regarded Judaism, or as Mormonism regards Christianity: a necessary precursor, the best parts absorbed and the rest disavowed.

The Revheaded Strangers had enjoyed two full decades of schismatic freedom. Now, with the reboot viable, the threat of official canon was imminent. When *Rev Beach* came back (if it came back) whatever we put on TV would instantly render apocryphal the work on which, it is no exaggeration to say, they had spent their entire adult lives. All their mythos development and plot-hole backfilling, their spin-offs and alternate timelines, prequels and sequels and crossover orgies with the *Dawson's* cast—obsolete in an instant. They didn't want to be the last pagans born to purgation, watching Messiah lead the saved souls to heaven from the fringe of limbo. But they also didn't want to convert.

Their solution was to oppose the reboot itself. Their methods were diverse, if predictable. They tweeted a lot. They started a Change.org petition, which took all the original language of the mid-aughts reboot petition and inverted it line for line. In the same way that Satan is the most devout Christian, because the terms of his rebellion confirm all God's claims, so too did the deranged persistence of the Revheaded Strangers legitimize *Rev Beach*. It spoke well of our prospects for generating discourse. These people hated us so much, they'd probably stream every episode twelve times just to pick them apart. TikTok reactions über alles, whole podcasts devoted to taking us down. They would, in fine, give the rest of the fans something to unite in opposing, a way to heal the enthusiast/convergencer rift, to make the body of the fandom whole.

That was one way it might go. The other way it might go was that one of the Revheaded Strangers would snap, come to a convention like this one, and stand in my fan line and take my hand in his and then, with a grim glimmer in his glassy eye, straight up fucking murder me.

It was a small but real concern. And getting smaller by the minute, as my time at the signing table wound down. A few minutes more and I'd be free. Free and paid.

It was something to be.

Back in the green room, I rubbed my hands with the Purell first and then the lotion. I took two Advil for the pain in my autograph hand and a zinc pill just to be safe. My handler led me through the gray guts of the convention center. We emerged through a side door, where I expected to find another black car, but instead there was a champagne Audi SUV with a corporate logo emblazoned on its hood: the six-sided diamond scored with lines that broke its body up into triangles (fourteen), and this whole mess inscribed inside a circle, well, almost a circle: the top and bottom tips of the diamond broke the planes of the ring so that the diamond actually looked a bit like it was between parentheses, which might have been a truly wild reclamation of the antisemitic online thing except that I happened to know (just as I knew without counting how many triangles there were inside the diamond) that Ty Travis had designed it himself a long, long time ago. It was originally for his production company. Now it was the Travis family crest.

Maybe the online antisemites and/or media Jews had gotten the idea from him?

"It's good to see you again, Mr. Crader," Craig Lelyveld said, his naturally deep and deliberately neutral voice pulling me out of my reverie. I knew for a fact that he did not mean this. He stood beside the car, his posture proprietary, though he did not lean on the vehicle. Indeed, I had never seen Lelyveld lean.

"Where's Grace?" I asked. "Did you send her for coffee?"

He favored me with a slight smile; coming from Lelyveld, this was a lot. He was Grace's head of scheduling and security. Ty had hired him for Grace on her fourteenth birthday after a men's-interest monthly put her on its "Countdown to Legality" watchlist. (This was two years before *Rev Beach* premiered.) Grace, unlike Shayne and me, had been a star her whole life. She was Ty Travis's daughter, after all. Her sonograms had sold at auction. She had her first certified gold record when she was nine.

"Ms. Travis is at the house," he said. I knew that by this he meant the Travis estate, a mansion and ample grounds.

"I have a flight," I said. "Which Grace is well aware of."

Lelyveld wore a crisp white shirt tucked into dark slacks. He wore his sport coat open and his aviators high on his nose. Ty had poached him from the Navy SEALs. I knew what he had used to bench-press, and though the stubble on his cheeks was white now, I doubted he'd cut back on his reps.

"Do I have a choice here?"

"You always have a choice, Mr. Crader."

I wondered whether that was true.

"The fires have caused some delays," Lelyveld continued. "We are monitoring your flight. If it departs, and you want to be on it, you will be. But we suspect that you'll be staying the night in Los Angeles."

I did not comment on his pointed use of the first-person plural, which I knew was not intended to assert the authority of his employer but simply to exclude me. There had been a time when, by virtue of my working for Ty and then being married to Grace, Craig Lelyveld had been much in my life and I in his. I was glad those days were gone and did not want to get into this car. On the other hand, what was my option? I could hire an Uber to take me to the airport, or, if what Lelyveld said was true, to a hotel. Something swank would be fun, and today was payday after all. But what are swank hotels for if not the very forms of fun I had foresworn? And would it really feel good to blow that kind of money, given the conversation I'd had yesterday with my other ex-wife and my sad-eyed, penny-pinching son? I should open a college fund for him. Maybe not feasible on a Saturday night but come Monday, yes, that's just what I'd do. And then there was this: if

Grace wanted my attention, she was going to have it, one way or another.

I looked uneasily at Lelyveld.

Lelyveld looked at me, inscrutable and unperturbed.

This man had seen me at some of my lower moments, moments that had been more like eras, and it was his opinion that I had treated shabbily the woman whose life it was his duty to keep free of complication and disgrace. He had not been wrong about me then, and I could hardly expect him to revise his opinion on such short notice. I had been the sort of problem that, if he'd had his druthers, he would have been granted discretion to resolve in his own way.

"All right," I said. "Let's get going. It's good to see you, too, Craig."

I extended my hand to him, though the last thing I wanted to do was shake one more hand. I need not have worried. Lelyveld had already turned away from me. He was walking around the car to the driver's side door and speaking in low tones into his jacket cuff. I turned to face my handler, who had silently gawped from the periphery of this freighted exchange.

"Please don't tweet this," I said. He made the zipped-lip gesture at me, and I responded with a wink and a finger gun. I climbed into the back seat of the SUV and shut the door.

The leather was cool and without blemish. I settled in. The SUV eased onto the freeway, which was moving at a rapid clip. I pulled the Woodford from my pocket and cracked the seal. I savored maple notes and throat heat while Craig Lelyveld sped us through the actual dusk and onward into the burning hills.

· · ·

Grace was waiting when we pulled up. She stood on the snow-white steps of the Travis mansion, though at present they were gray with a layer of fallen soot. She wore a billowing silk-ish thing, white, that I first took for a robe but then thought might have been a pantsuit. Or also a pantsuit? It had a cloth belt and a neckline that plunged halfway down her chest, but I did not allow myself to believe this display was for my benefit. She was, as ever, on a red carpet somewhere in her mind.

She wore high-top sneakers the same champagne hue as the SUV that I was still sitting in. I opened my door before it could become obvious that Lelyveld wasn't going to come around and do it for me as he should have done, would have done for any other passenger. I stepped onto the gravel and walked toward Grace on her mansion's ashen steps.

"Hello, old friend," my ex-wife said, her arms wide. She had unhooked her blue particle mask from behind her ear so that she could kiss my cheek as we embraced. I lingered no longer than a second too long in the warmth and scent of her, adrift in the tide of a body that I had known well and that had known my own. I spoke her name very quietly into her hair.

She stepped back to assess me. I stood on display. She resecured her own mask and then, from a pocket or fold of the pantsuit or robe, produced a second mask. She proffered this to me and I put it on, noting the oddness of my breath bouncing around inside the little tent that was now pitched on my face. A strange sensation that had become second nature during lockdown only to have since become, thankfully, strange again.

In the stew of my own trapped humidity I smelled Woodford and felt ashamed.

"Let's walk," Grace said, "and talk."

"Sorkin style?" I said.

"Don't worry about your marks and angles," she said. "Just focus on delivery. I've got camera guys in the trees."

I smiled at the ease with which we were falling back into our repartee and thought to say something about it, but she had not waited for me and was already a ways up the path. I jogged to catch up.

The path led us around the main mansion, where she'd met me, along the edge of a lawn that boasted not one but two Louise Bourgeois spiders, which, from this angle, seemed to be scheming against the silver Koons dog cowering in the shadow of a weathered steel Serra plate. These were Ty's acquisitions, and I let myself miss him for a moment: his brashness and bombast, his love of scale and disregard for order. I knew that he was buried on the property and realized Grace was leading us to his hilltop grave.

The lawn gave way to a gentle grade that was not as gentle as I remembered. I was out of breath when I met her at the grave. She stood directly atop her father's plot but faced away from the stone, away from him. Her hands were clasped behind her as she surveyed the city, where the fires backlit the hills and smoke hung above us like a layer of insulation, trapping heat and light. I took a position at her side, or as close to it as I could get without treading on Ty.

"We walked but didn't talk," I said, still short of breath. "Or did I miss my cue? Was the first line mine?"

"How was your day?" she asked.

"Not bad. Easy flight down, good money for a few hours' work, which doesn't amount to much here on this hill, but back in my life—" I cleared my throat. "Oh, and I got to catch up with my old friend Craig, which is always such a pleasure. I mean a real pleasure and joy, riding in a car with Craig. How was your day?"

"I took meetings. People asked me for money to fund things: movies, foundations, a school I think, though it might have been a website. An online school or a school for people who make websites. I gave them some money. I took some staged casuals in support of my line of personal-care products. We can't all be Gwyneth or Busy, but we do what we can. I monitored the fires. I mean I had people monitor the fires. I posted the staged casuals to my social media accounts. I watched the numbers tumble upward through five and six figures. Likes and reposts, RT and QT. Those are Twitter terms. The other sites have other terms. A man—well, I assume it was a man—who goes by BigDiogenesEnergy speculated at some length about my connections to Mossad and also my foot size. He was wrong on both counts, but closer on the feet. I've got big feet for a girl my size, as you know."

"The Mossad thing again?" I said. It was a recurring theme in Grace's story. They said Lelyveld was a double agent, like Jonathan Pollard, though to believe that, I thought, you'd have to believe Craig still worked for the US military, to say nothing of having ever worked for Israel's. I knew for a fact that Ty had doubled his salary and matched his pension when the Travises stole him from the SEALs. Lelyveld didn't need a dime from G-men or Jews—Jews other than the Travises, that is.

"It's not a secret that we're Jewish," Grace said. "Or I mean that Ty was. There's a star on his headstone, as you can plainly see. But he didn't raise me as anything. I'm as American as a

Philip Roth novel. But my middle name is 'Merkavah,' which means 'wheels of the chariot.' Grace Merkavah Travis—it's ridiculous. He almost named me Shekhinah, for fuck's sake, except he didn't think it would look good on a marquee. He was a dabbler who name-checked whatever he liked or happened to remember. Cole is short for Coleridge, which is how Will got named Will—as in Wordsworth. Little Easter eggs all throughout his work, but it isn't a code, it's a casserole."

"Easter eggs," I said, stress on the first word. "Sam Kirchner's the same way. He's a walking mood board."

"The problem with these conspiracy people is they spend half their lives uncovering what nobody's trying to hide. If Ty had secrets, I'd have sold them through Sotheby's by now. He was just a very successful entertainment mogul who read Martin Buber at a formative age, and that's why our stupid logo is a riff on the ten sefirot, minus malkhut, of course, but only because he didn't want a dick hanging off his diamond, which would have wrecked the feng shui of the logo, feng shui being a not precisely Jewish precept, but still. What I mean is he was pragmatic. It was 1967, and everyone was getting blow jobs except for guys named Morty Greenstein. That's the only reason he changed the family name to Travis and started going by Ty instead of Mort. Why is that so hard for people to understand?"

"People believe what they want to believe."

"My staff tells me that I don't have to read this stuff, follow the discourse like I do. My staff would really rather I didn't. They oppose it in emphatic terms."

"Someone who works for you opposes you? Pics or it didn't happen."

"They have their ways of making their positions known. They don't like it that I want to read the comments. It makes them worried. They say it gets me into a—headspace, sometimes, where I become less than my most effective. And there is the question of what my time is worth. More than BigDiogenesEnergy's, it seems fair to assume. But how is such a thing measured anyway? Time as money. I've always thought frankly that the adage has it backward: time isn't money, money is time. Let's say it costs twenty thousand dollars for me to spend fifteen minutes reading backward through BigD's timeline, really boning up on his disputations with Russiagate, his valorous opposition to the Clinton murder machine, all the other women whose feet he's guessed at. Let's say all this costs twenty thousand dollars—but to whom? Who pays that money and who receives it? Or are we speaking in the abstract, the theoretical, as in the twenty thousand dollars I could have made by, say, posting more photos in support of my personal-care line, which would have spurred sales in the amount of et cetera? Is that what we mean, what is meant? And how much can anyone really bemoan the nonexistence, as opposed to the loss, of this money? Who is haunted by the ghosts of these unrealized futures? It's only money, and only time. I have plenty of both."

There were reasons I had loved her once. Here was one of them.

"How's Henry?" she asked, switching subjects.

"Good, for the most part. He's on a polar bear kick. We went to the zoo yesterday." I thought about my son's money anxiety, about Amber's terseness, about her aging mother and their small house and the way I'd reveled in my offer of largesse, a few hundred bucks, a few thousand. All that seemed extremely far away from the top of this hill. Plenty of money, plenty of time. Grace could buy and sell me a dozen times over with the money in her checking account. With Lelyveld's petty cash, probably. I wondered whether she was planning to do exactly this, and why.

"The terms would be generous," she said, apparently satisfied with the update on my son and ready to get back to her real concern. "The commitment would be limited. Say eight episodes, maybe ten. I want to write and direct. I want that Lena Dunham treatment where people get so obsessed with you and what you represent about your generation that they forget about the hundred other names that roll during the credits."

"Why would you want that? Why would anyone want that? Not even Lena wanted that, or she didn't anymore as soon as she got it."

Grace ignored me. "If the first season does okay, season two's a no-brainer. After that, who knows. Maybe we keep going, or maybe we sit back and platform it. Spin-off, movie, some app thing. Our faces plastered across YA novels from here to eternity. You'll be able to open a trust for your son."

"I have a trust for my son."

"A less modest trust."

"You make this all sound so simple," I said. "Or inevitable."

"I'm just talking, David, sharing some feelings I have. That's what women do, you know, we share our feelings. Here I am standing on my father's grave while the world burns. It's a soulful moment. A lot's possible. And it was your idea. Your literal dream come true, if I recall your voice mail correctly. But we need Shayne Glade."

"Well," I said, "keep me posted on your progress with that."

"You're really going to make me say it?" she said.

"I am absolutely going to make you say it. In fact, take off your mask for a second, I want to see your face while you plead. I don't think I've ever seen you plead before."

That wasn't true, and we both knew it, but she let it pass, which was lucky for me (i.e., merciful of her) because in my snideness I had overplayed my hand. She had done more than her share of pleading in the last months of our marriage, and she had never entirely forgiven herself for ending it, even though it was (I can admit this now) the right thing, the only thing for her to do. Subconsciously, and then consciously, I had conspired to have her cut me loose, left her no other choice, not because I hadn't wanted her anymore but because I hadn't wanted to keep living in her world: the world of money and time. Fame Island. I would have died there, and I left in order to save myself. The fact that after leaving I spent the next several years almost dying in obscurity was ironic, sure, but it didn't negate the truth of my original instinct. And anyway, here I was, alive, standing beside her at Ty's grave.

I still barely believed that Ty was dead. My one-time boss and father-in-law had not, broadly speaking, gotten along with his daughter. Oh sure, she was the apple of his eye and the star of his show and all that shit, but on a day-to-day basis? Please. The whole Travis family was as prone to betrayal and madness as any of the grand sick dynasties of Europe, only it wasn't genes that had corrupted them but money. Money and fame, of a kind and degree that's hard for me to describe except as another cavern measureless to man. The Travises did not have crossed eyes or hydrocephalus. They were, if anything, alarmingly resilient and robust. Grace was, and Ty had been, and so were all his ex-wives and their second and third husbands and all the half and step- and otherwise semi and pseudo siblings racked up along the way. Even the adopted ones got it into their DNA: genetics transmogrified by fiat, science slapped back in its place not by money but by wealth, not by celebrity but by fame, which you should understand sounds like status but isn't. Celebrity is status. It can be won and lost, doubled down on or stripped away—intrigue and happenstance, fate in conspiracy with chance. It can even be forsaken, as I had more or less done with mine. Fame, on the other hand, is territory. It's land. An island nation where a coconut-scented breeze is always tousling your hair and the light of the money god shines ceaseless and grim on the blinding white sand. (Maybe Fame Island was what I'd dreamed of when I'd dreamed of Corey, only the sand hadn't been blinding white in the dream, it had been dead and gray as the *Langoliers*-like sky.) The Travis clan would all live to be raving centenarians, attacking one another in the press and in court over outrages real and imagined.

Or so I'd always imagined, by which I mean feared. But here we were with Ty dead and Grace downright solicitous. What did she want from me, from this moment? And moreover, what did I want?

What didn't I want? I wanted to jump from this hill and free dive into the fires. I wanted to beg Grace for unqualified forgiveness for having screwed up, for having crashed the show the first time, and later our marriage, and several of our cars. I wanted her to tell me that she forgave me for everything, and also that there was nothing I needed to be forgiven for. That we could do it again, and right this time. A real reboot. I wanted to be very rich but not have to be famous, but maybe—yes—I also wanted to be famous again. I wanted to be famous without going insane. Time, strength, and cash—what else was worth wanting? I couldn't think of anything. And as long as I was taking moon shots and making wishes, I wanted to rip my ex-wife's baffling outfit from her honeyed person and fuck her on her father's grave amid the ash that fell like snow falling faintly and faintly falling through the universe . . . Mostly, I wanted to go gin blind, because if I did, then everything that followed would be the gin's decision, an evil breed of freedom, the purest I'd ever known.

Grace slipped her mask off like I'd asked her to do. Seeing her face made her and all of this real in a way that it hadn't been before. The way her smile lent further light to her already high-wattage emerald eyes. She was a world-class smizer who was also smiling at me. Wide.

"We both know Shayne doesn't take me seriously," she said. "But he really does love you, and he's always hoped you'd get to work together again. He'll listen. Find out what he wants, and try to make what he wants be something we can actually give him."

"What if he won't do it?" I said. "Assume for a second that he's out of the picture. What's your calculus now?"

"No show without Shayne," she said, and slipped the mask back on so I could once again see only her searing eyes.

"Does the same go for me?" I said. "And Corey? And what

about Catherine Higley and Alex Nichols? Or is it only Mr. Indie Darling who's indispensable?"

She touched my shoulder. "Higley and Nichols already said yes," she said. "I called them earlier. They're excited. And of course you're indispensable, too. Always were and always will be—at least as far as *Rev Beach* is concerned."

I noted the hasty emendation.

"But the thing, and I'm not sure if this is another moment where you want me to take my mask off so you can watch me say it—"

"Might as well," I said.

She obliged me.

"Look me in the mouth, David, not the eyes. I took this mask off so you could watch my mouth move. My lip gloss costs more than dinner at Noma. Read these lips."

I looked. I read.

"Shayne Glade is a famous actor, and you're a cartoon character who happens to have my phone number."

"Avatar," I retorted. "Video games aren't cartoons, they're computer graphics, and you call the main character an avatar because he's the player's point of access to the world of the game."

"Fascinating, David, I love learning. 'Splain some more, would you?"

"So okay, fine, Glade can be the white whale. I'll go spear him. What about Corey?"

"I mean, he was killed off in the original run, so—"

"Yeah, but it's a show about the supernatural. He could be a ghost."

"The grown-up ghost of a dead child? Hmm, let me put this

another way: don't ever say his name in my presence again. How about that?"

"Okay," I said. "I understand."

"Do you?"

Did I? I knew she hated him, which I thought was overdramatic—I mean what's a little slander in a self-published autobiography between old friends? He'd trashed me, too, and I didn't hate him, or I didn't think I did. I felt . . . pity for him, monster though he was. A bit of pity for the monster, amplified by a wounded brotherly estrangement. Or something. Some fucking thing I felt about him that I'd never really dealt with, and hopefully wouldn't have to, since it sounded like Grace wasn't going to let him anywhere near the reboot.

Guilt. Guilt was what I felt but wasn't saying. I carried guilt about how his life had turned out, and how it was our fault, mine and hers. I wanted to remind her that we owed him. Even if he didn't know that, even if nobody else knew that. We knew what we did.

"I don't like being taken for granted" is what I said instead.

"I'm not taking you for granted," she said. "I never took you for granted. It's just, well, you were always a bad negotiator, and you forgot to pretend you were ever on the fence."

Grace put her particle mask back on.

"I need to check my flight," I said.

"Your flight is canceled," she said. "It's not LA, it's Portland. The airport is shut down. Do you want to stay here, or do you want Craig to take you back into town?"

"Tempting," I said, "but probably better if I go. You wouldn't want it to get out that I was here, right? Who knows what BigDiogenesEnergy will think?"

She ignored me, got out her phone, clicked something, something else, then turned it around so I could see the photos of myself climbing into Lelyveld's car. The handler, of course, had sold me out, mere moments after promising me that he wouldn't. Grace herself had RT'd him before I got here, but that wasn't what she was showing me. It was Shayne. Shayne had RT'd this photo, too.

I studied myself in the image and was surprised and disheartened by what I saw. The David Crader I imagined myself as was not so different from the one my fans had in their mind: slim and dark-eyed, stylishly coiffured, designer everything but no brand names showing, clean-shaven and poreless, edge of seventeen. Who, then, was this schlub in dad jeans and scuffed sneakers? His hair, anyone could see, was getting thin. Why hadn't he tucked in his shirt? His fingernails looked bitten. Two, three days' beard growth, graying.

Also—and this was the worst part—I'd gotten fat.

"Yeah okay," I said. "I'll stay."

We walked back to the front of the house, where Lelyveld was waiting.

"It's a new era, Craig," she called to him. "We'll be saying goodbye to old grudges and seeing more of David around."

With silk sails of the robe/suit a-billow she led me up the ash-gray steps and into the house, directing me to an upstairs room that had been prepared for me.

"Dinner in an hour?" she said, already disappearing down some other hall.

"Sure," I called after her. "Just text me directions."

My bag had been brought in from the car and set at the foot of the bed, which had been turned down. On the pillow, where at a swank hotel one might expect to find a square of chocolate, there sat the empty plastic airplane bottle of Woodford, which I had slipped into the console trash in the car. Lelyveld had found it and had left it here for me to find.

I didn't have a change of clothes, but I decided to take a shower, freshen up, and this gave me enough time to have another flashback. Probably I should have reviewed my marriage to Grace, or my long and troubled friendship with Shayne—who I was now charged with convincing to take on a project that I myself wasn't sure I wanted to be involved with, dream of mine though it may originally have been. But I didn't think about any of those things. Being back in the company of my first ex-wife, who didn't really need my help but seemed improbably eager to have it, had gotten me thinking about my second ex-wife, the one who desperately needed my help but didn't want it. I was thinking about women and houses, which is another way of saying that I was thinking about money and time.

I set the showerhead to the rainfall setting and soaped myself and thought about the night that Amber and I first met.

We met at a music festival, but not the kind you're thinking of. This wasn't Coachella or Bonnaroo, or even Fyre. This was a three-day white-trash jamboree held in a dusty field owned by a local Indian tribe in southwest Washington State. A quarter mile of one-lane blacktop and a double row of lodgepole pines kept us veiled from the casino parking lot, which would, in the five-year development plan, extend across all this space. But the tribe wasn't ready to build yet and had been chuffed that the jamboree organizers didn't blink at their asking price. When people had had their fill of jamming, they took whores' baths at the porta-sink, then wandered up the road to gamble and graze the buffet.

This place was about an hour north of Portland, where my evening had begun two days earlier, at the bar I still then only part-owned, with some guys whose names I could by that point no longer summon, if I'd ever known them. Neither could I have recognized the car that I'd arrived in, assuming it was still around somewhere, which was far from certain. What I knew for certain was that I had a bag of powder in my pocket, which my flat wallet suggested I'd paid top dollar for, and which I was about to take a bump of, curious to find out whether this elevator would be heading up or down. It didn't matter what the answer was. My mouth tasted like cucumbers. Amber was wearing a tie-dyed onesie and doing dervish spins by the bonfire while a bluegrass combo massacred John Prine.

I was lucky she was there alone, she told me. She said she'd planned to come with her boyfriend, but he'd gotten a DUI two nights prior. Under normal circumstances she'd have sold some plasma and sprung him the next morning, but he had a couple of priors, and now it was a whole parole thing. She was trying, she said, to be free enough for both of them. I proffered my powder. She led me to her tent.

Soon enough I told her who I was and what my life had been, the shambles I felt like I'd made of it. She took the news in stride, impressed in an abstract way but uninterested in the particulars. I loved that. A baseline lack of interest in pop culture is a really healthy thing for a celebrity to have in a partner. If they're too enamored of it, you feel like you're taking advantage, or being taken advantage of, but if they're not at least a little wary about how the gears of the fame machine are greased then odds are you're both going to end up on the cover of one of those checkout-line magazines nobody wants to be on the cover of, at which point the thing doing the greasing is you—your blood for their gear oil. Not good.

Amber got it when I told her that I'd come back to Portland to figure out what my next steps were, what my true calling was supposed to be, and she sympathized when I admitted that it wasn't going well. Soon, I took to telling her that it hadn't been going well until she had come along, which I felt was a very sweet thing to say, and it made her so happy to hear it that she said the same thing back to me, and in this way we rapidly pushed our relationship to a point of intensity where marriage seemed like a valid whim. This was similar, come to think of it, to what Grace and I had done.

The only problem with our plan was that we were both out of control, a pair of copilots working in perfect harmony to navigate the Cessna of our relationship into a Mount Hood of pills and powder, a Columbia River of gin. We encouraged the worst in each other, and the thing was that we both really did need the encouragement. We weren't exactly addicts yet, only bender-prone people pleasers, eager to egg each other on. The more pleased we became the more eager we got for even more pleasing. The usual circuit breakers weren't breaking like they'd used to. Pleasure lessened as bender periodicity increased, but that only made us more and more eager to get back what we'd lost.

We had more money than we knew what to do with and nothing to fill our days, so we did the only thing we knew to do with money, and the days and nights were indeed filled with nothing, with nothingness. We became connoisseurs of obliteration, occasionally racked by seizures of remorse, which, on the blue moons when they did arrive, delivered their own kind of high.

We were living in one of the new luxe enclosures, and one night we both nodded out with a slab of salmon in the oven. The idea had been to turn over a new leaf, and we thought we'd start with eating better, then work our way toward more rigorous forms of clean living. This made perfect sense to us. We sniffed the sweet aroma of the roasting fish and snorted a couple of pills to make it through the otherwise unbearable twenty minutes still on the cooking timer. We washed the pills down with a hundred-dollar bottle of local pinot that I had poured evenly into two pint glasses. I remember that the pills—before we powdered them—were oval-shaped, and that the salmon was miso-glazed. The next thing we knew, men in gas masks were slapping us in the face.

Suffice it to say we did not turn over our new leaves just yet, but the difference in how Amber and I were each billed for our respective trips to the emergency room was enough to make a Marxist out of anyone. What is marriage but a commune? I paid off her debt, picked up a ring. I wanted her on my insurance, which I still had through SAG despite not having acted in anything in ages. (Sing it: Solidarity for-ehhh-ver, and the union makes us strong!) Really, the thing we were trying to avoid was ever again having to pay ten thousand dollars for a glass of orange juice and a shot in the arm.

Those of you who have been down this road yourself can see the subtext here. We had not yet scraped bottom nor been scared straight. Salmon contains omega-3 but not naloxone. Another OD was all but certain, and we knew it.

We left that luxe enclosure but ended up in another, a condo this time. Our reputation had preceded us, but I turned on that old star charm, wowed the board. It didn't hurt that we didn't have to wait for a mortgage to be approved. I paid cash. We moved in.

All addicts are romantics. In a sense it is romance itself to which we are addicted, or that's one thing it feels true to say when you're truly fucked up, fucking up, and fucked. Having made the decision for the sake of paperwork, we decided to try to mean it, and we mostly did. The pregnancy was not planned, but the decision to keep the kid was easy. Maybe it should not have been, but it was the easiest decision I have ever made, and I still believe that if I've only done one thing right in this world, it's having Hank. My bringing him into it, despite what a wreck it's become, and becoming, this slow-roll apocalypse that isn't so slow anymore. Humanity is an end-stage alcoholic. We're at the part of the movie where we finally let Jesus into our hearts, or else it's the part where our mothers weep over our coffins singing songs imploring Him to let us into His.

I felt refreshed after my shower, which made it a bit of a drag to put my old clothes back on. I wandered down the long hall and descended the grand spiral staircase, crossed the soccer-pitch-size foyer and headed down a hallway that led toward what I thought I remembered as the main dining room. Maybe a minute later I heard a voice behind me say, "This way," and I turned. There was an open doorway that I had walked past without noticing. The room I now entered was the open-plan living room and kitchen of the Jansen house—I mean the *actual* set from *Rev Beach,* the plaid couch and recliner and the four-seat Formica table and the red vinyl chairs, even the trompe l'oeil window over the kitchen sink with its view of the sun-kissed gulf—reinstalled here in the bowels of the Travis manse, a grotto of anachronism amid the mysteries of the measureless cavern that was Grace's estate, that was Grace's life.

The appliances functioned. She was microwaving Bagel Bites, which had been prominently product-placed on the show: Will Jansen's favorite, i.e., mine.

"You talk to Shayne?" she said.

"What? No. If this is going to work I need to make my case in person." That almost certainly wasn't true, but if Grace was going to twist my arm about twisting his arm, she was going to foot the bill for me to blow a few days in New York City with my friend. A little reboot for me and him, a prelude to his with her.

"If that's the way you want it," she said. "I'll let Craig know. He'll reschedule your ticket."

"And you'll cover the difference and the change fee."

"Such a hard bargainer," she said. "You want a pass to the sky lounge, too?"

"Sure," I said.

She laughed at me.

"No man of mine waits gateside," she said. "Now sit."

I sat. She brought the microwaved Bagel Bites to the table as I puzzled over her description of me as "her" man. This too could be chalked up to sentimentality if not sarcasm. And yet I felt something kindling, rekindling, between us. I wondered what my life would be now, if I had never left—left her, left here. Dead in a ditch, probably, or rather at the bottom of some canyon after having drunkenly bluffed a hairpin turn once too often, me and six figures' worth of Italian engineering up in smoke. That, or Hank would be her son. He could have two or three siblings. There'd be no Amber. I could have been years into hosting some Travel Channel show—one of those ones where the once-famous kid is a semi-famous adult, and even still sort of hot, so he gets to travel all over the world and go "Oh, wow," while bright-eyed locals ply him with expensive delicacies and swear that he is experiencing authenticity at its most authentic, that he—and his whole camera crew—are really and truly off the beaten path.

Off the Beaten Path with David Crader. Has a ring to it.

Grace could occasionally guest-star. When our kids got old enough, we could give them producer credits.

Could that really have been my life? Could it still be? If this reboot happened, if it went well . . .

But here I was running Grace's lines. I pulled myself out of my reverie and looked at her, said thank you for the food. She had changed into a blouse and jeans, some kind of magisterial house slipper. I would say something more descriptive here, but "blouse" is about the limit of my vocabulary vis-à-vis womenswear. The only other thing I knew for sure was that these items, to a discerning eye, were surely worth the four figures apiece that their designer charged, and that Grace had not paid anything for them. They had been gifts given in the hope of an Instagram cameo. Vain hope, in most cases.

With a blue plastic spatula, she carefully dislodged the Bagel Bites from their silver nuking tray and distributed them equitably across two Pfaltzgraff dinner plates. You know the kind I mean, with the cornflower emblem in the center and the blue ring around the edge. This is what we, what our characters, ate off, all those years ago.

"Is the food vintage as well?" I asked as she set the plates down on the table. "Frozen for decades like the rest of this stuff?"

She took the seat across from mine. "Same basic recipe," she said, "but these are fair trade."

"Trade with who?" I said. "The Bagel Bite farmers?"

So we were flirting now. Maybe I wasn't as fat as I'd felt when I saw myself in that picture.

"Fair trade," she reiterated. "Also totally organic, no preservatives, and high GMO."

"You mean non-GMO, right?"

"Non-GMO is old hat; it's what aging white millennials tweet about from their nursing homes. Gen Z is solution-oriented, poptimistic. Our winery is doing this gamay from grapes we CRISPR'd with bioluminescent jellyfish enzymes. Earthy, big tannins, some fruit on the finish, and it glows the most eerie green when you pour it from the bottle. It's like something out of Harry Potter or one of those magical South American light-up lakes."

"The lakes aren't magic," I said. "They're full of algae. And Harry Potter is canceled, last I heard. Anyway, I don't drink."

"So *I* heard," she said, and I wondered whether we were still flirting. Or if we ever had been. Had Craig Lelyveld given her his intel, or had the empty bottle on my pillow been a message just for me? And why did I care what Grace thought? She was my ex-wife, my dead ex-boss's daughter, ambassador for any number of brands—including, apparently, Bagel Bites—that I did not consume. She was someone whose life had nothing to do with mine, a person to whom I owed nothing and who could ask nothing of me. Except here I was eating dinner with her in a life-size diorama of our shared real-fake past, which she'd had installed in the depths of her lonely mansion. Except that she was asking something of me: to go rope in my old friend to this big dumb project. And what's more, that I was going to do it—for the money, sure, but more than that, because I was lonely and bored and adrift in inclement middle age, and I wanted to spend time with my hot famous friends who had known me and pretended on TV to be my family back when I was hot and famous, too.

I had thought some more about what Grace said about wanting the Lena Dunham treatment. A slightly savvier person might have aspired to Greta Gerwig. Or maybe what was truly savvy about Grace was that she knew she didn't have an era-defining *Little Women* in her. Or she didn't, yet. Which was sad, because we were both past the point where anyone expected precocity of us. Nobody cared how we defined our era anymore, because our era was over.

Poor Grace. I don't say that sarcastically. She'd spent her childhood as a bobblehead doll, her adolescence as a pinup, and the last six years as a lifestyle guru. She was as bored, perhaps, as I was. Maybe *Rev Beach* was her Rosebud, or maybe she thought that it ought to be. This could all be part of some complicated grief for her father. I thought for a moment of my own father, and then of my mother, who lives in Florida, not far from the real town where we'd shot the second season of *Rev Beach*. I would say that there was some irony in that, but there wasn't. She'd met the man who became her second husband while we were living there. And anyway, a lot of people lived in Florida. Corey Burch lived there, too.

"Are you having an internal monologue?" Grace asked me. "Because you haven't said anything in four minutes, and your Bagel Bites are getting cold."

"Oh, just reminiscing," I said, "which I assume was the point of us having dinner here. I can't tell if you're trying to seduce me or just flaunt your power."

"Does it have to be one or the other?" she said.

I didn't know what to say to that and so, as a sort of filibuster, I quickly stuffed a whole Bagel Bite into my mouth. As it turned out, they had not yet begun to get cold, and I felt the skin on the roof of my mouth sear. I managed to chew and swallow, but barely. Grace saw my eyes go big as the fair-trade blaze ravaged my throat. She reached into her pocket. She pulled out a small square box, say half the size of an ALTOIDS tin. It was brushed metal and bore no label save the faint stamp of the Travis family crest on its silver face. She popped it open, plucked something small and white from within.

"Open wide," she said.

I gaped, my mouth still burning. She popped the pill—or mint or lozenge or wherever it was—in, then took my chin in her hand and pushed my jaw shut. A coolness, a vast thrilling chill, swept across my tongue, cheeks, and palate. It was like the rush of spearmint toothpaste but without the mint or the paste. It couldn't have taken two seconds to dissolve.

"What do the GMOs in this one do?" I asked.

"Your burn will heal by morning," she said. "And you'll be able to breathe underwater, but only for about the next hour or so. It depends on your metabolism, so don't push your luck."

"Funny," I said. "My little video game self gets the exact same ability when he takes his power-up. I wonder if you've played."

"I don't game much," she said, "but it's an interesting concept. Craig liked the numbers we ran, so I bought the option."

"On . . . what?" I asked, suspecting I already knew, assuming (which I couldn't) that she was serious.

"All of it," she said. "Film, TV, podcast, and opera. How's that for flaunting my power?"

"Seductive," I said.

"It's good to see you," she said, and got up from the table, leaving the plates where they were.

She walked toward the door. Not the door I'd come in through but one which I had not noticed earlier. She led me down an unfamiliar hallway, narrow and unadorned. For a moment I felt like I was back in the guts of the convention center. Then a featureless panel of wall split like a Star Trek door and we stepped through the opening into a room I knew well. Her bedroom, formerly ours. She had led me like Orpheus leads Eurydice, only Grace hadn't been tempted even momentarily to look back and make sure that I was still there, either because she took it as a given or because she didn't care. Grace was, in her way, a paragon of perfect faith, a true believer. This was another reason I had loved her. Why I perhaps still did.

Precisely what she saw in me, then or now, was obscure to me, but that's because I mostly hate myself. Therapy had taught me to say that plainly, but I was still working out what to do about it. *You are worthy of love,* I thought to myself, as the recessed panel reestablished itself and Grace stepped out of her jeans.

"Yeah, duh," Grace said. "But thanks for clarifying."

"Sorry," I said. "I said the quiet part loud. And I didn't mean you. But I mean of course you are, too. We all are."

"I know you've had a hard time," she said. "I've had a hard time, too. And I know this is random and weird. But can we just, for the next little while, focus on the subject at hand?"

"Yes," I said. The roof of my mouth was atingle—GMO healing? I hoped so. It didn't seem like I was going to bleed when we kissed at least. Maybe the burn hadn't been that bad after all. I pulled off my shirt, hopefully sexily. We met each other in the middle of the room, fumbled and tumbled, familiarly, rebooting. I focused. The subject was at hand.

In the R-rated film version—or the HBO prestige series— you'd get the swelling music and the nude scene now. But Grace has clauses in her contract about this kind of thing, and I (as mentioned earlier) was dealing with my own body-image shit. Suffice it to say, we both had reservations about exposing our mood-lit tits. Skip the nude scene. Draw the decorous curtain. We slept entangled like old times, me in and out of fitful dreams, her like a stone. But I suppose I must have caught some delta waves at some point, because suddenly it was mid-morning and I was in bed alone.

I put my now day-old clothes back on and wandered through the halls of the house, hoping to find the main entryway, from which point I would be able to find the guest bedroom where I had not spent the night, where the recriminatory bottle surely sat undisturbed on my still-fresh pillow and my bag and phone needed retrieving. Gradually, with only a few false starts and one inexplicable dead end into what seemed to be a chapel, I made my way.

When I arrived back at the guest room, I saw several days' worth of clothes had been laid out for me on the bed, and the bottle disposed of, presumably because the house elves didn't have the same inborn hatred of me that Craig Lelyveld did. And next to the clothes, a bottle of high-GMO magic light-up wine. There was an explanatory text message from Grace on my phone, which some thoughtful elf had plugged in for me, either last night or earlier this morning. It was fully charged.

"In meetings all day," the text said. "Sorry can't see you off but you look cute when you're sleeping. Hope the clothes fit, wardrobe did their best not knowing yr current sizes. re last night: fun times but pls dont make weird we have work to do. Craig has your ticket and here's a link to my nyc apartment you can use. It's a secure download of our app. Upload a photo so the front door will recognize you. Give Shayne the wine from me & keep me posted on progress. Sorry for the long text, hope mouth feels better, left u the tin in case u need another boost. Xo"

It was a long text. My mouth did feel better. So much better, in fact, that I wondered whether Grace had been serious about the underwater-breathing thing. Should I pop another power-up, stick my head in the toilet for a test? Better, I thought, to change into the new clothes, which looked very much like the clothes I had worn back in *Rev Beach* days: Bedford cargoes with a drawstring and distressed baggy jeans, long-sleeve polos and plain white T-shirts—I looked, in short, like the 2003 American Eagle back-to-school catalog, but off-brand, because the company had rejected our proposal for product placement, so wardrobe had just aped the style as best they could. Why they had aped it again, in the narrative present, was anyone's guess. Was Grace having a joke at my expense, albeit an elaborate one she would have had to have started planning days if not weeks ago, which would have required her knowing in advance that I would come here and how the whole night would go, which, if that was the case— I couldn't finish the thought. And if not, then did she truly believe that the grown adults of the *Rev Beach* reboot would dress the way that they had as teenagers, that the whole world of the show would be frozen in time, or out of time, timeless, like a David Lynch fifties thing but for the early aughts?

Probably the simplest answer was the right one: somewhere in the measureless cavern of this mansion was a room full of fashionistas and data quants who had determined that baggy pants and ring tees with faded numbers across the chest were due to come back in style, just like mustaches and Hawaiian shirts had. And so *Rev Beach* would get in on the trend, perhaps help set it. Think of the branding opportunities, the tie-in deals. Surely American Eagle, if they still existed, wouldn't reject us this time round. But then again, we hardly needed them. Grace had her own line at the store that my mother still thought it was funny to call Tar-jay.

I put on one of the long-sleeve polos, opted for the distressed jeans because I wasn't ready to be so fashion-forward as to attempt to bring back drawstring cargo pants. Despite their bagginess through the legs and rear, the jeans required a little gut-suck to get the button shut. That didn't help with my overall self-image, but I un-sucked as they settled and it seemed okay. There was something stretchy woven into the waistband; elastic probably, or fibers of the muscle that allows a boa constrictor to swallow a dog. Were the jeans pro-GMO like the wine and the Bagel Bites? No telling. But it wasn't going to be a full day of suck-in, and for that I was grateful, because I had a cross-country flight ahead of me, which probably meant more deep retrospection, and then there was the task that awaited me in the city, the enticement of Shayne Glade, who would be actively hostile to all the things about *Rev Beach* that I was merely ambivalent about, and unlike me did not need money or to be in Grace's good graces, where I thought it would be nice to wake up again someday, like tomorrow—and tomorrow and tomorrow and tomorrow until the last syllable of recorded time.

But, of course, I only knew this snatch of the Macbeth soliloquy because "the big school play" had been a plot point in a very special Halloween episode of *Rev Beach*. I couldn't have told you the next line, or who said it, or why. And Grace had warned me to not make things weird. I could manage that much, couldn't I? I thought so. I wanted to think so. If you will it, it is no dream, as John Goodman once said.

No airplane drinks today.

I did not stick my head in the toilet to test the underwater-breathing pills. I packed my new clothes and the wine into my bag, which was now bulging. I'd text Shayne today, try to see him tomorrow. And I hoped that my flight wasn't too early, because now that I'd spent the night in LA there was an errand I wanted to run before I left. A visit I wanted, maybe needed, to pay, in order to fortify myself for the task that lay ahead.

Lelyveld was waiting at the front door. "There's an Uber outside," he said.

"You mean I don't get the pleasure of your company again?"

"It's a weekday," he said. "And some of us, believe it or not, Mr. Crader, have jobs."

"Just give me what Grace left for me," I said.

He handed over the ticket. I eyed the flight itinerary.

"She made sure there's time," Craig said. "Just don't dawdle."

"How did she know?" I stammered. Then: "Of course she knew." It was, I thought, the most frightening thing in this world, to know somebody and be known in turn. To be fully comprehended and made plain to them, for them to read you like a book and upon completion say, "Yeah, that book was good; I'd read it again; I won't put it in the box that's going to Goodwill—I'd rather have it here." To be accepted for all that you were, all that I was—ex-addict, ex-husband, occasional lover, once and future colleague. I could have wept and, in fact, was about to start.

"Save your weeping for your Uber," Lelyveld said. "And quit burning daylight." He walked off down yet another hallway. I stepped outside into the California morning, reminded by Craig's parting comment that I had no idea what the status of the fires was. Contained, I guessed, if the planes were flying again. The wind had blown most of the ash off the front steps of the mansion. The sky seemed an okay color, a little hazy, but nothing like the doom vibes of the day before. One more apocalypse averted, then. Or at least avoided. Or at least, as per usual, avoided by me.

I climbed into the back seat of my idling Uber.

"They gave you the address?" I asked the driver, and he read it back to me for confirmation, and sure enough, Grace had known where I needed to go. The driver eased out of the turnaround and onto the long private drive. He hit the nav start button, told me about my options as far as AC and radio, directed my attention to the water bottle and KIND bar in the seatback pocket, to which I should help myself. He told me about how important it is for guys like him to get five-star ratings so if I felt like his service was good to please be sure and et cetera. It wasn't until we had to stop and wait for the front gate to retract itself that he glanced into the rearview mirror and saw me—I mean really saw me.

"Oh snap," he said. "It's you."

Down here, far from the hills, the scent of smoke from yesterday's fires was more pronounced. Yesterday's fires, I should say, were also today's fires; contained, per the NPR app, but not extinguished. I stood on the sidewalk where the driver had dropped me, at the front gate of an apartment complex: Rising Star Estates, medium- and long-term rentals, mostly studios and singles, a few two-bedrooms.

When I say "gate" I mean "archway." No obstacle stood between me and the Rising Star parking lot.

I had lived here once. So had a lot of people, and that wasn't the only way that Rising Star was like Florida. It was a place that drew dreamers and scammers in equal measure, ambitious wide-eyed neophytes and cynical last-ditch low-lifes. Our parents were all these things, one or the other or each in turn. As for us, well, we were kids. Children. We did what was asked of us, what was begged or demanded. We did what we thought we wanted to do, what we were told we were born for. Me and Shayne met here. Corey, too. Once upon a time, we were all rising stars.

A dry wind blew grit across the asphalt as I walked through the Rising Star parking lot, crossed over onto the fresh-cut grass, still agleam from having been watered that morning. There was a big central lawn with low-rise apartment blocks on three of its four sides. There was a playground for the young kids, some barbecues set up, trees here and there. Around the back of Building C, I knew, was a tennis court, and behind B there was a pool. Building A had the multipurpose center: classroom, playhouse, concert hall, birthday party venue. It was a big empty room you could rent by the hour or half day. It was whatever you wanted, provided that what you wanted involved folding chairs, card tables, and a modest PA system to which no more than two microphones could be attached. Sometimes auditions were held there.

I was headed for the western sycamore. It was a big old proud tree, older than the apartment complex, older than Hollywood. Kids climbed it. Shayne had been sitting on one of its long sturdy limbs the first time I met him. My folks and I had just moved in. They were getting the apartment set up and had encouraged me to take a walk around the grounds. Get used to the place and out of their hair for a while. They kept telling me how great things were going to be, how much better than Portland, all the opportunity that awaited us.

I thought it was bright, hot, and boring. I crossed beneath the tree branch (in the flashback, I mean) and Shayne called down to me: "Hey, kid!"

I looked up and there he was, in OshKosh shorts with his hair slicked back and a blue-and-white-striped T-shirt with ringed sleeves and collar. He was wearing sandals and holding a Game Boy. I was ten, he was eleven.

"Can you catch this?" he said. "I need to get down." He meant the Game Boy.

"I don't know," I said.

"Here, try this," he said, and let a sandal drop from a foot. I snagged it, held it high so he could see.

"You want to try again to be sure," he said, "or are you ready?"

"I don't know," I said.

"Well, decide," he said. "My dad says being decisive is more important than being right."

"I just don't want to break your Game Boy."

"I just want to get out of this tree."

"Okay," I said, and as soon as he heard me say it—or, maybe, before he heard me—he had let go of the Game Boy and it was falling through the air. I felt my fingers touch the smooth plastic. It was a hot day (not as hot as today), and my hands were slick with sweat, and I was sure I was going to drop it, but I didn't. I bobbled a bit but finally caught it and held the thing up triumphantly so Shayne could see. He flashed a grin, gave me a thumbs-up. And then he jumped.

It couldn't have been a ten-foot drop, so there was no real risk of him hurting himself. He landed cleanly, then dove forward into a tuck and roll for show. When he had stood up and brushed himself off, he found me still standing there, not dumbfounded exactly, but certainly impressed. He was taller than I was, prettier. I understood immediately that he would be my competition, that we would want all the same things and most of the time only one of us would get them. That we would eye each other from across crowded waiting rooms, each pretending not to notice that the other was there. But maybe, I thought, we could still come play by this tree sometime, be friends in real life if not in that other. I was already a little bit in love with him. He had that effect on people. I didn't and don't. Only Grace Travis ever really liked me just the way I was.

Rising Star was a desperate place, bloodthirsty and cheerful, an extended-stay hotel full of kids who could sing and tap-dance and launch into monologues at the drop of a hat, watched over by groups of mothers on second mortgages who traded tips about talent agents and drank white wine all afternoon.

Us kids came in types: wannabe beauty queens, fat freckled redheads bound for comic relief and/or very special episodes about bullying. I quickly learned how to see through the particular kid to the type of kid he was, which begs the question—I can feel you wanting to ask it—what type of kid was I? But you already know the answer to that; you just want to hear me say it.

I was on the slight side, short but not a pipsqueak, with green eyes and light brown hair that was almost blond after a day in the sun. America's fantasy of American boyhood: Smalls in *The Sandlot*, Gordie LaChance in *Stand By Me*, Dawson in

Dawson's Creek. Will Jansen of the Jansen boys of *Rev Beach.*
I was the boy the country wanted to believe it had been when
it was young, or had grown up next door to, or might have for
a son of its own someday. Nostalgia blurring into promise, as
the future blurs into the past. And I too aspired to be this boy,
to achieve my archetype, to find the me-shaped doorway and
walk through it.

Some families ran out of money. Some kids lost interest in
the work (and had parents who actually listened to them).
Some missed their siblings back home, the father who had
stayed behind to foot the bills. Because it was mostly moms
who came to stage-parent. There were only a handful of men
in the whole complex. Married couples were vanishingly rare.
All kinds of plans put on hiatus, families risked and shattered,
for the sake of dreams such as these.

I remember how the quitters, the failures, would say their
tearful goodbyes to those of us who were staying. They always
listed their reasons; they wanted to be validated and consoled.
But our sympathy was chilly. We kept our bon voyages brief,
stood stiffly in the grip of farewell hugs, afraid their loser mojo
would rub off.

I include myself in the "we" because I behaved the way I
was expected to, the way I wished I really felt and sometimes
did. There was a part of me that loved what I was doing, the
hunger and drive of it, the feeling that my parents needed
me—needed me to be good enough, and to keep getting better, bigger. Everything was riding on this, on me, or it seemed
to be. I squashed down that part of myself that would have

been relieved to be in the back seat of any of those station wagons, surrounded by battered suitcases, headed home.

Some people, when they left, didn't say goodbye at all. They disappeared into the first light of morning and were gone. You'd amble over to unit 3b or whichever it was, looking for Kylie or Dustin or Justin or Brooklynne, and you'd see through the front blinds that it was empty. Not empty of furniture, obviously—that the places came furnished was half their allure—but of personal effects and human energy. The way a vacated hospital bed or prison cell announces its emptiness to the world. Somebody else would show up later that same day and fill the space.

Is this enough origin myth for the moment? It's going to have to be. Shayne and I became friends. We did a few commercials together, a play. Our families moved out of Rising Star as soon as we were able to afford better, and we saw less of each other after that, but we stayed friends. Years went by. When we went up against each other for a part, I always lost. He woke up one day a young heartthrob, a regular *Teen Beat* pinup, whereas I was just a slim kid getting taller but not quite tall enough, good at memorizing lines but a little less good at carrying a scene. I wasn't your leading man, but I wasn't your Screech, either. I wasn't your fat kid. I grew into the faithful sidekick, the best friend. Which is another way of saying the also-ran.

They cast him on *Rev Beach*, the same part I'd read for. Hadn't even gotten a callback. But they were trying to build an ensemble for their *Buffy/Dawson's* knockoff dramedy, and they were struggling to find the ensemble. They had all their rubber monster suits ready to go and no teens to run screaming through the night. Shayne suggested me for the second billing, his half brother and sometimes rival—but ultimately, of course, best friend. That part, I could read for. I got my offer on the spot.

Corey Burch was, as Molly Webster so succinctly and cruelly put it in her explainer, our Designated Fat Kid. Jerry O'Connell in *Stand By Me* or Jeff Cohen in *The Goonies*. You get it. His casting, as it happens, had come at my recommendation.

Rising Star was always bugging its successful alums to come back and visit with its current residents. Our existence was proof that this wasn't all pipe dreams. That these lives were possible: we were living them. I didn't have much interest in showing myself off because I wasn't sure that what I did, who I was, amounted to much, but Shayne took an outsize pride in his achievements. This was before *Rev Beach*. We were still just sparkly tweens doing one-offs on Nickelodeon sitcoms, maybe a TGIF show if we were lucky, two minutes of screen time in some movie, five lines total. We were the kid who finds the body in the cold open and then is never seen again, because the movie isn't about the kid or the body. It's about the harried cop.

But that was plenty for Rising Star. They wanted us. I thought it sounded like homework, but Shayne said we should go and so we did.

Corey was funny. We would have been about fourteen then, so he'd have been twelve. Puberty hadn't touched him. He was big-boned, round-faced, and shameless. By this last what I mean is that his entire life was shame. His parents hounded him about his weight, his peers ignored or bullied him, casting agents asked him to do the Truffle Shuffle. His life was miserable. His shame was so pervasive and unrelenting he didn't question it anymore. I almost said he didn't even feel it anymore, but I'm sure that isn't true. The upshot was that he would do anything, say anything, to get a laugh. To get a dose of approval. Three minutes of relief from the misery of being himself. Remember that I am speaking from the narrative present, years of hard personal experience as well as the public record and Corey's self-published autobiography, which I've read. It's slanderous, pornographic, obsessive, deranged—in short, a fan fiction or RPF. (That stands for "real-people fiction," the most cursed corner of AO3, which you're welcome to google if you want to, but I'm not going to say another word about.) His book was an act of revenge for a whole host of imaginary outrages, and the one thing that isn't in there is the one thing I actually feel guilty over, which is how I know he doesn't know it happened.

Still not gonna talk about that. Not yet.

So David Crader and Shayne Glade made their mission of mercy to Rising Star. We spent an afternoon in the multipurpose center, told our war stories, gave sage advice, watched the kids do their bits. Dance steps, monologues, light judo, a magic trick. We offered feedback and encouragement. Afterward there was cake and bug juice. Some dumbshit who at the time thought he was hot stuff because he'd booked a spot for Frosted Flakes or something, dared Corey to smash his face in the cake, which had been left unattended on a card table.

"Ten bucks says you won't," Dumbshit dared.

"You don't have ten bucks," Corey said.

"Do it and see," Dumbshit said.

Me and Shayne were listening in, drifting closer. This was interesting.

"I don't think you should do it," Shayne said. "For the record. But if you do, I'll put twenty on top of this kid's ten."

"Twenty from me, too," I said. We had the money, and they knew it.

"Sold," Corey said, and his face was in the cake even faster than Shayne had jumped out of the tree.

In his memoir, Corey claims we stiffed him. That isn't true. We gave him the twenties we'd promised, plus we covered Dumbshit's ten. But Corey also says that he got in massive trouble with the Rising Star people for "setting a bad example in front of the special guests," e.g., us, and that the staff reported him to his parents and his dad beat the hell out of him for making a scene. I'm sure that part is true. Corey had it hard. But his parents should have praised him for his effort. We thought it was about the funniest thing we'd ever seen, him getting led out of the room by an irate assistant manager, frosting smeared across his face, weighing down his ringlet curls, grinning like an idiot, like a champion, our money tight in his fist. Shayne and I laughed about it the whole ride home. We never forgot him. When *Rev Beach* came around, and when we had everyone but our buffoon, I told Ty Travis about Corey Burch, who at that point we hadn't laid eyes on in over a year. Shayne backed me up. Even though I barely knew Corey, I wanted to do something for him like what Shayne had done for me. "If he's still around," we said, "you should at least try to see him." And he was still around, still an unknown, still sleeping on the foldout couch in the living room of the one-bedroom his parents were still renting at Rising Star.

So sue me, I did some more origin myth after all. Well, what else had I come here for, if not to make this journey to the past? I was grateful to be thinking about these guys, because it meant I wasn't dwelling on my own parents, which is usually what I did when I came here. Brood on my fractured family, how alone I feel, and how that's probably why I drink—drank—and why I rushed headlong into, and then out of, not one but two marriages. Why I thought about my son constantly but was terrified whenever I was in his company, as though protracted exposure to me would somehow ruin him. Had I ruined Corey's life? Did Shayne still care about me? Enough to help me do this thing for Grace? And what did she really want to reboot *Rev Beach* for? And what did I want, other than to feel needed by her? Hadn't she played me like a fiddle, making the Shayne thing into my problem, knowing that the only feeling I craved more strongly than oblivion was that of being needed?

These were questions I couldn't answer, wasn't sure I wanted answered. But whatever matrix of motive had brought me here, there was one purely pragmatic reason why I had come. A plot device, if you will, meant to move the story forward and set up act 2.

I took a selfie in the shade of the western sycamore, Shayne's long sturdy limb looming above me. I texted it to him.

"Good old days," I wrote.

"Two truths and a lie," he replied a few minutes later, by which point I was in an Uber headed for LAX.

"Wait, which is the lie?" I replied, not taking the bait. "That the days are old or that they were days?"

He didn't answer. I told him I'd be in the city. We made some arrangements. That settled, I pulled up Molly Webster's article, read it a second time. I noticed that the header image had been updated: no longer the *Rev Beach* screencap meme of Shayne. The latest iteration of "me/my anxiety" was yesterday's photo of me climbing into Grace's champagne Audi.

Given my ambivalence re: social media, as well as my fragile emotional state (sex with ex, threat of reboot, lure of fortune, fragile sobriety, reexposure to origin myth) you'd think that the last thing I'd have wanted was to be the subject of the internet's attention. White Helvetica slapped across the hood of the car as well as across my ass. (Lelyveld, true to form, had escaped capture, was invisible behind the tinted windows, behind the wheel.) So this was the new fame. Was I ready for it? I figured I had better get ready fast.

And yet for all that, I found Molly's essay soothing. Not least because it was billed as an "explainer." Some people don't like having their own lives explained to them. Me? I'd rarely wanted anything more.

As promised, my plane ticket came with access to the sky lounge, so that's where I went. I fixed myself a salad from the salad bar, a simple Caesar, light on the dressing, extra grilled chicken for the protein. I was going to start getting in shape, I thought. I was going to lean into this renewed-fame thing.

And to lean into it, I was going to get lean. I reached for the apple juice, thought better of the sugar, got grapefruit instead. I wondered if anyone in the sky lounge had noticed me. I was happy they hadn't, but also sort of wished someone would. There was a kid about my son's age sitting by himself playing a Switch, and I walked to a table on the other side of him, hoping to steal a glance at the game to see if it might be mine. It wasn't, which was fine, really. He was young for that anyway.

I ate my food, went back for seconds. Little more dressing this time, less chicken. A bit of pasta salad, for fortification. And a single sparerib from the steam tray, as a treat. I wiped my mouth, bused my own plate, looked at my half-finished grapefruit juice and wished for gin. The bar was right there. But I held myself firm. I was still doing my responsibility thing, and I was saving my daily allowance for the flight.

"How's it going?" I texted Amber. "Hank feeling better?"

She didn't answer right away, but that was nothing unusual. She was a busy single mother with an aging mother of her own to look after. Also, she didn't like me very much. I finished my grapefruit juice. They called my flight.

I settled into my seat, slid the window shade up so that when we lifted off I would see the glittering city and—if possible— the last of the fires. I wondered if I'd be able to tell the lights from the flames.

That was a stupid thing to say. It just felt, I don't know, poetic. What do you want from me? It had been a long day already, and I was sipping Scotch from a plastic cup, facing down six hours of uninterrupted flashback that, again, you'd think would have been about the guy I was going to see, but no. My text to Amber had still not been acknowledged, so it was with some reluctance that I honored my own policy of total in-flight disconnection and shut off my phone. I wanted to hear about Henry, but it was Amber herself I was thinking about. Our past, and hers before me, and by extension mine before her, i.e., with Grace. Shayne was in my immediate future, but he hardly bore thinking about. Shayne was Shayne, and we would deal with each other. We'd catch up, bro down. One way or another, I felt confident that we would come to terms.

Amber, then. In most ways a minor character, disconnected from the primary cast, more an element of my backstory than a character in her own right. But if there's one thing to be said in favor of television, I mean versus the movies, it's that the economies and pacing of TV allows for all kinds of sidetracks and cul-de-sacs that film doesn't. A film is sleek at ninety minutes, muscular at one hundred and twenty. Anything beyond that is Scorsese, bloat, or both. I know what you're going to say: *Stalker, Sátántangó, 2001*. Well, with all due respect, those movies are boring. They're genius, but they're boring. You haven't watched them since you were in college, and if you're being totally honest, you're not sure you've ever stayed awake through the middle hour of *2001*. Movies are like poems. You're supposed to experience them in a single sitting, then let them rattle around in your mind long after. TV is like reading a novel, or playing a video game, or having a roommate. It's this thing that's going to be around for a while. It always wants to keep going—to be more, to give more, to tell more. There's room for nooks and crannies. Bottle episodes. Winking callbacks across baffled time, like Amy Madison stuck as a rat for a whole season of *Buffy* or that one half-second shot of Superintendent Rawls in the crowd at the gay bar in *The Wire.*

I received my second Scotch and a minute later the flight departed. If the fires were visible from the plane, I couldn't distinguish them from the glow of the city, so maybe what I'd said hadn't been so stupid after all, or maybe they'd just finally been put out. I savored the smokiness of the Scotch, glad that it wasn't the smoke of acres of wilderness burning. Also, I wished it was gin. But that was a line I still wasn't crossing, so I took another swallow and slid the window shade down and settled in for a protracted flashback, Amber's bottle episode, something mostly self-contained that would nevertheless intrigue and provoke, and in its sidelong way serve to deepen the themes of the primary story, the A plot. If this went well, if people liked it, if Amber proved she could carry a lead, maybe a spin-off would be worth considering, or at least a bigger role in season 2. And if not, well, it would be a one-shot deal like the Brian Krakow episode of *My So-Called Life.* If absolutely nothing else, it would fill the time otherwise occupied by a static image of me half awake, sucking the dregs of the Scotch from the last of the ice cubes, six hours from Los Angeles to New York—just long enough, if you'd rather, to watch *Stalker* twice or *Sátántangó* once.

But we both know you wouldn't rather.

You want to fix yourself a drink to match mine, slide into your optimal couch slouch . . .

And watch this.

Amber's Bottle Episode

Amber grew up in the part of Portland that they used to call Felony Flats, where now there were bike lanes and vegan patisseries, a pan-Hispanic food cart pod with a robust Instagram presence, pour-over coffee shops on opposite corners of any given intersection. Every major pizza style was represented: New York, Chicago, Sicily, Naples, Detroit. All of it artisan, organic, and fair trade.

One thing about the bad old days was you could actually own a house. Little cinder-block number with a chain-link fence and postage-stamp yard went for twenty grand. Even someone with credit like Amber's mother could get a mortgage. The monthly payment would have been peanuts. Even after Amber's dad left (she was two years old) Nancy eked out the payments, hung on to the place. Nancy's philosophy was that as long as you owned the roof over your head and the ground under your feet, there was a limit to how much the world could fuck you over.

She waited tables and picked up night shifts cleaning offices downtown. She saw the sun rise from the fortieth floor of the U.S. Bancorp Tower. Big Pink, people called it. Tallest building in Portland at the time. Second tallest these days, which isn't bad considering downtown is choked

with tall buildings now; they shot up like weeds one night
when nobody was paying attention in 2015. But the pink is
distinct at least, even if some find it garish, tacky, disruptive.
Disrupting what, exactly? The latter-day tendency toward
Apple store austerity, this sans serif architecture that turned
the cityscape into acres of dull steel and polarized glass? A
long wall of freshman dorms is what it looks like, and maybe
I'm a little touchy about that because I never went to college,
but then again, maybe it just looks cheap. But the pink of
Big Pink is Spanish granite quarried special, windows tinted
to match. On a sunny day—and despite what you've heard,
we do have some of those—Big Pink shines like a new
penny. It's funny to think that this ugly artifact of the
corporate fever dream eighties is now helping to Keep
Portland Weird.

Where was Amber while Nancy was working nights?
Home alone with a box of Kraft and strict instructions,
mostly followed: wash your dishes after dinner and double-
check the stove is off; an hour of TV (she knew this really
meant two hours) as long as your homework's done; brush
your teeth and be in bed by eight thirty (this meant ten);
don't ever answer the door—I don't care who it is—and don't
ever not answer the phone, because it might be me. Amber
was seven, eight, nine years old.

Amber remembered the squeaky hitch on the front gate
of the chain fence, how it would wake her and she'd pretend
to be asleep because here came Mom to check up, to adjust
the tuck of the blanket and kiss her cheek. Leaving a young
daughter home alone wasn't Nancy at her best, sure, but
as Nancy herself often said: I'm not trying to get mother of

the year, I'm trying to get to the end of the month. And they always made it, somehow. Whatever else you might say about Nancy's parenting style, you had to give her that.

Nancy was careful about having men over at the house. Men were broody and unpredictable. And yet it felt good to have someone to cook for, especially someone who would really eat, unlike the picky wispish daughter who lived on boxes of Kraft and—because Nancy, who really was trying, insisted—the honest vitamins and fiber from two or three celery sticks, their gutters grouted in peanut butter and dotted with raisins: ants on a log, just like Amber makes for Hank now.

Fudgesicle for dessert, but only if you promise to shower and put on pajamas without dillydallying, because tomorrow's going to be another long day.

They were all long days.

And yet it could be special to lengthen such a day, for Nancy to extend her sense of labor to include the grocery store, the stove and oven, the soapy sink. To do this for a man who worked with his hands all day, laid tile or moved furniture, or maybe only stood around the shoe store at the Lloyd Center, sold sneakers to athletes despite having never broken a sweat in his life. (He swore he'd once fitted a young Tonya Harding for a pair of Air Jordans.) Even a man such as this was still a man, which meant that when he went for dinner at his girl's house, he showed up hungry, praised the preparation, and asked for seconds. He radiated gruff warm approval but probably forgot to ever actually say thank you.

Pork chops in apple cider brine, her own mother's recipe. Rib roast and potatoes, maybe with sweet carrots on the side. Three-cheese lasagna. Even something as simple as scrambled eggs, the mornings after those rarer and rarer nights when the men were invited to stay.

It felt good to cook, to serve, to nourish. Provided of course it was a week when you could afford the ingredients, had the time to do the shopping and get home to do the prep and the preheat and all of that. A few fat tips at the diner, or an extra shift of office-cleaning might mean miso-glazed salmon, the most exotic dish Nancy knew how to cook and which for Amber, kid palate notwithstanding, constituted the most coveted delicacy known to humankind. It was something unheard of in Felony Flats in the 1990s. Who even stocked miso? The girl at the Fred Meyer would look at you cross-eyed if you asked her. You had to go to Chinatown for a thing like that.

Miso-glazed salmon still had, for Amber, a Proustian quality. It was the recipe we'd been trying to re-create the night we almost died.

Another thing Nancy liked about men: they were without secrets. Oh sure, they lied and cheated, but that wasn't what she meant. She meant the small light of desire glowing like mellow coals in the braziers of their sated gazes. The way the tilt of a rocks glass in a hairy hand contained the half-fantastic hope of a reciprocated orgasm. How she'd bury her face in the pillow so her daughter wouldn't wake confused to her mother's cries.

The men wiped their plates, but did they help with the dishes? They pushed their chairs from the table, stretched their arms and scratched their bellies, sauntered to the living room. They took the good spot on the couch, spread their legs wide, turned the TV to the news or a football game, maybe flipped annoyingly back and forth. They made offhand remarks about Amber: that she needed more discipline, that Nancy coddled her. Which was maybe true, but who had asked them? And Nancy felt that if there were certain ways in which Amber was coddled, there were other ways in which she was anything but (double-check the stove is off, never answer the door) so it all evened out or got pretty close. That was what Nancy believed or hoped, that a greater balance was being achieved beneath the surface-level chaos and that they were living something like a normal life.

Nine, ten, eleven years old. Amber coming out of her room to say good night, freshly showered and smiling brightly in pink cotton unicorn pajamas or maybe shorts and a T-shirt, and the men let out a low whistle and said, "When that girl grows up, Nance, she'll be dangerous." And Nancy thought, *To who?* Maybe no more men sleeping over the house. Maybe no more men for dinner. It was a loss, but manageable: hardly a disaster. She missed having her hot food gobbled up in platefuls. She missed large arms around her middle on a chilly night. But in that greater balance, worth it. Men didn't wash dishes. They eyed your daughter funny over their fourth beers. They wouldn't watch your TV programs. They took sports losses personally and forgot to put the toilet seat down and before the night was over they wanted you to get on your aching knees and put their thing in your mouth. They said they couldn't sleep otherwise. Slightest undertone of aggression beneath the spoiled-boy pleading. The barest suggestion of a threat, which they maybe knew and maybe didn't know was hard-wired into the set of their stance, the tone they took, that small light from earlier now a full-blown blaze in greedy eyes.

It was a loss but not an insurmountable loss. A sadness but not a sorrow. Nancy already mostly slept alone, and slept fine. Who wouldn't? A day like she'd had, and another day like it tomorrow, and tomorrow, and tomorrow, and tomorrow.

Amber grew up. Overnight, it seemed to Nancy: a new body for her fourteenth birthday. Male classmates no longer capable of eye contact, and girls spreading rumors from the very first day of eighth grade. All because she'd worn her favorite dress to school without realizing what the three inches she grew over the summer had done to her hemline. Something her mother would have told her if she hadn't already left for work by the time Amber got up. (Or, also possible, wasn't quite home yet from wherever she'd been.) The math teacher stole glances at her tightly crossed thighs beneath her desk. An involuntary reflex action, she sensed, or hoped. Mostly involuntary. By the end of class her feet were throbbing with pins and needles because she'd been afraid to uncross her legs and recross them, afraid of putting on a show. She made a mental note: blue jeans and the back row from here on out. But it didn't matter. Talk had already started. Ghost touches, clammy and anonymous, in the hallways and the lunch line. By the end of the day, her fate had been sealed.

So she became who they wanted her to be, what they said she was. She did what she could to protect her mother from what was happening, because Nancy had problems of her own. Long-suffering Nancy with her Virginia Slims and graying hair, no man around in how long now, drinking more than she had used to—enough that she herself was no longer quite keeping track of it (*Did I buy this bottle Monday or Wednesday? Who remembers?*), which made it hard to confirm her suspicions about whether and how deeply her daughter was dipping into her supply.

The first time Nancy caught Amber with pot, she confiscated the joint and flushed it down the toilet. The second time, she smoked it alone in the bath. The message was less "just say no" than it was "remember who's in charge here."

One cool thing about being a girl was you never paid for pot or booze anyway. Never paid for anything really. You just asked for what you wanted or hung around until someone offered. It didn't take long. A hot girl all fucked up was a roulette wheel. She might do anything. Who wouldn't want to be the one to get her there?

The trick was to stay attuned to the vibe of the party, the undertone of the hangout. To know the essential yet unrevealed thing. You had to sense the hidden world pulsing beneath the surface world.

A good time to leave was when there were four or five people left, and ideally at least one other girl, because if it got down below that number you could find yourself left alone with one or two guys who felt they were maybe owed something. You were a cereal box with a prize inside. A gift about to be unwrapped roughly from its paper. Which, you know, was fine sometimes, even the goal sometimes, but not always. So you had to keep yourself attuned, with an eye on the door and a hand on your drink. You had to be able to see around the corners of the night.

Amber's burdens were the same as any other girl's, only scaled to mythical scope by what was said of her, truth and rumor swirling in the snow globe of high school. The way she moved through a room or sprawled out on a couch. Lip gloss sheen and I-dare-you eyes. Sophomore year, summer school, junior year. She conspired with her enemies in the construction of her image, struck a rock star pose in the backlit nimbus of her slut-goddess status, because this form of higher dying felt like fame—or it could for a while—and what else did she have? In what other circumstance would a small-boned girl from Felony Flats be invited to a party in a million-dollar mansion nestled in Kings Heights?

You know that lame Everclear song from '97, the one that starts, "Here is the money that I owe you" and has the line about "Welfare Christmas" and in the chorus the whiny blond guy sings, "I will buy you that big house / Way up in the West Hills"?

These were those hills.

At first light she slipped out of the bed of the boy whose parents hadn't been home in weeks—they were in Tahoe, or maybe Switzerland—and padded through the empty house to stand at the enormous window that took up a whole wall of the sunken living room. She looked out over downtown and saw the first stirs of morning life, buses and vagrants, and Big Pink caught the sunrise and she wondered if her mother was still in there, or on her way home by now, assuming of course that she'd been there last night at all. Amber should go home, too. She knew the bus schedule. But maybe if she was patient the boy would wake up. She could offer to make breakfast. Maybe he would offer her a ride.

After high school, Amber held jobs like the ones her mother had, only she couldn't hold them. She called in sick a lot, and when she did work, especially if it was a closing shift, the cash drawer would sometimes come up short. Rarely enough to provoke a thorough inquiry, just enough to raise an eyebrow and leave a sour taste. She eked out an associate's degree—business management, of all things—at Portland Community College, and was supposedly going to matriculate to Portland State, but the paperwork was a hassle, and though it was cheap it wasn't free. She decided to wait.

This guy she was sort of seeing wanted to go to some two-day hippie concert up at the Gorge in Washington. He didn't care about the music but needed to unload some weak coke he'd gotten tricked into buying; it would have been an insult to sell this stuff to his regulars. Amber's job was to keep him company on the drive and, when they made it to the parking lot, help draw customers. She was wearing a tie-dyed tank top and a pair of jeans shorts with the legs cut so high that the pockets hung out. The skimpiness was normal for her— but the style? It might as well have been Halloween.

An ocean of ponchos and corduroy, bucket hats and serapes. What you do is pick out a guy walking by with a girl. Get his attention. And then right as the girlfriend's starting to get pissed, you throw them both a curveball by talking to her instead of him: compliment her headband or her

sandals or her skirt, that part doesn't matter. Just ignore him
a minute, then casually ask if there's anything they need for
tonight, because my boyfriend's got extra and we don't want
to drive back through Idaho with it. Oh, where you in from?
Cool, cool. Yeah, all we want is to get back what we paid.

One dude who wanted a gram was flying solo that night.
He was from Virginia originally, was supposed to have met
his friends there but they bailed so he had this pair of extra
tickets, which for some reason he was not trying to trade for
coke. Amber had assumed that barter was the point of the
story, but no, he paid cash on the barrelhead and then gave
them the tickets anyway. An unrelated matter. "Miracles" he
called them, which Amber learned later was hippie-speak
for "free tickets." Because there was this whole hidden world
here, this traveling gypsy circus, where money and material
things simply didn't figure. That was the dream these people
had managed to make real.

The problem with the dream was that it didn't work and
it wasn't true. Money was still the fuel in the tank of the
system, and most people didn't have nearly enough of it. In
that regard, Amber came to realize, this hidden world was
a lot like the visible one. The worlds were not opposites or
inversions. It was rather that the surface world was hollow
and there was this smaller one spinning within it, and the
funny thing was that the world within the world had a
hollow center, too. It was the empty stage and venue, all
those aisles and rows and the thousands of chairs bolted
into the buffed concrete of the sloped floor. Money was what
filled it with bodies and music, light and heat and noise. You

could curse money or you could say money was a curse, but
money brought the night to life. It was less true to say that
money fueled the dream world than it would have been to
say that all this was a dream that money itself was having:
money's dream of self-transcendence, of a utopia in which it
could shed its identity like an old dead skin. But nobody said
this or anything like it. They spoke in terms of community,
the gift economy, the temporary autonomous zone, while
in shadow and shame they did what they had to do. And
yet, however compromised this hidden world was, it still
contained a spark of goodness carried in the hollow reed
of human kindness, of solidarity and the will to slip free—
however briefly—from Moloch's silver claws.

The greatest miracle in the hidden world was simple.
Anyone could receive or bestow it. You gave when you had
and took when you needed. The sacrament of this secret
world was a free ticket to that night's show.

Amber's boyfriend didn't care about any of that. He turned
around and sold his miracle for twice face value, a sacrilege,
and retreated to the car. But Amber was curious, so she kept
hers and went inside. She ended up high on mushrooms near
the stage, ran into the guy from earlier, the Virginian, who
was—as her boyfriend had predicted—himself way too high
to notice how crappy the coke was. By the time she got back
to the car, it was gone, which in principle was pretty enraging
but in real life didn't matter because she'd only swung by
to say goodbye. To say goodbye to the guy and to real life
itself, so-called, or to redefine what those words—"real" and
"life"—were allowed to mean. There was a nitrous tank going,

and the Virginian had offered her the middle bench of his Microbus to sleep on. He slept on the back bench and didn't try to touch her until she reached over and touched him first. Tomorrow morning she'd work on tomorrow night's ticket. It was a world of miracles, of abounding grace.

While Amber was hitting the road with the Virginian, Grace and I were at our house, newly married and free of *Rev Beach*, the world still seeming like our oyster. I like to imagine this as a split screen, even if it isn't strictly true. I mean, the dates match, but they may not match exactly: check Wikipedia if you've really got to know.

Grace is reading Eve Babitz in a chaise by the pool, and I'm in the water, adrift on an inflatable chaise of my own, rattling my glass to shake loose any stray vodka particles hiding in the ice. She's dog-earing pages and talking to herself—biopic, no, no, limited series. But it couldn't be network, could it? Maybe Showtime would bite.

And so these were the days of our lives, even as Amber was crisscrossing the country, giving and receiving miracles, perfecting her hemp bracelet weave and her burrito fold, following whoever was touring, her life as large as the skyline and as small as the Microbus, which she inherited from the Virginian when, after about a year together, he decided it was time to go home.

"My kids must be getting big," he'd said one night as they were exiting the venue. He sounded circumspect and hopeful. It was the first time he'd said anything about kids, and Amber was speechless, appalled. She forbade him from telling her their names. To know the names would have been unbearable.

The Virginian went home. Amber was an old-school head now, a gypsy princess, shown due deference anywhere they knew her, from the Portland Coliseum to the Hampton Coliseum. Coral Sky and Red Rocks. Alpine Valley and Deer Creek.

Periodic proof-of-life calls home to Nancy.

And you're okay, really?

I'm fine, Ma; Ma, I'm fine.

Men came and went.

The road on the whole was safer than the Felony Flats of her childhood, if not the up-and-coming hipster enclave it had since become. She had to pull her knife now and then, sure, but she'd never needed to use it. Soldier Field and Boston Garden. Saratoga Performing Arts Center. Corporations buying up naming rights, so now the tour schedule said things like DICK'S Sporting Goods Park, Smoothie King Center, Citi Field. The archaic charm this instilled into suddenly venerable venue names such as Merriweather Post Pavilion, such as Madison Square Garden. The Salt Palace and the Dane County Expo Center. The Jesse Auditorium at the University of Missouri, midway between St. Louis and Kansas City. Amber knew I-70 like the back of her hand.

Decommissioned airstrips and fallow farms. Future parking lots, future suburbs, a former megachurch. Ample camping, hookups for electric but not for water. One after another, she drove the roads. In lot after lot, she sold what she had, bought or traded for what she needed, found her way through the gates come nightfall and arrived at the innermost world. Every day was an exercise in improbability and desperation, but there was always the promise waiting. All you had to do was get there. The promise of life at the hollow center, of heat and light and music, of thousands of bodies swaying and whirling, together and apart in another American night.

PART 2
SHELTER FROM THE STORM OF THE CENTURY OF THE WEEK

(Brooklyn & Manhattan)

New York was as humid as a gym sock, as a swamp. As Florida. It was a little after ten o'clock, another American night, and I was at the other end of America. Having slept a bit after Amber's bottle episode, and still on West Coast time, I was wired. I took the AirTrain to the taxi stand, but then changed my mind, stepped out of line. I hadn't been here in ages, and the prospect of another cab ride through the clenched teeth of traffic sounded horrible. I'd take the subway to Grace's place.

The subway was aboveground out here, in

what I thought of as the outer reaches of Brooklyn, though it was actually Queens. I lucked out and a train pulled in just as I stepped onto the platform. It wasn't crowded, but I didn't feel like sitting. I stood clear of the closing doors as the avuncular voice on the PA requested, powered my phone on as the A train rolled out of the station. The home screen loaded and I was pleased to see that I had service. Pleased, too, and then less pleased, to see that I had gotten a text message from Amber.

"Nice to hear from you, ASSHOLE. Did you srsly give OUR SON A HUNDRED DOLLAR BILL?????!!! The fucking fuck were you thinking, I don't even know but he took it to school and was showing it off and some bigger kids heard about it and beat him up. THEY JUMPED HIM YOU DUMBSHIT MOTHERFUCK he is very shaken up and before you ask no I don't need money for the doctor visit we don't need your money for anything. PS sorry for the long text. assHOLE."

This was not what I had been hoping to hear.

I frantically called Amber back, got no response. I sent several apology texts that I knew were only making things worse. The train had been aboveground for a while after the airport. Now we plunged into a tunnel. Even in the midst of panic, I was impressed that I still had service underground. I thumbed dumbly around my screen, hoping Amber would answer me, send a photo of Hank not looking so bad after all. Or something. Anything. I wanted anything. To distract myself, I reread Molly Webster's explainer for a third time, and it struck me, as I reached the end again, that she was probably at her bartending gig tonight. I wondered how hard it would be to figure out where she worked.

It wasn't hard at all. She advertised her shifts on her Instagram: a place in Gowanus overlooking the canal. I flipped through some pictures. It looked like its former life, its pre-hipster life, had been as a driving school. In fact it was called Driving School; white backlit plastic sign that had clearly come with the lease. Classic gentrification move. The new bar names itself for the business it's replacing. The irony is easy, the name is memorable, and you don't have to pay to replace the sign. Bloodred swing door with an inset diamond window, wire mesh gridding the glass.

I decided to go see her. I had fucked up enough of my own life for one day. Maybe I could be somewhat useful to somebody else. I would go see Molly, give her juicy quotes that would yield another article. I could confirm the reboot, make it her news to break, earn her those bonus bucks. Eighty dollars for all that work! What a cruel, stupid industry. It was less than I'd parted with on an idiot whim in my ill-fated attempt to soothe my son.

And what would I say when Molly asked about Shayne? That was easy. I'd just tell her that he'd already said yes.

The A train was making great time. Trouble hit at Hoyt-Schermerhorn, where I had to transfer to the G. I waited and waited, and the G didn't come. The hour was late, but not that late. City that never sleeps, right? So what the hell. I was antsy, impatient to inaugurate my indirect redemption by entering the life of this person who, just as a side note and not remotely the reason I was doing this, would be extremely excited to meet me. Where was the goddamn train? I thought about texting Shayne. Grace's place, where I ultimately needed to end up, was in Tribeca, but Shayne lived near the bar. I knew he'd had a show earlier. He was playing Benno Levin in the stage musical adaptation of David Cronenberg's film adaptation of Don DeLillo's *Cosmopolis*. But odds were that he was free by now and would meet me if I told him where I was.

Shayne was appearing onstage six nights a week in the *Cosmopolis* musical. He would have liked to play the part of Eric Packer, the twenty-eight-year-old billionaire star, but he was a bit old for that role and frankly not committed enough to memorize that many songs. Instead he played Packer's assassin, a man who only ever appears in short interludes during the main body of the play (and the film it was adapted from, and the novel it was adapted from), isolated from the rest of what's going on. He's a rumor, a ghost. But he's also the final destination at the end of Packer's journey, the siren song of true oblivion that draws him dreamlike across the length of the novel, and the full width of midtown Manhattan. It is Levin who makes it possible for Packer, a man he has never met, to fulfill his deepest desire, which is to travel back to the site of his own origin myth, and then to—in a grim and final sense—transcend it.

(Is that a spoiler? Sorry, I guess, but come on, the book came out in 2003 for God's sake. It's as old as *Rev Beach*. Even the movie is a decade old now, and the show has been on Broadway for months.)

The thing about Levin is that "Levin" is not his real name. To become the lone-wolf killer, the world-historical course-shifter, he must first reimagine himself as someone capable of vision and violence on the scale required. Richard Sheets renames himself Benno Levin, and it is Levin who waits in the abandoned warehouse, who sings the oblivion song, who pulls the trigger and slows down time so that the last thing you see is the bullet frozen, marooned in original space.

Shayne played Sheets/Levin as a comic figure, a holy fool like something out of Beckett, rather than as a blithering puddle of David Mamet rage like Paul Giamatti did in the Cronenberg film. His performance divided critics, which I think ended up fueling ticket sales, because everyone wanted to see it and decide for themselves. Or maybe he was too famous for the quality of his performance to matter. They just wanted to see him.

My finger hovered above his contact icon. I clicked the phone asleep instead. I wanted to make an impression on Molly Webster, and if I brought Shayne along, he would outshine me. Mr. Indie Darling. He'd hog the attention, pose for the selfies, give the quotable quote.

Where was my G train? The tunnel was dark, no whiff of train breeze, just the buzz of the fluorescent lights and the scuttling of the rats, those unacknowledged janitors of the depths. It occurred to me that the subway system was basically a Hollow Earth situation, and I wondered if there was something to be done with that in *CM2M*, like something I could tell Sam Kirchner that he would think was cool. But come on. I wasn't a design savant or even a game nerd. The last thing Sam needed was his ventriloquist's dummy trying to become a real boy. It was stupid and it was making me feel bad to think about. So I exercised a bit of what Grace's pervy reply guy might have called Big CBT Energy and shut down that whole line of thinking.

I clicked my phone awake again. According to the map app, Driving School was less than twenty minutes on foot from where I was standing. What was I waiting for? I jogged up the stairs, excited, my bag bumping against my side. I stopped for a second to catch my breath. A second, a minute, whatever. Two minutes. I felt better. I walked up the next set of stairs, emerged into the surface world like at the end of the *Inferno*. *Shibboleth Gold* had made me something of an expert on Hollow Earth narratives, but believe it or not, Shib's journey to the center was not my first.

Ask me sometime about the Koreshan Unity cult, defunct now but in the late-nineteenth and early twentieth centuries a significant presence in Guiding Star, Florida, the Gulf Coast town where we shot *Rev Beach*. They were the originators of the phrase "We Live Inside," borrowed without attribution by Sam Kirchner as the tagline for the (supposedly) forthcoming *CM2M*, because there were no Koreshans left to protect the IP, though some of our sleuthier, stannier fans had taken it for yet another Easter egg, or rather, cosmogonic egg, as in the phrase "Vitellus of the Cosmogonic Egg," which is what Cyrus Teed—the cult's founder and leader, who called himself Koresh a hundred years before David did in Waco—deemed the town of Guiding Star, back when it was still mostly marshland that he'd swindled from a hard-up homesteader circa 1893.

I wasn't sure where all of this stuff would fall on a Venn diagram of rumor, fanfic, and straight-up trolling, but word on the street (i.e., the boards, the chans) was that neo-crypto Koreshans lived among us even today, and Sam Kirchner had been born into the cult and later defected; they said that his game was his revenge on it. Then there were those galaxy brains who theorized that he was still in the cult, that the game served as stealth propaganda for the neo-crypto Koreshans, who believed that the earth was hollow but, more important, that we live on its inner concave surface, and so what we think of as outer space is inner space, and therefore up is down. What we think of as gravity is actually centrifugal force.

That's what the Koreshans believed. Increasingly, I was given to wonder whether some of our hardest-core fans, our stans, believed it, too. There were guys who played obsessively, often live on Twitch, or devoted countless hours to unpacking secret symbolism, debating esoterica on subthreads, finding the keys to the conspiracy. Just as the magic weapon you need to defeat the last boss of the dungeon must always be locked in a chest somewhere in that same dungeon, these people took it for granted that if they spent enough time playing the game, they'd find what they needed to unmask and destroy its creator, a sci-fi nerd from Jersey whose only connection to global conspiracy was that he happened to be Jewish. This particular breed of antagonistic superfan tended also to be a Stay (((Gold))) power-poster. They terrified me. I'd been through all this before. The faction that would give anything to have us back. The faction that would do anything to keep us from coming back, so as to preserve us in a state of perpetual becoming in their hive mind. All these people whose affection was functionally indistinct from their enmity, whose love bled seamlessly into their hate.

But Sam Kirchner loved Stay (((Gold))). He had an alt account and checked the thread daily, contributed often. He was stealing their craziest ideas about the original *SG* and incorporating them into the sequel. He sometimes leaked rough animations, storyboard panels. Rather than recognize that they were being ripped off, or force-fed their own bullshit through the feeding tube of a Discord channel, the superfans went wild with joy. The prophecies! The prophecies were coming true!

And that's why I was thinking about Dante as I stepped onto Bond Street and into the proper Brooklyn night.

I turned south with a spring in my step, lungs no longer burning. I wasn't even sweating (much) when I got to the bar a mere fifteen minutes later and, as it was now just after midnight, officially a new day. I could put my mistakes behind me. Also, my drink limit was reset, so I wouldn't have to sit there like a derp and order soda. I pushed open the bloodred swing door and crossed the threshold.

I stopped short. I looked again.

Shayne was sitting at the bar. He stood when he saw me. He was grinning. "You're late," he said, shouting over the crowd and music, waving me over.

I moved like a man in a dream. It felt like the floor was moving rather than my feet. It felt like my shirt was sweatier than I'd thought it was a minute ago. It stuck to my wet belly. I felt fat. I fought the urge to do that nervous thing (like the *I Think You Should Leave* sketch) where you grab your shirt by the hem and tug it away from your gut so it looks like you don't have a gut. Because all that does is draw attention to the gut that you definitely do have, and if your shirt is also sweaty, then it showcases the wet spot on the shirt. Everyone gets to see it slap back into place: wet fabric on wet gut. The gesture is compulsive, almost obligatory. I fought. I focused. I wasn't going to do it. I didn't do it. I wasn't fat! I was in better shape than probably 90 percent of men my age. Or, I don't know, 80. My beautiful celebrity ex-wife had deigned to have sex with me yesterday—or, wait, okay, two days ago now—and I might have been a matter of convenience for her, but I was hardly the object of her pity. Grace didn't have an ounce of pity in her. It was one thing I loved about her and also what had wrecked us, because I was someone who, at sudden and unexpected moments, needed to be pitied in a deep and ugly way.

But I wasn't in one of those moments now, or I didn't have to be. Psychology! I thought. Big CBT Energy.

Control, control.

I was in a strange bar, confronted with my oldest friend, my perennial unmet standard of ideal masculinity, whose face was unlined and whose hairline held firm and whose abs you could have cast in bronze, who was standing here happy to see me but also directly between me and what I had come here for, which was Molly Webster, who was standing behind the bar, at first watching us and then, when she noticed me notice her, turning toward the bottles, giving me and Shayne our moment while she mixed up a couple of cocktails and set them before us, at the space Shayne had been saving. I was about to have a very different night than the one I'd been planning on having. Maybe that would be okay? It would have to be. Shayne threw his strong arms around my sloped shoulders, squeezed me tight.

"It's good to see you!" he screamed, over what must have

been Guided by Voices, which must have been his pick. He'd always wanted to play Robert Pollard in what he believed could be Ohio's answer to *Love & Mercy*. So far, he'd had to settle for playing Conor Oberst in the Phoebe Bridgers reboot of *I'm Not There*.

"Come sit," he continued. "And let me introduce you to Molly. And hey, it's gin, right?!" He was a god among men, yes, but he was also just a puppy. A pure spirit, maybe still my best friend—if only because I had so few. It was not his fault he made me hate myself, or that when he got excited, he sprayed charisma all over the floor.

"Gin's my favorite," I said. "You remembered." I sat. I was going to take a dramatic first sip but then instead I took a nondramatic gulp. Oblivion tastes like cucumbers.

Molly Webster was down at the far end of the bar, serving other customers. Some people had noticed us but, this being Brooklyn, nobody would cop to caring. They might tweet or whatever, but they'd leave us alone.

"Let's not talk work," he said. So we didn't. We drank our drinks and he asked about Henry and I told him about the trip to the zoo, eliding only the dispiriting details: his money concerns, Amber's disdain for me, the air-quality alert, the fires, the mistake I'd made giving the kid the hundo. So mostly I talked about the polar bear. Fresh cocktails appeared as quickly as we drank them. It had been humid outside of the bar, but the inside was a sauna. I was sweating like crazy, my soaked hair sticking to my head. I could hardly imagine what I looked like, but then I wasn't imagining much at the moment. The gin had brought its blessed blinders down, and I was focused on what was in front of me. The trick, I knew, would be to keep that focus. I was a few over my limit and wrote myself a mental IOU for the days ahead, when I wouldn't drink at all, so this week would average out to me having met my limit, even though that wasn't exactly—wasn't remotely—how this was supposed to work.

"We need to talk for serious," I slurred to Shayne.

"Tomorrow," he said. "And stop shouting."

He was right. The crowd had thinned out, the music was lower and softer. Guided by Voices was gone. This was a solo singer-songwriter, just voice and guitar, singing and strumming, the music sweet and sad and yet, at the same time, joyous. It felt to me in that moment like the sound of salvation itself. I didn't know what it was or who had put it on.

"Molly did," Shayne said. "It's the closing-time music. It's Jerry Garcia covering 'Goodnight, Irene.'"

"You're a regular," I said. "The article was planted. Your tweet was a conspiracy."

Shayne was laughing. "I mean that's one way of putting it, but . . ."

"John Cleves Symmes lived in Cincinnati," I said. "He was from New Jersey like Sam, but he ended up in Cincinnati. He was William Henry Harrison's cousin."

"I don't know what you're talking about."

"Cincinnati's like an hour from Dayton. I mean for your movie. It's all connected. I get it now. We really do live inside. Maybe that's where the voices are guiding us. I can prove it. This is why Grace gave me power-ups. I have enough for all of us. I was never going to get to give the quote. You always knew that. Fuck. You guys were always so much better at all of this. Reddit was right, I guess."

"Dude, please slow down, I can't—and that's . . ."

"No, no, it's fine," I said, waving away his concerns, wishing he could see things in the golden light of truth as I saw them. Molly came by with a last round of drinks for us.

"On the house," she said.

"Hey, actually—" Shayne started to say to her, but I waved this away, too, grabbed my glass from the bar.

"All this has happened before, and all this will happen again," I said, which of course you're thinking is exactly what an addict in relapse would say. But in the moment, all I meant was the prophecy from *Battlestar Galactica*—not the original show, but the late aughts reboot, the one where (spoiler alert) it turns out the humans and their Cylon enemies were the same all along, so the prophecy had been a kind of ironized or mistaken interpretation of this universal truth, the eternal return, which was what we were trapped inside, and might as well make the most of, is what I think I was thinking. Something like that. Actually, I'd never seen the show, I'd just read some recaps after Molly mentioned it in her explainer. Molly, who was meanwhile rushing back and forth behind the bar, closing out tabs and gently urging everyone who wasn't us to get out the door. Shayne was realizing he'd made a mistake giving me gin, but he was still coming to terms with the size of it. For my own part, I was still seeing things with crystal clarity. In absolute lucidity I pounded my drink, dropped the glass on the floor, and kicked my stool away as I stood.

"Stay gold!" I shouted at him and then ran out the front door of the bar.

. . .

Carroll Street crossed the Gowanus here. The road became a small flat bridge. I wanted to show Shayne that Grace's power-ups would protect us. I was climbing the concrete wall, planning to dive, and maybe I would have made it, but then I remembered that I had forgotten to take the pill, so I had to stop and dig the tin out of my pocket and pop the power-up and I felt the cool, crisp neutral burst of it dissolving and now I was ready to dive into the black water but instead I was falling away from the water, back toward the bridge, because Shayne was pulling me from the ledge, holding me down on the ground, telling me to get control of myself.

"There could be a passage here," I said. "You don't know."

"I know that it's a Superfund site," he said.

"The thing about Hollow Earth theory," I said, still pinned to the ground, "is that it's played out. Poe, Verne, Edgar Rice Burroughs, Symmes holes—it's all colonialist bullshit, empire's fantasy of limitless expansion, manifest destiny, dusky natives, new Edens to strip-mine and clear-cut."

"You're really scaring me, man."

"Are people taking pictures of us?" I asked meekly. "Does my outfit look okay?"

I was out of breath, out of mania, far from home, awake for way too long. The weight of Shayne pinning me down was comforting, and even though there was gravel and asphalt against my back and maybe some broken glass pressing into my scalp, I felt safe beneath the heat of him, made real by his exasperation. There were people in the street, their phones out.

"We're going to win the internet tomorrow, aren't we?" I said.

"Can't promise a win," he said. "But it'll be an honor just to be nominated." He was lifting me now, his shoulder in my armpit, holding me upright, making me move. I wasn't going to find out tonight if I could breathe underwater, and I wasn't going to see Grace's Tribeca apartment. Molly hustled the last stragglers out of Driving School as Shayne brought me back inside. There was a glass of water waiting. I felt sleepy but knew what I had to do. I knew because Shayne was telling me. Drink the water, he said, and we'd go back to his place. Tomorrow would be tomorrow's problem. And tomorrow, and tomorrow, and tomorrow, until the last streamed rerun of rebooted time!

"My ex is pissed at me," I slurred, putting the glass down after I'd drank about half.

"If she isn't yet, she will be soon," Shayne said. "Lelyveld is probably already on his way here."

"Not her, the other."

"Ahh, well you're two for two, then. Drink your water, bud, okay?"

I obliged him. I finished everything in the pint glass, wiped my flushed face with the back of my hand. Molly was turning off lights.

"I don't think he ate dinner," he was saying to her. "And he was probably pretty dehydrated between the airplane and the subway and then walking here. Still, I guess the gin was a bad call."

"You guess?"

I didn't love that they were talking about me like this. I wanted to be back in the conversation.

"I never gave you my quote," I said. I felt my dashed hopes

throbbing in my heart and saw my son's bruised face behind my eyes when I closed them, which I was trying to avoid doing because it made my head spin, but it was hard to avoid closing them because I was very, very tired.

"We can do that tomorrow," she said, her voice perfectly calibrated to express sympathy and authority, the Mother-is-losing-patience voice of bartenders everywhere.

"No," I said. "It's why I came here. It isn't fair they only gave you eighty dollars."

"Okay," she said. "Give me the quote and then let's get you home."

"It's great to be back," I said. "That's the first thing. After all this time it's just great to be back, and to get the chance to bring this character, this story, to life again. It's a privilege to serve the fans this way, so many of whom have kept the faith for so long. Our whole lives, really. They're who this is for. But having said that, Molly, I have to say, too, that it's great to be working with Shayne and Grace and Corey again. We've had our ups and downs over the years, and we don't need to go over all that right now, everyone knows the stories, or they think they know, but forget that. These are the people I came up with. They're my oldest friends in the world, my family really. Me and Shayne played brothers, but we all became a family. I love them so much, and here we are together again. It's perfect. I think about everything it took to get here, all the struggle and uncertainty, and I just think, *You know, this was all in the plan. It all makes sense.* I look around and I see my friends and I think, *Hey, who's got it better than me?*"

I took a breath.

"How was that?" I asked. "Was it good?"

"Perfect," she said.

"Great," I said, secure in the knowledge that I'd done this one thing right today, and perhaps redeemed myself after all, maybe not completely but in part, yes, a small down payment on redemption that I made this day, whatever day it was, and now I could rest. So I rested. I let the last of the gin madness drain out of my body, and I let the gin dark fall in its place. Shayne would make sure I got home. All this had happened before, and here it was happening again.

I dreamed of Higley and Nichols. They were on the stage in the multipurpose room at Rising Star, which made no sense because neither of them had lived there. They'd probably never set foot in that room in their lives. I stood in the audience, though there was no audience except for me. The walls of the room were thick red curtains, floor to ceiling, like the Black Lodge in *Twin Peaks*. I looked around half expecting to see Michael J. Anderson and Sheryl Lee, but they weren't there. It was only Catherine Higley and Alex Nichols, who had rounded out the *Rev Beach* main cast for all three seasons it aired. They had never lobbied for more screen time, just showed up to work, cashed their checks, smiled brightly in promo photos, always at opposite ends of the ensemble shot, like the castles on a chessboard.

While the rest of us hustled and squabbled and threw tantrums and booked movies and courted disaster, they were quietly falling in love with each other—and with improv comedy, which they practiced on the side. Like Grace and I, they married shortly after *Rev Beach* was canceled. Unlike us, they were still together. They operated a small successful theater in Minneapolis, performing nightly and offering classes to the public. Thanks to their judicious stewardship, the Twin Cities had become something of a regional improv mecca. They weren't exactly an *SNL* farm team, but scouts flew out for their annual showcase. Their troupe was called Secret Handshake, and they were going to use the *Rev Beach* money to finance its first feature film, a Christopher Guest homage set in the world of competitive speech and debate.

All of that was backstory about them, by the way, not the content of my dream.

In the dream, Alex Nichols was wearing a white dinner jacket like Sean Connery in *Goldfinger* (or Daniel Craig in *Spectre*). He sat on a black bench before a black baby grand piano in the center of the multipurpose room stage. (The actual multipurpose room at Rising Star had a Casio keyboard on a card table.) Catherine Higley stood beside him with her hand on his shoulder, her eyes closed. She was dressed like Wednesday Addams, but had Uma Thurman's *Pulp Fiction* haircut. Alex, whose back was to me, was playing the changes for the Springfields' "Silver Threads and Golden Needles," though I knew that song mostly from the Tammy, Loretta, and Dolly version on *Honky Tonk Angels,* because Shayne had gone through a country phase during one of his authenticity kicks. Alex sang the verses, and Catherine harmonized on the chorus. They had slowed the song down and distilled it to its essence, turned it from a defiant anthem to a forlorn weeper: "You can't buy my love with money, for I never was that kind . . ."

I approached the lip of the stage, not wanting to interrupt but excited to talk to them, to reconnect. Catherine kept her left hand on Alex's shoulder but lifted her right. She put her hand up flat in a gesture of warning. I stopped walking. She opened her eyes. They were a radiant gold. The chorus ended and they stopped singing. Alex played the bridge.

"That gum you like is going to come back in style," Catherine said.

"I don't chew gum," I said. "Never have. I think you're thinking of Shayne."

She was about to say something else, but there wasn't time. Her radiant eye-light consumed the room, a total gold eclipse. A gilt apocalypse. They dissolved into the radiance and so did I.

I awoke in a great perplexity to a pounding headache and a lot of questions. Where was I? Who was I? What was I doing here? Where was here exactly? And what smelled like bacon?

I sat up, surveyed the vast redbrick-walled room in which I found myself. I was on a couch, covered by a thin blanket, fully dressed except for my shoes, which were by the front door next to another pair of shoes that I recognized as Shayne's. This was Shayne's loft. The bacon smell was bacon. He was making breakfast. A wave of gratitude swept through me; gratitude and nausea. So much for my Big CBT Energy. I stood on tentative legs like a newborn doe, shuffled from the couch to the open-plan kitchen. Other than the toilet, the division between rooms was strictly conceptual.

"I'm so sorry," I said.

"Me too," he said. "I never should have gotten you going. But I thought you were doing the moderation thing."

"I was," I said. "Am. This was a one-off. You took me by surprise being at the bar. Not that I wasn't happy to see you, but."

"I'd love to know what you thought you were going to do there, if not run into me."

"I'd love to know why you didn't tell me you knew Molly Webster. Is it fair to assume that you're already excited about this project and I didn't need to come out here to lure you?"

"Yeah, *Cosmopolis the Musical* is nearing the end of its run, and this MCU thing I was gonna do next is on hiatus. Director's having one of those sex-cannibal scandals, and they're trying to keep it quiet, which actually, shit, forget I said anything. I already signed the NDA. And I'm still hurting from COVID losses. I can't pay rent or tour my jam band with Olivier Assayas's esteem for me. And I never should have tried to produce and direct and star in a shot-for-shot remake of *The King of Marvin Gardens*. When you're watching the movie, you think the hard role to live up to is Bruce Dern, so you take Nicholson to make things a little easier on yourself, but then you realize . . . and having James Franco as Dern was not a great call. Dano had said he'd do it, but James had already grown the mustache. Now Zendaya's pissed at me because she did the Ellen Burstyn part, and obviously this movie is never seeing the light of day. And I really don't want Grace to know all of this, so please don't tell her I'm hard-up, but between us, old pal, I'm ready to hit reboot. I'd love to spend some quality time with you, and Higley and Nichols. I'm going to present a position of strength and take Grace for every penny I can, but in the end I'm going to let her do her worst to me—product placements, press junkets, whatever the fuck it is *you're* wearing. Basically, anything this side of Bill Maher. Do you think

John Oliver is still doing that joke about how he wants Adam Driver to step on his throat? Maybe I could audition for the next season of that joke. Anyway, don't think of this as a wasted trip. Think of it as an easy victory. You can go back to Hollywood a hero."

My stomach was still unsettled, and I wasn't sure whether Shayne's speech was helping or hurting its prospects. I also wasn't sure I wanted to go back to Hollywood. This was news I could easily deliver by phone or text. On the other hand, if I went back to Grace's I could see Grace.

"I'm glad to be here," I said. "It's not a wasted trip. Now where's my phone, and is there coffee?"

The first spatters of rain hit the windows.

"Molly's getting coffee from the place down the block," he said. "I haven't seen your phone. It's either in your bag, which is next to the couch, or it's at the bottom of the Gowanus Canal."

I returned to the couch zone, found my bulging bag. My phone, small mercy, was not in the canal. The bottle of Travis wine was still in bubble wrap, nestled among my horrible new old clothes. I checked my messages. There were none. No Grace, and worse, no Amber.

"So what's with you and our intrepid reporter?" I asked, returning to the kitchen zone. "Might as well cut to the chase before she gets back with the coffee and you have to start showboating again."

"We're friends," he said. "Good friends."

"How good?"

"She has a key to the apartment. She feeds my cat when I travel. I like her ideas about politics and culture. Also, I like the way she tends bar. I'm not her ex-boyfriend's favorite person, but then he's not mine, either, so it evens out."

"Can't imagine why he'd have a grudge against you," I said. "Can't imagine why her leaving him for you would result in his feeling a little inadequate, a little sore."

"He's a jealous prick, and he wasn't nice to her. Also, she didn't leave him 'for' me. There was no overlap there."

"Not even a little? C'mon, Shayne."

"A week, two weeks maybe. It was over. Trust me, he sucks."

"You don't have a cat."

"I could get one any day now. Look, I care about her, we're figuring our shit out, and what are you anyway, my dad?"

Now I knew I was on dangerous ground. I would have backed off, but there was still a lot that I wanted to know.

"In her article she literally poses the question 'What is Shayne Glade thinking?' and then answers herself, 'I have no idea.' Which seems, in light of her having a key to your apartment, and your pants, like that question and its answer were a bit of a false flag."

"We thought it made sense to not emphasize the fact of our acquaintance."

"I guess I wrecked that for you."

"Spilled milk. And gin."

"And gin, yes."

"Here, breakfast is ready."

He handed me a plate piled high with eggs and bacon, a hot buttered English muffin.

"Jesus, this is good," I said, chewing a mouthful of muffin while I broke up the bacon with my fork.

"Thanks, I made it from scratch."

"I didn't even know that was possible."

"It was a long quarantine."

"But I mean, wow, man. You could have a cooking show!"

"If *Rev Beach* doesn't come through, I might have to."

We ate and watched the rain, which was picking up. I was thinking that his cooking show could be a nice lead-in for my travel show—or, in all likelihood, my show a just-okay lead-in for his.

"Hey," I said, "you have a shirt I can borrow?" I still had clean clothes from Grace, of course, but I was increasingly embarrassed by them, and anyway, I thought borrowing a garment could only accelerate our bonding, which was already happily in high gear given everything that he'd just confided.

"Sure," he said. "Let me go check." He got up, retreated to the hinterland of the loft, his bedroom zone, to try to find something that would fit me. We were the same size except I was several inches shorter and out of shape, which was what I assumed was slowing him down. I tried not to think about that, thought about my son instead. Hopefully he was healing. Hopefully it hadn't been too bad, the whole thing overblown by Amber. Hopefully I'd be allowed to see him again. This wasn't a great line of thought, either.

I texted Grace: "Sorry for the photo op last night. I'm at Shayne's. He's being a jerk but I think I'm making progress. Keep you posted."

She texted back immediately. "So you met Molly, too. What's she like? Lelyveld did a little digging; he likes her vibe."

I stared at my phone, dumbfounded. I'd already finished my serving of bacon but reached across the breakfast bar to Shayne's plate to grab a piece of his. I stuffed the whole thing in my mouth, relishing the crunch and grease of it. Bacon was as much a restorative, a power-up, as Grace's magic beans.

"We didn't get to talk much," I texted back, "and I'm not expecting to see her again but if I do, I'll let you know."

Just then Molly opened the front door of the apartment. She was holding an umbrella in one hand and a tray of coffee in the other. The keys were in her teeth, and the umbrella seemed to have done her little good.

"'Come in,' she said, 'I'll give ya shelter from the storm,'" Molly sang through key-gripping teeth.

"You live nearby?"

"LOL," she said. "I could never afford this neighborhood. Shit, Shayne can barely afford it. I live in Red Hook. With three roommates, in a place half this size. I just talked to them and the power's out. I had been planning to drop these off and split, but I guess with the lights off at home, I'll hole up here awhile. That is if you don't mind me crashing your reunion special."

"Sucks," I said. "About the power." I was impressed that she'd managed this whole speech with the keys still in her mouth. It was the kind of trick they taught you in acting class. I walked over to help, but taking the keys out of her mouth seemed too familiar a gesture, so I relieved her of the coffee tray instead. Also, I desperately needed coffee. Now that I could smell it, every second I went without drinking it was shaving a year off my life.

"Are you hungry?" I asked. "That's Shayne's plate, but I'm sure he wouldn't mind. I don't know why he didn't fix you one, maybe he ran out of bacon?"

"I don't eat bacon for moral reasons," she said, slipping off her jacket. There were dark words tattooed up her pale forearm. "And bread and dairy are worse for you than cigarettes. Shayne made me a smoothie before I went for the coffee."

"There was a blender running in this room this morning? I guess I slept through it."

"That and the three orgasms he gave me as repayment for my putting up with you last night."

She popped the lid off her coffee, sipped, seemed to be considering something. "Power goes out at my place every time it rains like this," she said. "Lines go down or a pole gets washed away. The subway floods, and the tunnels take days to drain. And they fix it, sure, but they never fix it all the way, so each time it's always a little worse than last time. Storm of the century of the week."

"What can you do?" I said, attempting sympathy. "It's New York."

"I could leave New York," she said. "You need a bartender?"

"Actually—"

"Kidding. Didn't you read my article? I have an MFA."

"I don't know what that is."

"Sixty-eight thousand dollars with a minus sign next to it. My degree's in speculative nonfiction, but I'm also just enough younger than you to have come of age during the first golden era of online fanfic, the message boards, the LiveJournals, the shipping. I've written more *Rev Beach* headcanon and RPF than you can imagine. The things I've described you and Shayne doing to—"

"You?"

"Each other. I mean talk about orgasms."

"You don't need to tell me."

"I wasn't going to. Google it if you're curious."

"What does your tattoo say?" I asked. "Or should I google that, too?"

"'To whom we lend fate from the very border of fate,'" she said. "It's Rilke."

I stared at her.

"He's a poet."

"I don't have an MFA."

"It sounds better in German."

"I wouldn't doubt it," I said. A beat. "So are we cool, then?"

"I think you're a decent guy, David, or I think you might be, or Shayne thinks you are and I want to be on his side about this. But you made a huge ass of yourself last night, caused a scene at my bar, and scared the shit out of our mutual friend. He won't ever say this, because you're both dumb boys, but he's worried about you. And now there's a whole faction of Revheads out there who think I'm Yoko'ing this reunion, when that's the furthest thing from true. Because first of all, Yoko is a misunderstood and wrongly maligned woman who everyone is wrong about, and second because the last thing I want is for this reboot to not happen."

"Noted," I said. "So what do you want?"

"Seat in the writers' room," she said. "Or weren't you listening when I said the thing about the sixty-eight thousand dollars and the minus sign?"

"I heard the words 'speculative' and 'nonfiction,' but I don't get how they relate. It's what, you're inventing what the truth might be? Like what you think it should be, or just what you wish it was?"

"Yes and, as the improv kids say."

"And they give degrees for this?"

"Degrees and variable-interest loans, which are also a form of speculative nonfiction. I mean they're always changing based on someone's speculations. But they never get less real."

Shayne entered from stage right, doing a slow clap, my loaner shirt draped across a forearm. It was a plain gray T-shirt boasting the Cannes Palme d'Whatever logo, below which it read, "Official Selection 2009."

"Glad you guys have kissed and made up," he said. "We're gonna be a happy family."

He tossed the shirt to me. I caught it. A Game Boy flashing before my bleary eyes.

"I really am sorry," I said to them both. "About last night. Maybe that goes without saying—"

"It does," Shayne said at the same time Molly said, "It doesn't."

"But I wanted to say it."

"Well, thank you," she said. "Luckily there's an easy way you can make it up to me."

A bright blue light flashed outside the living room window: a shower of sparks flew from the transformer box at the top of the power pole. The apartment went dark. I heard the fridge motor clunk out. The rain picked up some more. The wind, as Bob Dylan once said, began to howl.

"Shit," Shayne said. "First time that's happened at my place."

"The future is here, it's just unevenly distributed," Molly said. "But the redistribution is on its way."

"Is that speculative nonfiction?" I asked.

"More poetry," she said. "By the Bronx-born poet Ocasio-Cortez.'"

"I don't know his work," Shayne said.

"No," Molly said, "I didn't suppose you would."

"I've got an idea," I said.

Shayne and Molly both looked surprised.

"Don't look so surprised," I said. "The thing you said about the future reminded me. How it's uneven and we need to get some for ourselves?"

"That's not exactly what I meant."

"Grace lives in the future," I continued. "Or her apartment does. I was supposed to stay there. Red Hook might be drowning, but how much you wanna bet they're still doing DoorDash in Tribeca?"

"This is morally sus as fuck," Molly said. "I mean just for the record. But beggars can't be choosers. We'll take my car."

"You have a car?" I asked, shock in my voice.

"I'm the working poor," she said. "Of course I do. How do you think you got back here last night?"

"I didn't think about it," I said.

"That's right," she said.

"Okay," Shayne said. "Enough of that. We all agree that Bernie woulda. Give me two minutes to put some clothes in a bag and we can hit the road. Let's go get us some shelter from the storm!"

Molly's car was parked out front. It was a silver Ford Fiesta that apparently predated keyless entry. She hopped across the small but rising stream of water that rushed along the curb toward a storm drain, went around to the driver's side, let herself in, shut the door behind her, reached across what I saw was a no-bullshit stick shift and pushed the shotgun-side door open from the inside.

"Be my guest," Shayne said, gesturing.

"Nah."

"Suit yourself." He got into the car, shut the door, twisted around in the seat to toss his bag into the seat behind Molly, and then opened the door behind his seat for me. I had my own bag with me, threw it in on top of his, shut the door, and buckled up. Molly revved the engine while Shayne fiddled with his phone, trying to get Google Maps to render a clear verdict on the Battery Tunnel versus the Brooklyn Bridge.

The Fiesta's interior was as gray as a Béla Tarr movie, save for fabric inlays in the seats that had a confetti-colored dot pattern like bowling alley carpet, like something on which you could spill nacho cheese or stub out a cigarette without disrupting the general vibe. The driver's side sun visor was missing, the roof fabric drooped—I could feel it nuzzling my hair—but the biggest tell was the tape deck.

"How old is this thing?" I asked.

"It's a 2001," Molly said. "Same age as 9/11."

"Jesus Christ," I said. "Why would you say that?"

"My dad died on Flight Ninety-Three," she said. "This was his car and now it's mine, and the rule is when we're in it I get to say whatever I want."

"Sorry," I said, and buried my face in my phone.

I texted Shayne from the back seat: "Is that true???"

He replied on text: "Not the plane part but the rest yea. He was a firefighter who got lung cancer from working on the pile."

Out loud he said, "So I think we should take the tunnel. Maps says it's open and there's not too much traffic."

Another text to me: "She was six. It's the origin myth of her socialism as well as her sarcasm, and the one thing she never ever writes about, so maybe don't push it?"

"Oh boy," she said, pulling out of the parking spot and into the street, glancing into the rearview and catching my eye. "He's not texting you my origin myth is he? Now you'll know what my weaknesses are."

"You caught us," I said. "But the good news for you is he says you don't have any."

"If that were true," Molly said, "you boys would be in a cab."

"Uber," I said.

"Lyft," Shayne said. "Uber's business practices are execrable. We boycott."

"She's good for you," I said, and then added, experimentally but (I hoped) meaningfully, "bro."

The streets were empty. Potholes were already full with rainwater, spilling over their ragged mouths into the puddles that would eventually merge with the fast-flowing gutter streams, top the curbs and cover the sidewalks, turn the whole borough into a lake. This was prime flood zone, the watch already upgraded to a warning. On the news (e.g., Twitter) there was speculation about whether, and when, evacuation orders would come. Was it wrong to wait when we all knew where this was headed? Or was it wrong to tell people that they had to leave, just so the city could say it had said so, when we all knew that most of the people who would be most affected wouldn't have any way to get out or anywhere to go if they did?

Court Street south to Ninth Street, quick right on Ninth to Hamilton, which looped us around so we faced the city, what little of it we could see through the driving rain. Freedom Tower faintly visible against a sky the same color as Molly's car seats (sans confetti). The speed limit was twenty, but there wasn't much traffic on our side. Outbound, however, was bumper to bumper. Some people, it seemed, had somewhere to go, and were going—Lexus, Audi, Lexus, Greyhound, Beamer, Tesla, Tesla, city bus.

The mouth of the tunnel was, as ever, under construction. Orange traffic barriers, the round trash-can-size kind with reflective white stripes and black rubber skirts, nudged us out of a mysteriously closed center lane, forcing us across one of those solid white stripes you're not supposed to cross. Above the mouth of the tunnel, set back just enough that it didn't quite loom, was the ventilation building, squat and square as a medieval fortress, redbrick with raw concrete accents, no windows that I could see. We passed a parked police prowler, lights on but siren off, seemingly there for no reason but to let its presence be felt. On the left side, the rotund orange barriers gave way to slender white ones. On the right side, a bronze plaque the size of a backyard swimming pool read EXCELSIOR and EVER UPWARD, respectively, above and below the borough seal. Above the tunnel mouth an LED sign shifted between the speed limit and DO NOT PASS.

The tunnel felt at once over- and underlit. The traffic barriers were blue now. The walls were tile: white with yellow stripes, blue at the base. Double track of boxy lights as far as the eye could see, curling around the corner. There was water on the road, I could hear it sloshing in the Fiesta's under-carriage, could see it being sprayed back at us from the black Taurus SUV we were trapped behind. And through the Tau-rus's rear window I also saw a boy about my son's age watch-ing cartoons on a portable DVD player. I squinted, tried to see what the show was, and let's say it was that effort that caused my eyes to water a little. And let's say it was Thomas the Tank Engine, because that's a Hank favorite, and if it wasn't, who would ever know the difference? Nobody, including me. I cleared my throat.

"Anyone hungry?" I asked. "We can order Seamless and have it meet us."

"Sounds good to me," Shayne said. "Sushi?"

"Perfect, let me see if I have service." I waved my phone around. We cruised along at the limit. The outbound lane continued to stutter and crawl. Shayne dug around in a pile of tapes at his feet, came up with *Blood on the Tracks,* which he showed to Molly.

"Bit on the nose, don't you think?" she said.

He put it down, resurfaced holding *After the Gold Rush,* popped it in.

"Well, I dreamed I saw the knights in armor," Neil said, "saying something about a queen . . ." When he got to the part about Mother Nature on the run, we were still in the tunnel, but I had found service. I picked a place, pulled up a menu, chose what I wanted, then handed my phone to Shayne. By the time Neil saw the silver spaceships lying in the yellow haze of the sun we were on Trinity Place, which turns into Church Street after the intersection with Liberty Street, aka the northwest corner of Zuccotti Park.

Just as I had nonfictionally speculated, Tribeca had power. Grace owned the penthouse of a thirty-story building with an infinity pool on its rooftop patio. The building had a private parking garage, and I had updated Grace about our plan after placing the food order. She'd had Molly, Shayne, and the Ford Fiesta all registered with the building's app. The front door of both the building and the unit would recognize them now. Inside the unit, we could control our own microclimates, and the espresso machine would remember our preferences. We could also come and go as we pleased, not that anyone was going anywhere. The weather was getting worse and worse. The sushi arrived twenty minutes after we did. Molly confined herself to vegetarian rolls but consented to taste a piece of Shayne's octopus nigiri and grudgingly admitted that it was very good, however morally indefensible. Shayne said he'd never tried octopus until he'd starred in the Whit Stillman adaptation of *10:04*.

We knew that if the rain kept coming it was likely there would be delays and closures, and Grace's fridge was empty, so as I mopped up the last of the soy sauce with the last piece of my spicy salmon roll, Shayne put together a Whole Foods order: pasta, eggs, steaks for dinner for me and him, some other stuff Shayne wanted, assorted vegetarian shit for Molly, and a pallet of bottled water just to be safe.

Molly was messing around with *Rev Beach* script ideas,

and I was trying to help, but I could tell she was distracted. She kept tabbing back over to social media to see the news from Red Hook, where there was already a foot of water in the streets.

"Okay, what about this?" I said. "Cole Jansen comes back to town after a long time away. His career, whatever that was, is kind of fallen apart. Maybe his wife has left him, whatever. So he has to get a job working at Will's bar, bar and grill actually. Restaurant. Will has this very successful restaurant right on the beach. It's the hot spot in town, you know, more for locals than tourists, but there's also a stage on the patio deck where bands play. Plenty of cameo potential. Anyway, Will's life is going great, and Cole has to come crawling back, not the golden child anymore. Long way from football camp, you know what I mean?"

"Yeah," Shayne said, "we get it."

"Anyway, unbeknownst to the Jansen boys, well, to anyone really, there's this uh, not hellmouth, I guess we still can't say hellmouth—"

"Wouldn't want to," Molly interjected. "Whedon's canceled."

"Right, yeah. So it's something else. I don't know, a cave. Cavern. Not directly under the restaurant but nearby, down the beach a ways, an opening at the base of the cliffs."

"The Florida cliffs?" Molly again.

"Okay, that was dumb. I mean it might be funny, actually, to do that. Just CGI a cliff in there and never explain it. Has a ring don't you think, 'the Florida Cliffs'?"

"Sounds like a jam band," Shayne said, not unhappily, which in turn made me worried. I was already worried I was giving him too much rope with the house band at the restaurant.

"Forget it, no cliffs. What about a cypress dome—aren't those a thing?"

"They're a thing, yeah," Molly said. She sounded distracted.

"Like what kind of thing?" I asked. "Because it doesn't super matter, there just has to be some origin point for where the monsters are coming from, or something they want, some reason why they would— You're not listening."

"I'm listening," Shayne said. "I just don't know what you're talking about. Or care, honestly. Isn't all of this Grace's problem? Or the twelve people she's going to hire to write the show?"

"Of whom our friend here wishes to be one," I reminded him. Reminded her, really. "Besides, it would be good for us to have some ideas to bring to the table. A sense of what we want our character arcs to be."

"I shouldn't have left them," Molly said. The words hung in the perfect-temperature apartment air while tropical storm rains continued to batter the soundproof windows, soundlessly. It took a second to realize she meant her Red Hook roommates.

"I'm sure they're fine," I said. "Try to focus. Let's think about Grace, I mean Misty. What's her story? She's married to Will, right? That's obvious. They have a couple of kids, or maybe just one kid, say he's six. Is that old enough where you can get one kid instead of having to hire twins? Make a note to ask. Kid could be older. So they've got this perfect life, but now Cole comes back into the picture—Grace's old flame, Will's old rival. Cole could never tear apart what they have, of course, and in the end he wouldn't want to because he loves his brother, but let's say it sort of psychically stirs things up. Lots of drama. Misunderstandings. We can do a new version of the crying-blood meme. Internet would love that."

"Internet will roast you for a try-hard," Molly said. Still barely paying attention to me, and yet somehow capable of dissing my kick-ass ideas in the most offhand and (I hated to admit it) obviously right way.

I had been pacing the room while I talked all this out, but I paused now to peer over her shoulder and see what she was looking at on the laptop on which she was definitely not taking notes on all my ideas. She was looking at her roommate's Instagram Live, in which gray water was seeping through the ceiling of their living room. The roommate panned the camera down the wall to a large and growing puddle on the floor. Just outside the frame, a cat could be heard mewling.

"They should really get out of there," I said.

"And go where?" she asked.

"I don't know, they must have friends, right? Red Hook seems pretty bad right now, but it can't be every building. I'd say they should come here, but I'm not sure Grace would be cool with that, I mean we're already sort of pushing it. Still, if you think—"

"They'll never make it," Shayne cut in. "The water's too deep in the streets. Everyone's gonna be where they are for the duration of whatever this is."

"Let's hope the Whole Foods delivery guy doesn't feel that way," I said.

"I think we're still a little in the future here, should be fine. Maybe we can't save the world, but we're sitting pretty."

"Story of your life," Molly muttered.

She quickly checked herself. "Sorry," she said. "But this is pretty stressful. I mean these people aren't my best friends, but I do live with them, and everything I own other than my car and this laptop is in that apartment."

"I'm sure your renter's insurance will cover it," I said.

"The two of you," she said. "Sometimes I think the planet you live on is at least adjacent to mine in the solar system, but that isn't true, is it? I mean where the fuck am I right now?"

"Two miles from where we were an hour ago," I said. I was starting to get annoyed with her constant ragging on me, on us. Who can help that his life is what it is? Shayne had to be Shayne and I had to be me and Grace was Grace and Molly was— Who was Molly? Some writer, some chip-shouldered wannabe class warrior who nevertheless had proven rather adept at cozying up to power, as evidenced by the fact that she was here in Grace's apartment with me and Shayne. If I hadn't still been so ashamed about last night, I might have said some of this out loud. But I was, so I didn't.

"One upside," Shayne said, "is that by the time this storm is over, nobody's going to remember our little adventure."

"It'll only be a day," I said.

"That's eons in internet time," Molly said. "The only person who will still be thinking about it at all is Corey Burch, who by the way takes great exception to my quote unquote defamation of his character. He has been fundraising off me as a 'media elite' and 'rootless cosmopolitan' for days now. And this guy BigDiogenesEnergy has been on my timeline all morning with some really weird shit."

"Is it feet?" I asked. "Because if so, you're in good company."

"I don't know where I am," she said.

"You already said that," I said.

"Bears repeating," she said, turning back to her laptop, clicking open a Google doc. She sang "Drifting Too Far from the Shore" under her breath as she worked or pretended to work.

I walked away from both of them and stood by the floor-to-ceiling windows. Rain lashed across the balcony, across the glass. We were on the West Side, and I could see the roiling Hudson. There were a lot of dark spots in the Jersey skyline. And you know what? I didn't think that Bernie woulda. Or shoulda! Okay sure, in '16 maybe. But '20? I was a Buttigieg guy. I liked that he was our age. Furthermore, I figured that since his first two careers had been working on regime change around Africa for the CIA and fixing Canadian bread prices for McKinsey, he'd probably keep inflation down and not start more than one or two small wars. Now that I was the sole proprietor of a small business, the price of gas and probability of supply shock were serious concerns for me. In the end, it hadn't mattered enough to me to go vote in the primary or the general. But here we were, and things seemed like they'd more or less worked out. I mean give or take a pandemic, an insurrection, a rash of wildfires, and a superstorm.

"Hey! Earth to Crader!" Shayne was beside me at the window.

"What?"

"Last call before I place the order. Should we do surf 'n' turf? Some shrimp to top the steaks?"

"Sure," I said. "I think your little Jacobin has already got our names on her kill list, so we might as well have a nice last meal."

"She has written for *Jacobin*, actually," he said. "But please don't be a dick to her. I like her, she's having a hard time—and she's right." He meant about *Rev Beach,* I think, though it could have been Bernie—or both. But she was right about more than that. It wouldn't stop raining for two full days. Red Hook would be declared a disaster zone; Molly would lose everything she owned to floodwater. Her roommates would escape, but barely. I don't know where they went. Somewhere. Wherever people go when the water takes their building and they have nowhere to go.

But we didn't yet know that all of that would happen. We placed our Whole Foods order, and it arrived within an hour, delivered by a soaked-through Chinese guy who I had to meet downstairs because the concierge wouldn't let him up, wet as he was, because the storm had tied up the building mainte-nance staff with other projects for the foreseeable future. The delivery guy stood in the middle of the slate-floored lobby, dripping, his Mets cap covered by a plastic THANK YOU bag with its handles tied below his chin like the strings of a bonnet. The motor on his e-bike had shorted. His sneakers squeaked when he walked. I figured him for about my age. I signed Shayne's name on the slip. He nodded, turned, wheeled the bike toward the automatic doors beyond which the storm raged. We—the concierge and me—heard the wind and thun-der when the doors opened, then silence was restored as soon as they slid shut.

"Sorry for the bother," said the concierge.

"It's nothing," I said. The truest words I'd spoken all day.

Given last night's performance, I wasn't going to drink tonight, which meant I couldn't bring out Grace's gift of high-GMO wine. Shayne cooked, we toasted with Topo Chico. After dinner Molly busted out her vape pen, and soon we were all sprawled on the living room couches talking about our dream projects, or, I don't know, bullshitting one another about what our dreams were. I was a little too high to tell whether we were kidding, or if the fact that we were serious was part of the joke.

"Gender-swapped *The King of Comedy*," Shayne said. "Kristen Stewart as Rupert Pupkin, Paula Poundstone as Jerry Langford, I'm Sandra Bernhard's character, and Daniel Kaluuya as Rita." He passed the vape to me.

"Sequel to *Ghost World*," I said on my exhale. "Get Birch, Buscemi, and ScarJo back. Like a 'Where are they now?' sort of thing. Just like what we're doing."

I passed the vape to Molly with a hand that felt rubbery, weightless. I was in a pleasing fug and barely missed alcohol at all.

"But what part would you play?" Shayne asked.

"I don't need a part," I said.

"Defeats the purpose of the game, doesn't it?"

"Does it?"

"Okay," Molly said. "But why does everything have to be recycled IP? Do either of you have an original idea?"

"Derivative ideas are original," Shayne said. "That's like saying children aren't original because they have parents. You just have to push things far enough. It's like, what's the word I want here—"

"Evolution?" I offered.

"Exactly!" Shayne said. "God, I've missed you, David."

"Well, what's an example?" Molly asked. True to form, Shayne had one in mind.

"Shot-for-shot remake of *Vanya on 42nd Street,* but set in the MCU. Both the New York exteriors and the busted theater are, like, illusions of the Holodeck—"

"That's Star Trek," I said, but he wasn't listening.

"And all the actors are from *Guardians of the Galaxy.* And the premise is they're killing time while they travel from wherever to wherever, between two of the main movies. So they're bored on the ship and decide to do this play to pass the time."

"That's the plot of *Mansfield Park,*" Molly said, but he wasn't listening to her, either.

"So you've got Chris Pratt as Vanya, Zoe Saldana as Yelena, Vin Diesel as Dr. Astrov, Elizabeth Debicki as the nanny, that CGI raccoon as Andre Gregory. The rest will figure itself out."

"Are you finished?" Molly asked.

"That depends," Shayne said. "Do you believe me now?"

They may have started kissing after that, but my eyes were closed. I let myself drift as though the couch were a small boat out at sea, or fording the river of Canal Street, though I guess Canal Street would be a canal and not a river, however flooded it was at this point, and also the couch was maybe not a boat but a massage chair, one of those vibrating coin-op beds they have in cheap motels. Because it was shaking, or I was. Maybe I was having a heavy body high, vibing my face off here in this luxe enclosure with my old friend and my new frenemy, tucked away from the apocalypse in the safety of the future. Then the shaking stopped.

"Shit, sorry," Shayne said. "I tried to turn on my massager with the apartment app, but I think I hit yours instead."

"No big," I said, though in fact the stillness was rather

jarring. The cessation of shaking had left me shaken. I was really high.

Control, control, I thought, and saw the word float by on the movie screen of my still-shut eyelids, bright as cinema.

I opened my eyes, scooched up to a sit.

"What about you?" I asked Molly. "You haven't said yours yet."

"Well, I'm not an actor," she said.

"You're a *writer*," I said, hoping she heard the sarcastic backspin I put on that word, but also hoping she wouldn't take it as too sarcastic.

"You must be full of ideas," I said.

"I'd love to write a Wordsworth and Coleridge movie," Molly said. "Costume drama. Real steamy. Basically, take as a given Coleridge's suspicion that Wordsworth is banging both Mary and Sara Hutchinson. That scene from the Holmes biography where he walks in on the three of them in bed. For Coleridge, that's like the primal scene: the most destructive, shattering shit. But it's complicated because Coleridge of course has his own wife, couple of kids, and they're all together out by the lakes—"

"Oh," I said. "Is that why Taylor Swift has that line about how she wants you to take her to 'the lakes where all the poets went to die'?"

"I think she kind of screwed that line up, actually," Molly said. "I think she means the Gulf of La Spezia in Italy, where Shelley drowned because Byron made him feel like a pussy because he couldn't swim. And then Byron died, too, but later, in Greece, of malaria. Kind of both Trelawny's fault, to be honest. But I guess she could have meant something else, I just don't know what. Anyway, Coleridge. So you know how he was a heroin addict?"

"No," I said. But now she was on a Shayne-grade roll.

"Well, opium, but still. So, I figure that that's the frame story. He's older, maybe deathbed, looking back over his life, and he's going through it all one last time. Or maybe he's putting together his collected poems and when he rereads all the Asra poems he thinks about her."

"Asra?" Shayne and I said at the same time, and then got the giggles, which Molly didn't think was funny.

"That was his code name for Sara. Sara Hutchinson. Haven't you guys been listening to me?"

"So wait," I said, choking down laughter. "His code was to switch the first two letters of her first name around?"

"Yeah," she said, glum. She still had the vape pen. A sullen puff was followed by a fluffy cloud. "I'm not saying it was the fucking Enigma machine. I mean everybody knew. And that's sort of what the movie is about. How you're young and you think you have all these secrets but for the most part people are seeing right through you and it doesn't matter anyway. And how your real friends are the ones who take you back no matter what, even when you don't deserve it. Maybe especially then. When Coleridge was old and sick and trying to kick dope, he went back to live with the Wordsworths, and they let him stay even though he was a pain in the ass. I might be garbling the timeline a bit because I'm pretty high, but I think I've got the broad strokes down. Anyway, that's the movie I'd write. You guys can be in it if you want."

"Did he ever get with Asra?" Shayne asked.

"That's your question?" Molly said. "And no, I don't think so."

"Well, he'd have to in this version. At least once. Like out on the moors or something."

"That's *Wuthering Heights*!"

"I'm just saying," Shayne said, "that if they hook up once, then they're star-crossed lovers and there's your movie. If it's just two and a half hours of a hophead poet jerking it to some guy's wife's sister—that's, I don't know. It'll never get made."

"We were just sharing dreams," I said, a little off-put myself, now, and wanting, I wasn't sure why, to defend both Molly's vision of her obviously unmakeable period drama and Coleridge's—Shayne's own character's namesake's—dignity. Poor schmuck. Sounded to me like he'd done the best he could with the hand he was dealt.

Shayne got off his high horse, assuming he'd been on one, which, again, given how high I was, I really couldn't. Had he been lashing out at Molly or trying to help her? Did she want help? Where was the vape pen? When would this storm end? What were my exes up to right now—right this very instant? Was my kid okay?

"So what do we call this movie?" Shayne asked.

"*Duty Surviving Self-Love*," Molly said.

"Doesn't really roll off the tongue," I said, as gently as I could.

"Yeah, but it's the title of one of his poems," she said. "My favorite one. It's this sonnet that I think he wrote around the same time as 'The Pains of Sleep,' which in objective terms is the far better poem, but I just can't get over this one, I

memorized it, hang on"—a vape puff; so she had the pen still—
"okay, here goes." She put on an air of seriousness before recit-
ing the poem.

> *Unchanged within, to see all changed without,*
> *Is a blank lot and hard to bear, no doubt.*
> *Yet why at others' wanings should'st thou fret?*
> *Then only might'st thou feel a just regret,*
> *Hadst thou withheld thy love or hid thy light*
> *In selfish forethought of neglect and slight.*
> *O wiselier then, from feeble yearnings freed,*
> *While, and on whom, thou may'st—shine on! nor heed*
> *Whether the object by reflected light*
> *Return thy radiance or absorb it quite:*
> *And though thou notest from thy safe recess*
> *Old Friends burn dim, like lamps in noisome air,*
> *Love them for what they are; nor love them less,*
> *Because to thee they are not what they were.*

Neither Shayne nor I said anything. Out of respect for her
recitation, we had each sat up, but then it had become somehow too much to watch her while she spoke (her own eyes
closed) and so we'd ended up looking at each other, staring
into each others' eyes like a scene in some cheesy movie about
semi-estranged old friends who end up trapped in a house
together and come to realize that they're still as much brothers as they ever were, but what they can't tell is whether that
matters anymore. If it's going to be enough.

"So what did you think?" Molly said finally. Her voice was
lower now, timid and eager.

"Well, I really liked it," I said, rubbing my eyes because they were red and dry from the pot or possibly from rubbing them because her poem had made me cry a little, and I wanted her to think I was rubbing my eyes because of the pot. "That line about old friends burning dim was really something. And what kind of air was it?"

"Noisome," she said. "It means smoky, or bad. Bad air, you know, like if the oil in your oil lamp isn't very good quality so your wick isn't burning clean."

"Or if there were massive wildfires and it hurt to go outside," I said. "Half the reason I came out here was to get away from the West Coast's noisome air. Speaking of which." I reached for the vape pen. She relinquished. My praise was worth something to her, but it was Shayne's assessment she was waiting on.

"Great poem," he said. "Bum title for a movie. You could call it *The Asra Poems*. That has a ring. Little bit like *The Meyerowitz Stories,* but not too much. I bet if you don't tell Taylor she was wrong about the lakes, she'd do a song for the soundtrack. Ask Grace to ask her. It's a good idea, really. But I don't see how it makes your original point, about doing something original. Didn't you say this was someone's life that you read about in some book?"

"I read Richard Holmes's two-volume biography of Coleridge, if that's what you're asking," Molly said, her face falling. "It's one of several worthwhile source texts, including Dorothy Wordsworth's own journals and John Livingstone Lowes's *The Road to Xanadu.*"

"Xanadu like the 'caverns measureless to man' guy?" I asked.

"Like *Citizen Kane*," Shayne said.

"Oh my god," Molly said. "This is really happening. I'm really trapped here with the two of you. Don't either of you know anything about the namesakes of the characters that made you famous? Will, Cole, the *Rev Beach* fucking Mariners—any of it?"

"So," I said, suavely switching subjects. "You know all this stuff about poetry, and you obviously love it, but you said your degree is in nonfiction. Why?"

Molly started laughing. She didn't stop. It got a little scary. I mean she was doubled over. Tears big as the raindrops hitting the windows were streaming down her face. I was still holding the vape pen and quickly located the power button. Shayne hoisted himself off the couch and went to get her a glass of water. When he returned with it, she was still laughing. He held it until she was ready. She took the glass, sipped, sipped, coughed, sipped, handed it back to Shayne. She composed herself, looked right at me.

"I wanted," she said, "to study something that would lead to a stable career."

The mood in the morning was subdued. Shayne spent it playing the grand piano in the solarium. He ran through standard takes on "After the Gold Rush," "Celluloid Heroes," "She Don't Use Jelly," "Life on Mars?," and Taylor's lake song, then he launched into Guided by Voices' "Gold Star for Robot Boy" and jammed it out for a solid twenty minutes, which is no easy (or advisable) feat on solo piano. Molly sat at the breakfast bar trying to draft a "How I Spent My Superstorm" essay, which she had pitched to her editor while we were high last night. (The apartment had an office, which Grace had given us leave to use, but Molly said her best ideas only came to her when she was playing hooky from an office, so she'd left a notebook and a mug of tea in the office proper and then come out here to work.) Her idea was a split screen, sort of a double portrait of her roommates in Red Hook versus her and us holed up here.

"Memoir only works if the author is willing to indict herself as much as all the other characters," she'd said to me that morning.

I didn't know what she meant by that and hadn't been about to ask.

I was staying as sane as I could under the circumstances. I was watching the hard rain fall.

The internet had—as promised—forgotten all about my drunken escapade and Shayne's brave saving of me. Only Corey Burch was still ranting and fuming about it, and *Rev Beach*, and Molly's article, and now *Shibboleth Gold* as well, which seemed to have become a new front for the culture war, even as people were divided about the grounds of their objection. Some took the old conservative line that video games were brain-rotting and immoral, endorsed by Satan and quite possibly authored by him. (They'd said the same of *Rev Beach* once upon a time, though now those same factions rated us part of the "good old days," when teen dramas were still anti-sex and had no Black characters.) Others, meanwhile—the younger and more pilled reactionaries on whom Corey's mayoral candidacy would ultimately rely—had grown up gaming, so this didn't hold any water with them. Their objection to the *SG* series was that *CM2M* had been so long delayed. They thought that a *Rev Beach* reboot would further delay *CM2M* by taking up my time, and possibly Sam Kirchner's, if our nostalgia trip extended to bringing him back aboard as well—a thought that had not crossed my mind but which wasn't a bad idea. I'd have to ask him. A little cameo or something. An Easter egg, yes. Or we could add him to the writers' room. Grace had told me she already had the option on his IP, and even if that had just been dirty talk it could easily be made true. We could join our houses, so to speak. Expand the universe, pursue Shayne's dream of originality by means of derivation and remix. Context collapse like a new big bang. Maybe the convergencers were right. Maybe I would read that biography of Coleridge.

On the other hand, if it really was reboot versus sequel, the fans had to assume that *Rev Beach,* with an anniversary to shoot for and Grace Travis behind it, would take priority, which left the gamers feeling sidelined and disrespected. "Marginalized" they said, in what Molly had to explain to me and Shayne was yet another example of the online right co-opting the very language of identity politics it was forever denouncing in the online left. The angry gamers also suspected that the new game was being made woke, or woker, since it was already, in their view, too woke, insofar as its focus on iterative adventure was so absolute that there were no sexy tentacle women to ogle and murder. The tentacle women existed only in an X-rated fan art subreddit loosely affiliated with Stay (((Gold))). Here was Grace's old antagonist leading the charge of grievance:

@**BigDiogenesEnergy** MAKE THE SMOKY GOD GREAT
AGAIN!!!

@**BigDiogenesEnergy** BURCH + SYMMES 2024!!!

@**BigDiogenesEnergy** CELLULAR COSMOGONY IS AN
((((INSIDE))) JOB

@**BigDiogenesEnergy** WE WANT HYPERBOREA
NOW!!!

BDE was on a roll. Corey likely didn't know what any of
this stuff meant, but he had RT'd the 2024 tweet, presumably
because it had him in the top slot on the prospective ticket.
Would I have to go to Florida to serve as his explainer? Would
I be the one to tell him that John Cleves Symmes had died in
1829?

There was something exciting in all of this. It had been
many years since I had found myself in any kind of demand,
much less at the center of a fandom rivalry. I had spent so
much time dwelling on the toxic effects of fame, the ways
it had warped and deranged and humiliated me, and how
lucky I had felt to leave it behind and to still be alive, that I
had forgotten a small but important truth: the pleasure, the
glory, the thrill of being the center of attention, the star of the
show, the grinning headshot ripped from the magazine and
taped to the bedroom wall. The desktop background, the lock
screen. Maybe this wasn't so terrifying.

Let the fandoms fight!

Let the shipping commence, the wild rumpus start, et
cetera.

Let the stans stan as hard as they could stand.

.   .   .

It occurs to me that some of you are probably not dedicated archivists of internet microculture or the real history of fake science, and therefore much of what you just read must have sounded like gibberish. But unlike the video game gibberish I was slinging earlier, this actually does sort of matter. While it's tempting to say something flip about how we all have super-computers in our pockets and anyone can look up anything on a moment's notice, we both know you're not going to do that, and I don't blame you, so let me take a minute here to disambiguate a few choice morsels of crucial lunacy. I'm tempted to try out my best Molly impersonation and whip up my own incisive, intelligent, perfectly cutting "explainer." But who am I kidding? I could never match that exquisite blend of casual authority, sneering sarcasm, and shitposter's glee. I'll have to settle for telling you what I know—some of which I learned on the set of *Rev Beach* back in the day, some during bull sessions with Sam Kirchner, and some on this very morning in question, because Molly, who'd had her fill of BDE, logged off social media and onto Wikipedia, where she learned a lot of what I'm about to tell you while I read along over her shoulder, gleaning what I could, which wasn't easy because she reads so much faster than I do.

First up, *The Smoky God*, a book published in 1908 by a guy named Willis George Emerson. Born just before the Civil War, Emerson became a newspaperman in Chicago, also practiced law and dabbled in politics, later founded a copper-mining company in Wyoming, ended up in Los Angeles, living not far from where the Rising Star apartments now stand. *The Smoky God* is a novel that insists it is not a novel but rather a kind of tell-all, the deathbed confession of a Norwegian sailor named Olaf Jansen, whose "voyage journey to the inner earth" took him through a hole in the North Pole and brought him to a lost continent, where he spent two years living with a race of benevolent giants in a sophisticated utopia complete with high-speed trains. The book is titled for the hazy secret sun that lights their hidden world and which, for all their wisdom and futuristic tech, they are happy to worship as a deity. I don't know whether Ty Travis found this book himself, or if it was someone in the writers' room who got hold of it, but Will and Cole are named Jansen in Olaf's honor. Another little Easter egg that, if you've been huffing the forum and feed fumes for long enough, starts to feel like a capital-c Clue.

I already gave a decent rundown on John Cleves Symmes, and Hyperborea is an ancient Greek myth thing, so if you want to know more about either of those you really will have to google them. Which brings us to cellular cosmogony, and to Cyrus Teed, my personal favorite rogue in this gallery, who died in 1908, the same year that *The Smoky God* was published. Another coincidence? I'm just asking questions, man.

Teed was born in 1839 and grew up in Utica, New York, which is in Oneida County, which is the part of the state that had for decades been so consistently racked by religious awakenings, revivals, and crazes that people called it "the burned-over district." The Great Disappointment of the Millerites occurred when Teed was five. The Oneida community was founded when he was nine. By the time he was eleven, he was working as a mule driver on the Erie Canal. Supposedly he worked as an army medic during the Civil War, too, though it isn't clear whether he ever had any training or made it as far as a battlefield. In any case, he called himself a doctor and

treated patients for all kinds of problems, real and otherwise—
often with electricity. This was cutting-edge science at the
time, about a step removed from alchemy, which of course
Teed also practiced. It was during an electrical alchemical
experiment that he shocked himself unconscious, and it was
during his knockout that God appeared and told him he was
the Messiah. He changed his name to Koresh, started writing
books, giving lectures, and attracting followers. Also controversy: many members of his newfound fandom were wealthy
married women who were giving him gobs of their husbands'
money. He moved to Chicago and made a go of things there
for a while, but the angry husband problem persisted. Under
threat of public tar-and-feathering in 1894, Teed decided that
the Koreshan Unity ought to relocate to Florida.

Why all the women? And why Florida? Well, the first thing
you'll want to remember is that all cults either start or end as
sex cults, and there are only two kinds of those: the kind where
the master fucks everybody, and the kind where nobody fucks
anybody. Teed's cult was the second kind. He preached celibacy
as well as gender equality, and he really meant both things.
This in an era when divorce was almost impossible, especially
if initiated by a woman, who, even if successful, would probably end up broke and socially shunned. Much easier, therefore, to have a religious awakening, give all your money to an
affable maniac who had already made clear he wasn't trying to
fuck you, and who was going to spend it on you anyway in the
form of a utopian community he wanted to build in Southwest
Florida, which was at that time as isolated and wild as any of
the lost continents imagined by Symmes, Jansen, et al. It was a
place where your bad husband was probably not going to find

you and getting there was worth pretending to believe—or maybe, over time, coming to *actually* believe—that there is no such thing as outer space, and that we all live on the inner surface of a planet built like a hollow egg.

Teed spent more time and money trying to prove the scientific truth of his theory than he spent on anything else the Koreshans did. And they did a lot! They cleared huge swaths of swamp and wilderness. They built the region's first electrical plant, ran a bakery, a grocery store, a printing press, and a machine shop. They had their own orchestra and theater company. They published multiple newspapers and all of Teed's books. By 1900, they owned about a hundred miles of land. You can see why people were ready to believe Teed's boasts of a New Jerusalem. Also, why it was easy enough to just roll with the whole cosmogonic egg thing.

Your average hollow-earther believes that the earth has a hollow *center,* accessible by cave or polar hole, or whatever. They still see the earth as *mostly* solid. Others imagine earths like Russian nesting dolls: there's an inner world below us, a tiny planet, and an outer world above us, which, if we could reach it, would be so large as to make *us* seem the tiny planet. You'd have to first fly a ship far enough into space to hit the inside lining of that larger world, then figure out how to get through to its surface.

Teed's theory was more bespoke than either of these. He imagined the earth as an eggshell or a basketball and that the spinning of the planet kept us firmly planted on the inside of the O rather than sliding down its curved vertical face. The sky, stars, and outer space are all illusions, by-products of atmospheric phenomena happening in the empty center. A powerful enough telescope, Teed thought, could be pointed straight up in the air and see what was happening on the other side of the world. It was an idea that could only have taken root in the decades between the completion of the industrial revolution and the beginning of the age of air (and, later, space) travel, which is to say that Teed was a perfect messiah *for* his times, but also *of* his times.

The two big problems the Koreshan Unity had were that (1) as a celibacy cult, there was no second generation being raised to take over, and (2) as South Florida became more developed, they started having to deal with a lot of freaked-out normie neighbors. Teed tried to protect the Koreshans' interests by exercising the community's political muscle. The Koreshan Unity started voting as a bloc and running candidates for local office against the Democratic Party. Then things got very ugly very fast, in that very special Florida way. In 1906, Teed and a few of his boys got jumped at the train station in Fort Myers. The goons pistol-whipped his ass in broad daylight, beating him so badly that he never fully recovered. He died on December 22, 1908.

Because this was three days before Christmas, and because Teed had always told his followers that his mortal body would be theomorphically translated into that of God, the Koreshans assumed that his death was the first step of a gestational process that would culminate in a divine rebirth on Christmas Day. They stuck him in a copper bathtub and sat there waiting for the divine Koresh to emerge like a butterfly from the cocoon of the corpse of Cyrus Teed. The messiah was at least a week late when the sheriff finally forced them to bury the rotting body. Grudgingly, they built a stone tomb out on a spit of beach and sat vigil for a few more weeks. When they gave up the watch, they were still faithful enough to leave a canoe by the tomb so that Teed, when he woke up, would have a convenient means of getting back to the commune. The tomb was lost in a hurricane in 1921, and nobody knows where it stood. If *Rev Beach* had gotten a fourth season, it would have dived deep into all of this. There would have been ghosts, time travel, period costumes, a secret society of modern-day Koreshans keeping the flame lit and (just maybe) guarding the secret of the cosmogonic egg.

Obviously, that did not happen. The Koreshans died out and so did *Rev Beach*, though we went a lot faster than they did. A lot of Koreshans defected after Teed died, but thirty or forty stayed on the grounds and kept things limping along for decades. Now, here's where it gets *really* funny—or if you're of a certain cast of mind, conspiratorial. Because of course it's time to bring in (((*the Jews*))). Specifically, a German Jewish woman named Hedwig Michel, who had fled the Nazis in 1940 and somehow ended up at the Koreshan Unity, where she did what refugee Jews have been doing since time immemorial: balance the books, open a bank branch, adopt the party line on the space egg, and try to keep everyone happy enough that you don't get murdered or kicked out.

It is entirely plausible, though probably unprovable, that Ty Travis, through his magpie dabbling in literature, philosophy, and religion, as well as his protracted agita over his heritage—let us recall that this man changed his own name from Greenstein to Travis, then named his daughter Grace Merkavah—read something about the Jewish refugee Hedwig Michel, discovered the Koreshan Unity through her rather than the other way round, and that this could be why *Rev Beach* was set in Guiding Star. We'll never know. Anyway, by the 1960s there were less than ten Koreshans left, so Hedwig negotiated with state officials to cede the land back to Florida on the conditions that the surviving members be allowed to live out their lives on the property, and that the grounds be maintained as a state park and site of historic interest.

When Hedwig Michel died in 1982, she was the last Koreshan left. She is the only person buried on the property, and they know exactly where her grave is. Somewhere in my mom's house there's a photograph, taken with a disposable camera, of me and Shayne standing by her marker, dressed in period costume (i.e., Abercrombie), making ironic peace signs, and looking bored out of our minds.

I hope the look on your face is less bored than the ones on ours in the photo. This turned into a way longer detour than expected, and I guess I ended up doing the whole "explainer" bit after all, but even if I've tried your patience, can you grant me at least that my Molly impression was pretty good?

I called Grace before dinner. I suspected this would be our last night at her place. After two days of rain, the storm was finally subsiding. I'd been coy with her up to this point, describing my negotiations with Shayne as tentative yet promising.

Shayne had been cooking all our meals. He'd made use of every appliance and tool in Grace's kitchen: the sous vide, the pasta bike, the electric dough riser. It seemed a little ridiculous that I owned a restaurant instead of him.

Since tasting the sushi on the first day, Molly's principles of ethical consumption had taken something of a beating. Shayne's cooking was exquisite, and the only break in the monotony of this new micro-neo-quarantine we were living through while the storm of the century of the week had the boroughs locked down. Also, I suspected her article wasn't going well. Her vegan powders and goos had been gathering dust in the corner, not that dust gathered in Grace's apartment, which was patrolled by two Roombas and an aerial vacuum drone. Molly ate Shayne's food, and he was happy and so was she. What were morals compared to new love, to a rib eye aged sixty days and then skillet-seared in butter and finished in the oven, still purple as a bruise on the inside, the bloody juice flooding the asparagus as surely as the Hudson had flooded the West Side Highway?

"Enough about what you're eating," Grace said. "How's it going?"

"Good," I said. "We're hard at work. Molly's cool; I like her. She and Shayne are a couple. Or they're something."

"Don't love that," she said.

"No, it's fine," I said. "It's good. She wants to write for the show, and she has all these ideas. I think in a way she's the one doing the heavy lifting here. This is exciting for her. Have you ever heard of an MFA?"

"Yes. And I see why she wants the work. Well, any port in a storm, right?"

"Port in a storm is right. Have you been following the news here?"

"I saw the video of the waterspout in the East River, and the tornado in Morningside Heights. Oh, and those women getting airlifted out of that building in Red Hook."

"That was Molly's block! She lives there. Or did. I guess nobody lives there now. And thank you, by the way, for letting her and Shayne crash. I know this wasn't the original plan."

"Just happy you're all safe. And wow, that's great to know that she knows that neighborhood. I already bought the option—"

"On what?"

"The cell phone video of the women getting rescued. *Rev Beach* is one thing, but those girls in that helicopter is like that guy who landed the plane on the river."

"No, it isn't."

"It will be if I want it to be."

"Touché. Look, there's one thing you're not going to like, and I'm sorry, but I don't think we have a choice." I stopped talking, let the silence build.

It built. I heard my ex-wife sighing. One of those long, low, ragged, marriage-ending sighs. I missed her. I missed us. At the same time, the one thing she wanted was for me to not make her ask, and for some reason that meant making her ask was the one thing that I absolutely had to do. We were either completely right for each other or completely wrong. I felt our fates entwining and was ambiguously thrilled—ecstasy or doom, whatever, just take me somewhere. Let all this come to something. I was horrified above all by the prospect of going back to Portland, my lonely luxe enclosure above the fog line, to sit and wait out the months until *Rev Beach* went into production, until Amber let me near Hank again, measuring my life in Netflix queues and bespoke grilled cheese, studiously avoiding cucumber oblivion, making myself a paragon of virtue and stability—

I wouldn't make it. This thought appeared so calmly in my consciousness it wasn't even scary. It was a simple truth: I was riding the tiger now, and if I had to stop, I was liable to either kill myself or get myself killed.

Grace did not sigh a second time, and yet I could hear her giving in. Or maybe I couldn't hear it, exactly, but rather could feel it in my bones.

"What's the one thing, David? Just tell me. And bear in mind before you speak that I have loved you more than any other person in this world besides your mother, and that there are certain narrow but supremely important contexts in which I know you better than you know yourself."

"I've always appreciated those things about you," I said.

"David," she said.

"Okay, sorry, yeah," I said, and launched into my lie. "The thing is Corey. Shayne says we have to at least reach out to him, mend the fence there. Shayne says we owe him. In the broad karmic sense. He won't say yes unless we promise to try, and for whatever it's worth to you, Molly thinks it's a good idea, too. She says she's got a great plan for how to write him into the show—not a full cast credit, just a one-off cameo. Fan service. Keep him happy. And get him to stop tweeting."

"Is her idea by any chance that Corey could be the grown-up ghost of a dead child because in this world, for whatever inane reason, the rules of the afterlife allow ghosts to age?"

"Right, exactly. It's this thing of, well, how can I say this? The idea of ghosts is usually that they're stuck forever as they were when they died, but what her version of the afterlife presupposes is what if the dead got to live some of the life they were robbed of? So, he has all these memories of the person that he might have been, and he looks like he thinks he would have if he'd become an adult—but everything's a little off because it's speculative, an adolescent fantasy of what an adult life would have been. And that becomes a major plot point in an episode. I don't know which one yet, she's working on it, maybe seven?"

"Is that out of ten or out of eight?"

"Not sure. Maybe twelve if we do a two-part Christmas special."

"You got Shayne to agree to a two-part Christmas special?"

"All he wants is this one thing. The olive branch for Corey. Oh, and for Molly to get a seat in the writers' room."

"Molly can have her seat in the room," Grace said. "And not as a favor to Shayne. The rest of this sounds frankly like a terrible idea. But you seem to be on a hot streak, so I'm going to let you try my patience. Is it fair to assume that the next thing you want is a ticket to Florida?"

"As soon as this storm ends and they drain the runways."

"Done. But one thing. Actually, no, two things. First, don't fuck this up by getting sucked into Corey's bullshit. We are here to reboot a beloved mid-aughts cult classic that is on the precipice of being embraced by a new generation of fans who would perhaps also like to become devoted patrons of my lifestyle brand and consumers of my high-GMO wine. We are not here to join the hashtag resistance or to resist the hashtag resistance. We have no politics or values. The words *woke* and *Q* are equally meaningless to us. Second, if you're going down there, visit your mother. I know you've been avoiding it, but it's far past time. You don't even hate her, so there's really no excuse. Corey hates his parents because his father beat him and his mother allowed it. Shayne hates his because they robbed him blind, and that's why he has to skip every other Kelly Reichardt movie he gets offered to instead go put on an army man costume and point a plastic gun at Spanish guys pretending to be Arabs. I hated Ty, because he was a domineering psychopath who mapped my whole life out for me the week I was conceived. I'm still stuck living in his stupid mansion and trading off his name, because what else can I do? But now that he's gone, I miss him. I even miss what I hated. Do you hear what I'm saying to you? I miss my dad. Why do you think I'm trying to reboot this stupid show that I hated and that I hated him for making me be on? The only bad thing your dad ever did to you was die, and the only thing your mom ever did was keep living. You want me to mend a fence with Corey? Fine. But it's sugar for sugar and salt for salt. No more nostalgic ex-sex until you sort out your family shit. I love you."

"I love you, too," I said.

Grace did the wise thing then. The brave thing. She hung up on me. I sat on the edge of her king bed and stared at the call log on my phone. Who says a life can't change in an instant? Now all I had to do was go back into the living room, eat another gourmet dinner, and lie to Molly and Shayne about the conversation I'd just had. I needed to convince them that the thing I'd told Grace they had demanded of her was the thing that she had demanded of me. Then I needed to go to Florida. I wished that the storm of the century of the week would never end.

. . .

The storm of the century of the week was ending. The tornadoes had subsided. I was pretty sure we'd seen the last of the lightning. Even the rain was easing up; drizzle through the night and clear by morning. So they said. Flights would fly again, swamped subway stations were being pumped. The disaster was winding down, the city switching into cleanup mode. The mayor was saying things were less bad than they looked but was also asking the governor for help. The governor was saying that things were far worse than the mayor was claiming, but also that New York was on its own. Things were getting back to normal. Our very special episode was coming back from its last commercial break. Sound guys were cuing up the learn-your-lesson music. I still didn't know what the lesson was but hoped I would be the one teaching it and not the one being taught.

"Nature is healing," Shayne joked. We were in the kitchen. He was pat-drying a spatchcocked free-range chicken with some paper towels. A bowl of fresh-ground spices sat ready for application: a dry rub. Quartered purple creamer potatoes were ready for roasting in the skillet along with the bird.

"Nature is still very much wounded," Molly said. "It's bleeding out while we make dinner." But her objections were half-hearted. Shayne obviously had not been referring to actual nature, which we all understood was deeply deranged and had spent the last two days trying to murder us. Rather, he'd been making a joke about state versus local gridlock, which I had favored with a laugh since it tracked with my own understanding of what constituted normality, and anyway I wanted to make sure he was in a good mood because I had all these lies to tell that I needed for him to believe.

As for Molly, she had her service industry allegiance and her Bernie-ish convictions, but she was still young enough to believe that the worst thing a cool person could do in this world was say something boring and obvious, even if it happened to be true. And though she knew that making earnestness uncool was part of the power structure's master plan to undermine social movements, which have no choice but to be earnest, she was enamored enough of her parents' (or would it have been her grandparents'?) generation to hold the fundamentally Gen X conviction that jaded irony was deathless. And she'd been living in high luxury at Grace Travis's apartment for the last forty-eight hours, eating steak and sushi while everyone else she knew was either staying with friends or in a literal flood shelter. So she knew she had lucked out, even if her luck was, in some vague commie sense, ill-gotten. Or maybe she was getting soft.

She was, to be certain, eyeing Grace's wine fridge. Unsure, I think, of whether we were allowed to open a bottle, and if we were, whether she ought to do so in front of old alcoholic me. Would she be the cause of my temptation and downfall? And if she did, and if I did, would I become a huge pain in her ass like I had the other night? Ruining that night had been one thing. In a roundabout way, it had gotten us here. But this was our last night together in the secret Eden we'd scored for ourselves. Nobody wanted to wreck that, least of all me.

Maybe Molly was in mourning. Maybe I was, too.

I brought out the bottle of Grace's magic wine.

"I've been saving this," I said. "Grace sent it. And don't worry. I'm good for a glass, but I won't freak out again. I have this system I stick to, and it really works. Ahem. Usually works.

It'll be fine." I was earning my honorary degree in speculative nonfiction. I found a corkscrew, plunged screw into cork.

The cork popped out easily, and its wet bottom lit up as soon as it hit the air. It was like a little green candle in my hand.

"The hell?" Molly said, the shock in her voice so stark and genuine that Shayne turned from his half-rubbed chicken to see what she was looking at. I grinned at them. I put the corkscrew down and picked up a decanter.

"You're going to want to watch this," I said. "We'll give it a minute to open before we drink it." I poured slowly, holding the bottle a good foot above the decanter so the liquid would blaze in a long arc before it hit the glass. The decanter looked like something out of a mad scientist's laboratory. The pouring wine was gorgeous and hypnotic, but I suddenly wasn't sure whether I wanted to drink it, or whether anyone else would. Or should. Still, I persevered.

"It'll mellow and won't be as glowy," I said. More speculative nonfiction on my part. We'd know soon if it was true.

"So you talked to Grace?" Shayne said. He was back to rubbing rub into the chicken skin. Molly looked like she'd been hit in the head with the skillet.

"I did," I said. And let the silence build.

But Shayne wasn't my ex-wife, and he wasn't going to prompt me, nor sigh about having to. I'd never successfully bluffed him in our whole lives, but there's a first time for everything, and I needed for this to be it.

"Grace will meet your conditions," I said. "And Molly's hired."

"Holy shit," Molly said softly. She shook her head.

I brought her a glass of the magic jellyfish wine, which I was pleased to see had mellowed like I'd said it would. It looked less like cartoon radioactive waste now. I brought Shayne a glass and then poured one, a small one, for myself.

"Grace does have one condition," I said. "And you're not going to like it, so let's toast the good news before I tell you the rest."

Like a lot of alcoholics, I felt that a toast was a kind of oath. I hoped that once we did it, they'd take the news about Grace wanting me to go see Corey as a minor annoyance rather than a deal-breaker. Not that either of them had any reason to find his involvement a deal-breaker. Grace was the only one who had real cause to hate him, and as far as she knew, his inclusion was their condition, because of what I'd said about the wishful logic of ghosts.

They raised their glasses to meet mine. I felt another wave of that ambiguous emotion I'd felt while on the phone with Grace. Was I the hero or the villain of this story? I was weaving webs of deceit, albeit in the name of a greater good. I wanted to save Molly from the service industry as well as elite media, both of which were dead-end fields that skated by on paying starvation wages. I wanted to reunite with Shayne. I wanted to love Grace again and be worthy of the love she had for me. I wanted all of us to help honor the memory of her father by rebooting this dumb TV show that had cost him a fortune and nearly wrecked all our careers. But maybe that same show could save us now. Maybe it couldn't have happened any other way. I still wasn't sure what Nietzsche's eternal return meant, but I wanted to rescue Corey Burch from the stupid purgatory where he'd cast himself, and for him to forgive me an old wrong he didn't even know that I'd done him, i.e., the thing I still haven't said. I wanted to do anything other than see my family in Florida, but I'd cross that bridge, or burn it, when I got there. One step at a time. One glass of wine and not seven. System works if you work it, as I'd heard people say in AA, though I was mostly thinking of that episode of *Halt and Catch Fire* where Donna says it and that's how Cameron figures out she's been going to meetings. Because Cameron's mom used to say it. Amber's mom says it, too.

I made for a complicated but redeemable antihero, someone who, despite all his flaws, or rather because of them, you want to root for. That, at any rate, was my present hope.

My wing and prayer.

Hear the crystal clink of our three glasses touching, that single pure perfect note. A freeze frame, bright eyes and big grins. Wouldn't it be great if we could call it quits here? If this was the end of the story: All of us happy and safe and together? If this was the last thing that you saw before the screen went black, like *The Sopranos* finale, and after a long beat the credits rolled?

Let's skip the scene where I convince them. Like a sex scene, it's more of me showing my ass than anyone needs to see. Suffice it to say, they were pissed. But I held fast, blamed it all on Grace. *Out of my hands! Truly! I'm powerless, guys. We all know she holds all the cards here. She says Higley and Nichols think it's the right thing to do as well.*

Molly and Shayne hated this plan. They registered their vociferous and, it must be admitted, reasonable objections. And then they relented. What else were they going to do? We had survived our apocalypse and taken our emotional blood oath, not to mention all the money on the line.

I reassured them to little effect. But the issue was settled. I booked my ticket for tomorrow. We scrolled through social media, catching up on the steady stream of flood refugee stories, videos, photos, testimonials, news about the cleanup. Despite being at the lip of the Gowanus, Driving School had survived, so Molly would still have work while we got things official with the reboot. We finished our magic wine and said good night to each other. They retreated down the hall together, and I was glad for them. I said I was going to stay up awhile, maybe read. I waited until I saw the line of light beneath the bedroom door flick off and then I went back to my own room to dig around in my bag for something. Then I left the apartment.

But I didn't go far.

I stood on the rooftop patio. The drizzle was still coming down. My mouth had that cool neutral coating from the power-up I'd just taken. I took off my shoes and socks, my jeans and shirt. I was about to slide my briefs down when I heard a decorous cough behind me. I turned to see Molly standing there, wearing a Travis-monogrammed bathrobe.

"Oh shit," I said. "I almost MeToo'd you. Or you me, I guess."

"That's reductive and not funny," she said. "Except, okay, it's a little funny. And I'm not going to MeToo you."

"That's a relief."

"Well, I mean, we're alone here. Are you going to YouToo me?"

"No. I came up here to be alone, and to see something. I can show you if it wouldn't be too weird."

"I guess that'll depend on what you want to show me."

"Not my dick, I promise. I was going to take my boxers off, but I don't have to."

"Great," she replied. "And before this conversation gets any weirder, let's just agree we are feeling relaxed and chaste, and that not all nudity is sexual. Please provide immediate verbal confirmation, because I'm also in my underwear underneath this robe."

"Roger that," I said. I turned away from her, less embarrassed by my awkwardness or almost having flashed her than by the ungainly fact of my body: pale and soft, furred over, so unlike the man she had waiting for her downstairs. Not that I wanted to be him, just, well—who wouldn't want to be him? I jumped into the water. I dove for the bottom and, when I got there, let out the breath I had been holding. I sucked in lungfuls and found that I was able to breathe—I won't say effortlessly, but without much effort. The chlorine taste was icky. The feeling of the fluid filling and then leaving my lungs was incredibly strange. A lot of liquid where no liquid was supposed to be, and yet my body accommodated.

I heard Molly enter the pool. I surfaced and saw her treading water in bra and panties, a vaguely sexy but basically blurred-out shape, like a movie censored for network. I assumed I looked about the same.

"You held your breath for a long time," she said. I spit a stream of lung water into the pool, coughed a few times as I shifted back to air-breathing.

"I'm a good swimmer," I said. "How's the article coming? You figure out your split screen yet?"

"That part's easy," she said, still looking away. "It's the ending. I've got everything except an ending."

"Because it isn't over," I said helpfully.

"Right," she said. "That's very helpful."

"I just mean we're still here, more stuff could still happen. Think about it this way: a TV show gets green-lit at a certain number of episodes per season, ten or twenty or six or whatever. But you know how many episodes you'll have in your season before you know what they're all going to be about, what all the big arcs and small arcs are going to be. Tomorrow everyone goes back to reality, or we each go to our own reality. That's an ending. Then you can find the story that fits the form."

"That actually is sort of helpful," she said. "Thank you. I'm calling it 'Storm of the Century of the Week.'"

"Good title."

"It'll never see the light of day. They'll probably call it 'Thirteen Weird Tricks I Learned Sleeping at Famous People's Apartments.' Hard to see how this doesn't end with me having to quit all social media and maybe my job."

"Would that be such a bad thing?"

"No. Everyone knows the highest expression of social media clout is deleting your account. But still, I need to see some hiring paperwork from Grace before I can stop bartending, because my minus sign isn't getting any smaller, and now I don't have anywhere to live. I can stay with Shayne for a while, but that's not a long-term plan. Which means, believe it or not, that I'm counting on you, David. Looks like everyone is."

"Is that why you followed me up here?"

"I didn't follow you. Shayne fell asleep, and I was bored and had the same thought you did, the one about how nice it is to take a solo swim at night in a light warm rain. I didn't know you were here until I got here. Okay, now you."

"It was in another lifetime," I began. "Five days ago, in a strange land called Fame Island where my ex-wife, your future boss, gave me a box of magic beans that let me breathe underwater. That's why I wanted to jump into the canal when I was drunk. I was trying to show Shayne. And when I say magic, I mean science. I mean, I don't know the science, but someone does. Her scientists. Same ones who jellyfished the wine. I wasn't sure if it would work, so I came up here to see for myself. I lied before, I suck at swimming. But watch this."

I opened my mouth wide and dropped below the surface of the water. I stayed under for the count of a full minute, then another, then another. I was starting to feel light-headed but still breathing fine. I counted off a fourth and final minute, then I rose.

"Okay," Molly said, when I resurfaced. "That's cool, this parlor trick you learned or whatever it is she pumped you full of. I guess I'm not as impressed as I should be. Sorry. I got my first cell phone when I was nine."

"Right," I said. "It probably isn't that impressive from your perspective. But if you could feel what I felt, the way you can go under and feel totally at peace and alive down there, well, I just had to know that it was possible."

"It's still good you didn't go in the Gowanus," she said. "Assuming it is science and not magic, then it stands to reason that the usual rules apply as far as your body absorbing the pollutants that are in the substance you're consuming. So, the Gowanus would be lungfuls of cancer and human shit. Even here, you're mainlining quite a bit of chlorine."

"I hadn't thought of that. I do feel kind of light-headed."

"Yeah, maybe come out of the water and sit on the edge for a bit? For your modesty's sake, I'll keep my eyes on the skyline, which is what I came up here to see."

I pulled myself out of the water. "There are worlds and there are worlds," I said. "That sounds like mystic mumbo jumbo, but it isn't. Grace lives in a different realm than the rest of us. I've been there before, and I'm frankly a little trepidatious, maybe more than a little, about going back. Even though it's exciting. Maybe especially because it is."

"And you want me to, what—know what I'm getting into? I can't tell if you're trying to entice me or scare me off."

"I'm not trying to do either."

"That's bullshit. But it doesn't matter. I know you need to feel like you're at the center of all of this, and I can mostly vibe with that, even if I don't get why. I'm still trying to like you, but you're a weird dude, and desperate, which makes me wary. Also, I know you're lying about Corey Burch."

"Wait, what? How? I mean, no I'm not."

"Sure you are. Anyone who has ever read the kind of garbage culture websites I write for knows how much Grace hates that guy. She isn't making you do this. Also, I talked to her and she told me."

"Since when are you talking to Grace? How did you get hold of her?"

"That Craig guy called. You think she gave me a job based on your ultimatum? We had a nice long phone call yesterday."

"Does Shayne know?"

"About the call, of course, but not that you lied. I care about him a lot, but I have a rule I live by, which is never get in the middle of other people's family drama."

"Me and Grace, you mean? We're not a family anymore."

"You and Shayne and Corey. Whatever happened to the three of you at that child actor factory farm you all come from. You're obviously on this mission to un-fracture the family, de-estrange everyone, and all I can say is good luck, and I hope you don't relapse when it blows up in your face. So go to Florida and get your shit sorted with Corey. And your mom."

"Why are women always talking to me like this?"

"Because we're socialized our whole lives to respond to the needs of men," she said. She paddled over to the steps and made her way out of the pool, no longer caring if I watched her, maybe hoping I would.

"Also," she said, "Grace told me. She knows you extremely well and still seems to like you a lot, which is something worth considering."

"You're telling me," I said.

"Be a good guy, David Crader," she said. "Don't drink any more chlorine. Or gin. It's tempting to believe the scientists when they say that science will solve all the problems science has caused, but you just learned the truth firsthand:

underwater breathing is worthless if the water is full of poison."

She slipped into her robe again, set off for the elevator. I went back into the water but didn't tempt fate with another long submersion. I stared at the skyline as she had done, the jagged mountain range of light punctuated here and there by unaccustomed dark. The water was warm, and the falling rain was warm, and I felt at peace. The aftermath of Molly's exposure of my lies and her commitment to keeping my secret had turned her into a kind of confidant, an unlikely ally. Or I hoped it had. I floated on my back and felt good with raindrops hitting my face and stared into the gray sky with its low lid of clouds. I imagined those clouds as the innermost layer of the crust of the next world above ours, someplace we could someday escape to and start over, leave this world behind like the old, totaled car that we had made of it. Solar power and organic gardening. Uncollapsed fisheries, virgin forests, starlings to darken the sky for days and endless buffalo roaming the endless plain.

But my vision didn't last long. It was hard to feel utopian with chlorine in my blood.

What was this future we were flailing toward, with its fires and floods? Its rolling blackouts and tornadoes? Where was the reboot on this? The plot twist, the science fiction dream turned real scientific breakthrough, that would make everything okay? Where were the venture capitalists with their cold fusion and their wind farms? Their plastic-digesting bacteria? Their CRISPR-driven vaccination platforms? Their cancer-curing pills? Were we all really just going to keep fumbling along through these storms of the centuries of the weeks?

What would it look like when the power went out for the last time? When there was no one left to put the poles and wires back up? All those empty unlit rooms, all the rats and pigeons starving, and the subway tunnels full of water, a new species of blind shark taking dominion of the thousands of miles of man-made sea caves, reefs in the stalled cars whose windows had shattered under the pressure of all that water, and the broken glass worn smooth by time, and all the subway stairs become oyster beds, anemone tendrils adrift in the current—all those gorgeous impossible colors, a true new Eden, except of course that it would all be happening in absolute darkness, with nobody there to bear it witness, to register the beauty and terror of nature repairing itself. Who would rub the condensation from his dive mask and stare stupefied? Who would catch the silver gleam of scale or white teeth full of bloody shredded spoil in a dive-rated flashlight's sun-bright beam?

I got out of the pool, dried off, went downstairs, took a quick rinse, drank some water, and got into bed, whereupon I fell fast asleep and into uneasy chlorine dreams.

But I woke up feeling rested and refreshed. In the light of day, from the vantage of Grace's penthouse, swaddled in her one-thousand-thread count sheets, my nightmare of the flooded subway seemed cool, even exciting, like something we could do for *CM2M*. I reached for my phone, texted Sam.

"Hey you know what would be cool," I typed, "is if Shib comes up from the center of the earth and the apocalypse has happened and he has to fight in the flooded subways under New York. Imagine union square station as a whole biome, all the platforms and tunnels, and the boss is like a megashark that's blind and hunts by sound so shib can't use his guns?"

He wrote back: "Dude who gives a shit about the game I got doxed this morning. Had to tell my wife and kid to go stay with her mom. They're making Shib into the next Pepe. This. Is. Fucked."

"Give me a day," I wrote back. "Maybe two days. Also what are you talking about?"

He didn't write back again.

I went to the bathroom, brushed my teeth, took a long hot shower, got dressed, checked my phone again. Still nothing from Sam.

"But seriously," I wrote him. "What do you think of my idea?"

I put the phone in my pocket and walked out into the living room. Molly was drinking fresh-squeezed orange juice, a homemade English muffin buttered on her plate. She was wearing a high-necked yet sleeveless prairie hipster dress, sherbet orange, with ruffled shoulder fringe and red braid trim like suspenders down the front.

"Aha," I said. "The explainer. Can you tell me what the hell is going on?"

"You're canceled," she said. "I tweeted a picture of you with your dick peeking out of your boxers when we were at the pool."

"Are you serious?"

"No."

"Oh . . . But then what, um, actually happened?"

She handed me her phone, the clip already queued up. It was Corey.

Because of course it was Corey. Looking for all the world like a younger and almost as buff Kyle Chandler in *Bloodline:* pale blue shirt with the top two buttons undone and the sleeves rolled up, khaki pants, brown leather loafers, pistol in a holster, standing beside a palm tree with what looked like a plantation house (but was almost certainly a hotel) out of focus in the background.

"I'm standing here," he said, "to share something about myself that I have never shared before. A few years ago, just before she died, my mother told me that, before she married my father, she was Jewish. I never knew that before. Neither of them had ever said anything about it. Now, you all know me. I was raised a Lutheran, and then I had my wild years, the temptations of Hollywood and cetera, on which I shall not dwell, and then I was born again. I was saved by the precious blood of Jesus and *that*, friends, is what I still believe. But I have been learning about my, what you call it, heritage, and you know that part of my platform on which why I am running for mayor of this Florida beach town is to be a friend to Israel and our Jewish brothers and sisters, of which I am also one. The best friend they ever had. No daylight there. And cetera. And when it came to my attention earlier this week that there was talk of rebooting the TV show on which I appeared so many years ago, my first thought—my very first thought—was of what that money could do for this community and how it might raise our profile, bring the tourists on which I know so much of the local economy depends. It has been a hard few years here. I don't need to tell any of you that. We've had it tough in Florida, what with the red tides, the oil spill, the other oil spill, the sinkholes, the microplastics, the hurricanes,

Zika, COVID, Obamacare, Piney Point, Matt Gaetz, and now we have the federal overreach of the so-called Green New Deal threatening our sugar planta—farmers. Our sugar-growing, job-providing friends who are not only our friends but our community, our brothers and neighbors and campaign financiers. Sisters and wives, too, I suppose. Not to say sister wives. So I know that anything that puts dollars into cash registers, lodgers into hotels, fishermen into fishing boats, ice cream into ice cream cones, and cetera, is to the good. We want to be a place that welcomes everyone and is a place where everyone wants to come. All-you-can-eat fried shrimp and cetera. I was even, to be personal a moment, looking forward to seeing my old friends again. Some better friends than others, it is true, but we learn in the church that forgiveness is one of the virtues, and I was ready to mend those fences, accept those apologies for old wrongs and move forward. But then I learned that my old friend, or who I thought was my friend, David Crader, has been profiting off of a video game built on the most pernicious of antisemitic stereotypes. He plays a creature called Shibboleth Gold, I mean how much clearer can it be, that is said to be somewhat of a secret lizard person. When I first learned this, I could hardly believe it. 'David?' I said. 'He wouldn't!' But my kids showed me the game. They had been playing it! Well, friends, they are not playing it now. And so long as I have any say about it, which if you vote for me, I will, Florida will roll out no welcome mat for this hatemonger and his band of rootless cosmopolitan fellow travelers. They can go peddle their smut elsewhere, as far as I'm concerned, and we can sell ice cream to each other. God bless the troops."

The clip ended.

"Shibboleth's not a lizard," I said. "He's a tentacle monster. And only half."

"A key distinction," Molly said. "Maybe you should tweet that."

"The game isn't antisemitic. Sam Kirchner is Jewish. And so am I! And so is Grace! And Corey isn't!"

"And so am I!" Molly said. "Christ, we really do run Hollywood, don't we? But setting that aside, why would Corey lie about this, especially if he's courting a shadow constituency of internet fascists?"

"People pretend to be Jewish for all kinds of reasons."

"Okay, true. Have you ever read *Operation Shylock*?"

"You're just being a dick with that question," I said.

"How about the *Seinfeld* episode where the dentist converts so he has license to tell Jewish jokes?"

"Tim Whatley. Played by Bryan Cranston! Long road from there to Walter White, much less LBJ."

"Great, yeah," Molly said. "Go with that. Anyway, nobody is going to believe this guy. Just look at him. He's about as Jewish as Kyle Chandler!"

"Are you saying he's hot?" I asked.

"Say what you will about fascism," Molly said, "but a commitment to severe aesthetics and bodily discipline does have its advantages."

"Noted," I said. "Where's Shayne? This mission of mercy just got weird."

"He isn't trying to shut down the show," Shayne said. He was half-asleep and grouchy, his English muffin still in the toaster.

"It's the opposite. He needs us, and he knows it. He'd love nothing more than to fundraise off us for the next five years. He just wants us on the defensive."

Now that the storm was past, the theater was open again and he had a performance tonight. The subways were running, but only at half capacity, long delays between trains because some of the tunnels were still flooded. Molly had work later, too. She had graciously (and, I assume, at Shayne's request) offered to drive me to JFK. Our little utopia was almost over.

"And it sounds like he's really buying into this fandom-rivalry thing," Molly said. "He's threatening to make *Rev Beach* hard to shoot in hopes that you'll come to him, hat in hand, begging for compromise. Then he asks you to step away from your little video game for stupid incel babies, and when you do, he gets to boast a culture war victory. He gets to be the hero who brought the local economy back, and he ensures that you're on his side, or at least in his pocket. No throwing fundraisers for whatever bag of meat the Democrats run against him. No errant tweets."

"You know, you really are great at explaining things," I said. "Though it would have been just as lucid without the crack about the *Shibboleth Gold* fanbase. Female gamers have it hard enough without you erasing their existence."

"Sorry," Molly said.

"No you're not," I said.

"No," she said. "I'm not."

"I'm glad you two are getting along," Shayne said as he buttered his muffin. "But what do we do?"

"Go down there anyway," I said. "Let Corey get his photo op, tell him that Sam is Jewish and that Hollywood is coming to

Guiding Star whether he likes it or not. Then we, I don't know, donate some money to AIPAC and tell him he can guest-star as the mayor."

"Just to be clear," Molly said, "if either of you donates a dime to AIPAC, I will destroy you both."

"With another explainer?" I was getting tired of Molly's politics. Not what her politics were so much as the fact that she had them. I thought about warning her about what Grace had said about steering clear of all that, then I thought, screw it, she'll find out soon enough. The hard way, I hoped.

"Okay, kids," Shayne cut in. "I guess I spoke too soon. But listen, we're all on the same side here. Nothing but blue skies."

"I wonder," Molly said.

"No, for real," Shayne said. "I checked the forecast."

"Not what I meant," Molly said.

She eyed me. I understood her. She had meant were we all really on the same side. And I had to give her credit—I didn't know.

Shayne set his half-eaten muffin down on his plate. "I gotta get ready," he said, and walked off toward the residential wing of the apartment, leaving Molly and me alone.

"Well, you must be thrilled," she said.

"Why would you think this thrills me?"

"You wanted a problem, now you've got one."

"I'm just trying to help you find an ending for your article."

"There is no article."

"You couldn't finish it?"

"I took my own advice." She held up her phone so I could see the new wide gap in her icon array. Twitter, Insta, and Tik-Tok were all missing; her accounts were gone.

. . .

I wanted new clothes. I was tired of Will Jansen's wardrobe,
also of Shayne's Cannes shirt. JFK had some nice stores, practically a mall there on the other side of security. I could go
shopping if I got to the airport early enough, or, failing that,
once I got to Florida. My plan was to land, rent a car, find a
store, buy an outfit like the one I'd seen Corey wearing in his
video, then head for my mother's house.

My mother, yeah. I haven't said much about her, have I?
That's been on purpose. Well, maybe it's time for a bottle episode of my own. Of her own. Or maybe it isn't quite time yet,
because there was my heartfelt goodbye with Shayne to get
through, and then there was me and Molly left alone, test-
ing the contours of our tentative peace but also knowing that,
with Shayne safely seen off, we were free to have it out with
each other if we wanted. If she wanted. I didn't want. Elevator hum as we rode down to the lobby. Sunlight gleaming on
wet pavement. Cars and pedestrians and cyclists: here was the
city, alive again. I was sorry to be leaving. It was a quiet ride to
the airport, just the two of us. I wanted to offer her gas money
but didn't have any cash because I'd spent my last physical
hundred ruining my son's life and hadn't had a reason to hit
an ATM since.

"If you stop at a bodega I'll get cash out," I said to Molly.
She waved me off.

"Shayne'll cover it," she said. "He'll owe me, and then you
can owe him."

"See?" I said. "This isn't other people's family. Like it or not,
you're one of us now."

"Why don't you put some music on?" she said, refusing to

glance in my direction, though I could see I'd put a smile on her face. The line of poetry tattooed across her pale arm was bright and blackly legible in the full sun of a perfect New York day as we changed over from the BQE to the LIE, turning our trajectory from north to east and leaving the last views of the city skyline behind us. I turned my gaze down to my phone, where neither Sam nor Amber had texted me back, where Corey Burch was blowing up the internet, or an internet—his or ours, it was too soon to tell.

I reached down into the mess of cassette tapes, put on *Blood on the Tracks,* which I remembered Molly rejecting on the drive in from Brooklyn. I was hoping that the tape would kick right in with "Shelter from the Storm." It's what would have happened in the movie version, but of course this was real life—or, at least, it wasn't a movie. We got "Idiot Wind," and all I could think was *Yes, well, that, too.*

The airport was a different place today than it had been a few days ago. I felt like I'd landed on a different planet, or fallen into an alternate universe. Some movie where the guy is the same but everything else has changed and he doesn't know why. But I did know why. I was an object of attention again, of fascination. Veneration and controversy. People saw me and they whipped their phones out. They waved or they whistled. Some booed. I wished I'd thought to wear a hat and sunglasses.

The *SG* hive was giving Corey hell online, and the Guiding Star Chamber of Commerce and Tourism Board weren't happy with him, either. The evangelicals and Israel-hawks were thrilled. The Q-pilled were split down the middle. How did the claim of unwitting crypto-Judaism square with the idea that all Jews were secret lizard people masterminding an intergalactic conspiracy? What it really came down to was one question, which the online hordes were now rabidly mooting: Could you be a secret lizard person and not even know?

Absolutely, said the game-theory guy, with a few qualified exceptions and maybes, glossed in a ten-tweet thread.

Absolutely not, retorted the assistant professor of composition who pretended to be a journalist. His was a full stop: no ifs, ands, or buts. And yet, the thread in which he took this position had ballooned to 106 installments and was still growing when I closed out the app.

As for @BigDiogenesEnergy, he was the only one who, to my mind, had made a good-faith effort to cram the camel of his hot take through the eye of the needle of the situation as it stood.

"Obviously, not all Jews are secret lizard people," he tweeted. "That's just stupid. But what if some of the secret lizard people are Jewish?"

It was hypnotic, watching the numbers tumble upward.

One tweet to rule them all, I thought. We deserve the world we're stuck in, as well as the apocalypse that shall consign said world to the void.

Had Corey overplayed his hand? I hoped so. A day was an eon in internet time, as Molly had told me after my unfortunate photo op at Driving School. And she had been right. But I wasn't sure Corey had a day. This thing was mutating fast.

By the time I went to see him, not today but tomorrow, maybe he would already be in retreat, would need my help more than I needed his. I reminded myself that I did not need his help for anything.

Help me help you, I imagined myself saying to him.

What would he say back? That was beyond my imagining, at least for the moment.

But then, I was awfully distracted with all these goddamn people taking photos of me as I made my way through the terminal. I still had an hour before my flight boarded, and no prospect of privacy at gateside. I made a beeline for the sky lounge. The frosted-glass doors slid open for me, their motion silent and seamless, no stutter or *whoosh,* only cool filtered air and soft music to welcome me into this secret world hidden inside the world.

I went behind the paywall.

I crossed the border of fate.

PART 3
WE LIVE INSIDE

(Florida & Florida)

The sign at gate C7 read WELCOME TO PALM BEACH INTERNATIONAL AIRPORT! ENJOY OUR PRISTINE BEACHES! NO POTABLE WATER! Little clip art palm tree at the bottom. Caution tape across the fountain by the bathroom, Dasani selling for four bucks a bottle at Hudson News.

I know what you're thinking: *Given that all my destinations were on the Gulf Coast, why fly into PBI?* Well, for one thing, this was the first flight out that I could get. And for another, it was the same two hours of drive time across the Everglades from the Atlantic side as it would have been down from Tampa. I was going to see Mom in Fort Myers today, and Corey in Guiding Star tomorrow.

Speaking of Corey. I checked my phone.

The chamber of commerce had not taken kindly to his principled rejection of Hollywood money. He himself had enumerated all the reasons: red tide, oil, our friends and allies in the sugar-growers association, "and cetera." The city was investing millions to raise roadbeds and houses in the hopes of staving off the rising gulf, but lately the water had presented them with an entirely different problem, one they couldn't build their way out of. Because the bedrock of South Florida is porous limestone, the ocean is as much under the land as beside it. (cf. *Buffy,* season 7, the Big Bad's catchphrase, "From beneath you it devours.") As the sea level rises, it breaches the water table, raising the saline content of the drinking water. Also, because so much of South Florida real estate was built so fast in the midcentury, construction ran well ahead of municipal services. Millions of houses still have septic tanks, which aren't closed containers like you might imagine. They're open at the bottom, and there are these layers of gravel that filter the waste. Eventually it decomposes and is reabsorbed into the soil. Except now the septic tanks were being breached by the water table when it rose up, and the toxins got absorbed into the water, and so when the level fell again the groundwater itself was toxic. The sanitation plants couldn't keep up.

Mercury in the swordfish steak, toxic algal bloom in Lake Okeechobee, the river of grass drained for Big Ag and retirement exurbs, the last panther shot on a golf course—all that, people could live with. Some of it they even rooted for. But now, Florida was drowning in its own brackish sewage. All these beach town economies were terminal, and the powers that be knew it, and here Corey Burch was risking their last round of palliative cash.

I rented a red Corvette on the logic that, if I was going to be under constant surveillance, I might as well be seen riding in style. I was thinking ahead to when all of this would be archival footage in the documentary. I imagined the oral history, the making-of, the bonus features. The future was certain, only the past was unpredictable. I wanted to attribute that quote to Lenin. In fact, it was something David Thewlis said as V. M. Varga, archvillain of the uneven third season of the TV reboot of the Coen brothers' movie *Fargo*. The attribution was Varga's, and if memory served, the person to whom he said it had questioned the veracity of the quote.

Who remembered this stuff, and did it matter?

Me, almost. And no.

Anyway, cost was no object. I was playing with house money, i.e., Grace's.

I put the Corvette into low gear, earned a whistle of approval from the guy at the checkout kiosk, eased over the backward spikes, and headed for the highway.

But I wasn't ready for the long drive just yet. I kept my eyes peeled for a suitable big-box store, took the exit as soon as I saw one.

Pack of boxers, pack of crew socks. Two gray tees and two white ones. A pale blue collared shirt and khakis so I could look like Corey looking like Kyle Chandler. Brown belt—hell, why not spring for loafers while I was at it, they were on sale. I

also picked out a pair of flip-flops and a pair of swim trunks—
blue board shorts with a white hibiscus print and drawstring
waist. My full Floridian gestalt was coming to blossom.

I felt like a whole new man and wondered if I would actually be one soon. Sure hoped so! I bought toothpaste and a
toothbrush, travel soap and shampoo, some face cream. Advil.
A little dopp kit to hold it all. A small, wheeled suitcase with
hard ridged sides and a retractable handle, teal as the gulf at
noon. I hauled my haul toward checkout, still noticing that
people were still noticing me. Phones poked up from behind
clothing racks and around the corners of endcaps. Any one
of them could have been a gun muzzle, one mechanized eye
versus another, this desperate culture of fame-sick loners, this
sun-damaged open-carry state. The target logo that was Target's logo never felt so ominous. I did self-checkout, paid with
plastic, jogged my cart to my car.

It was a straight shot west across the state, a long flat line
laid clear through the heart of the Everglades, which is to say
through brutally drained and cleared and planted land, where
it really did look like an apocalypse in progress. The grasses
were blond as sand, starved and dry. Heat rose from the road
in stupefying waveforms. A few miles outside of Clewiston,
whose motto was "America's Sweetest Town," I started to see
the sugar plantations, vast fields of cane with windowless
white industrial buildings like small islands in the oceanic
monocrop, sky braced by pillars of smoke from their fires.
Noisome air, I thought. Road signs warned to watch for wild-
life crossing, images of deer and alligator, but I saw no sign of

activity save for a few turkey buzzards picking at a flattened possum. Perhaps raccoon.

THE AIR OUT HERE IS CLEANER THAN IN CONGESTED URBAN AREAS, proclaimed billboards sponsored by U.S. Sugar. The billboards had pictures of blue skies. In Clewiston proper, the only signs of life were at a couple of dollar stores.

I probably should have had this protracted flashback on the plane, but I had spent that time rewatching episodes of *Twin Peaks: The Return* on the in-flight entertainment system, so instead I was having it now, as the desolate state road rolled by and I closed the distance between myself and my mother's house, the house in Fort Myers where she lived with her husband, a man I could not bring myself to call my stepfather, not that he'd ever asked me to. I called her on her birthday, texted him on his—or better, texted her to tell him that I sent my best wishes—and sometimes I sent them a picture of Hank if I thought of it (and only after Amber thought to send me one). But mostly what we had between us was years of silence. There had been no great falling-out. There was no singular betrayal. As Grace had reminded me. (As if I'd needed reminding.) They hadn't abused me like Corey's parents had, nor stolen my earnings like Shayne's had. I had never petitioned for emancipation, nor tried to run away from home. There was only the trauma of my father's loss, that radiant fact, that beacon in time, shining brighter the farther I drifted from it so it never dimmed or slipped from view.

Gerald, Mom's husband, was a good guy. He was her second chance, long-awaited and well-deserved: her reboot. She was happy, and I knew that. And yet there was this other part of me, the long-suffering and unappeasable inner child hidden deep in the hollow of my heart, begging for a disbelief that was never granted, and so still stuck believing that Mom and/or I could have done something different, that there was some alternate universe, some fanfic, in which Dad was still alive and we were still a happy family.

Every therapist I've ever had has told me, some more gently than others, how ridiculous this was. A sweet but impossible dream, the archetypal childhood fantasy of a parent's possessing godlike authority (*Control, control*) that I, as a parent myself now, knew to be false. Where was my omnipotence, my transcendental wisdom, when I gave the fated Benjamin to my credulous, anxious son? What was the divine plan when I impregnated Amber? Or all those times Corey's father had drawn his hand back, closed it into a fist?

It was a self-inflicted curse to let the long shadow of a wounded child's wish cast itself over a grown man's life: his choices, his relationships, the only family he had left. That's what the therapists said. I'm sure they were right. You could say I was good at listening but bad at processing. A couple of them had said exactly that. I believed them, but what difference had it ever made? Could it make a difference now?

The bender that ended my first successful stint as a sober person was triggered by my mother's remarriage, her lovely wedding to lovely Gerald, who liked to be called Gerry and never held a bit of ill will toward me. It was a simple affair, family and a few friends, the middle of the afternoon on a

Saturday in their backyard, the backyard of the house where they still lived, where I had stood beside my mother and, at her request, gave her away, a sentimental gesture I had perhaps taken too seriously, or too literally. I mean, I grieved her loss. I conducted myself with dignity that whole weekend. Then I flew back to Portland, obsessed by the notion that, having relinquished her, I was an orphan now, alone and adrift, and so I decided to embrace obliteration and blew up my life. Out of those ashes came my second wife, my beloved son, my fourth and fifth second chances.

Honestly, when I put it all this way, it does sound like there might have been some divine plan at work, some secret higher intelligence calling the shots and saving my ass.

The full George Bailey.

I had not been back to this house since the wedding. The pandemic could be blamed for some of that, but my avoidance had well preceded the plague, and Grace knew it. To her, the idea that I would come here and be so close and yet not pay the visit I owed was abhorrent. I knew she was right. But if this were only done to placate her, it would be worthless, and she'd see through the false gesture immediately. Grace was what the venture capital tech bros call a unicorn: a sexually magnanimous kajillionaire with fierce loyalty and few hang-ups, who, after all these years, still thought I was funny, interesting, and cute. I was scared of loving her, because I trusted her so much, because I believed in her judgment, and so to accept her love meant accepting her vision of me. I could understand that vision as an intellectual proposition, but I could not share it. If she was right, and there was a decent guy—a suitable partner—somewhere inside of me, then why had I spent my entire adult life trying to drown him out? And sometimes to actually drown him? Here was perhaps the one and only IP worth rebooting, yet here I was, terrified to green-light it, because cancellation felt inevitable and even if I beat the long odds, I would still have to live with the fact of all my wasted time.

There is another saying. I don't think Varga said it, and it doesn't sound like Lenin, either. It's the thing about the direction that the angel of history faces, what it sees from where it's standing. Something about paradise and a storm. *I should google that,* I thought. *Or text Molly and ask her; she'd know.* But I didn't want to bother Molly, and maybe I didn't need to.

Paradise and a storm? Sounded like Florida.

Let's attribute the quote to Carl Hiaasen and move along.

I guess the rest of this won't make sense without my mother's bottle episode, mirror or echo of the one that I gave to Amber and her mother all those pages back. You'll have to believe me that I haven't been withholding this to be coy, or because I was scared to face this story, though it's possible that both those things are true. I've held off telling it because I believe that when you speak, you are always also listening—or you should be. You are trying, in a sense, to "overhear" yourself, and so to be changed by what you have heard yourself reveal no less than if someone other than yourself were the one revealing it to you. Revelation was what I was afraid of: self-knowledge and change. Molly said Harold Bloom said that this capacity for self-overhearing is what Shakespeare's characters do in their soliloquies—they listen to themselves, are changed, and then act based on that change—and that this is the foundation of modern human consciousness. Or something. I'm not saying I followed it all, but I did take the trouble later to peruse the relevant Wikis, where I learned that Bloom borrowed this idea from Hegel. Or maybe what I really did was hire Molly to ghostwrite this whole book for me, and here she is throwing in Easter eggs that reveal her unacknowledged legislation of my story. All these hifalutin references that I'd never have, modes of attention inorganic to my consciousness. She's my secret sharer, my infusion of GMO: the narrative equivalent of Grace's glow-in-the-dark wine. (And see what happens, just as a for instance, when I don't have her around to help—you get dumb TV references while the angel of history is left out in the rain.) Molly promised me that, by the time she was finished revising the text, nobody would be able to tell.

"It'll all sound like you," she said, which I suppose is a writer's version of "We'll fix it in post."

Reading these pages over now, I can see she has been as good as her word, give or take a few Easter eggs, like the part where I info-dumped all that Cyrus Teed history and now you get that it was her imitating me imitating her. And also— obviously—these paragraphs that you're reading now, which I haven't yet decided whether to ask her to cut or to thank her for including. She wrote this, not me, but the crisis over meaning is entirely mine. Her forgery of my perspective— through the power of sympathetic imagination and a few feats of narrative sleight of hand—has been transubstantiated into authenticity, into my truth, though I'm counting the victory less as Christian than Kafkan, or even Borgesian. Rothian. It doesn't matter. All I'm trying to say (all she's trying to say) is that this, what I'm saying now, is what I would have said, not "in my own words" but in these words, if only I had known them. If I possessed her ferocious fluency. What I lacked, she had, which was that fluency, that imagination. What I had, she lacked, which was sixty-eight thousand dollars. So, when we were in the car driving to the airport, right after "Idiot Wind" came on and she smiled at me, I propositioned her. It was crude, I admit it, which is why I left it out of that scene, or why I asked her to. But don't get the wrong idea. I didn't try to buy sex. First because I might be six kinds of asshole, but I'm not *that* kind of asshole. And second because that's just her messing with you (with me) again. She likes the #MeToo jokes because she knows how bad they scare me.

My proposition was simply that, if things went sideways with our reboot and she still wanted to get out of New York, she was welcome to come to Portland and work for me at Wing and Prayer.

"Thanks, but no thanks," she said. "One way or the other, my service industry days are done. But call me when you're ready to write your inevitable memoir. They're gonna hire some schmuck to do it for you, and it might as well be me."

"First refusal's yours," I said, and was as good as my word. As good as her word, really, since it was her idea. It was my favorite idea she ever had. To hire her to put these words in my mouth. To sell me my own story so that I could finally own it. So I could call it mine.

Mom's Bottle Episode

Lorrie Schwartz knew Don Crader because he was friends
with her older brother. He played bass in a bar band with
a standing gig at Mo's of Delray Beach, a small city on the
Atlantic side of Florida, sort of a mirror image (since we're
keeping track of those) of Guiding Star on the gulf side. (Or,
for that matter, of Rising Star and Guiding Star in California
and Florida, this story's other set of near-miss twins, like me
and Shayne.)

Lorrie's homelife was happy but chaotic. Her parents
struggled. She was the second of three. Her older brother,
my uncle Marvin, had dropped out of high school to work
in an auto shop. He was buying motorcycle parts piecemeal,
dreamed of cross-country travel: a belated hippie, aspiring.
He was murdered while working late one night. The place
was technically closed, but he had the light on and the garage
door rolled up for the ventilation. Low music on the radio,
whatever was coming in on FM, Skynyrd and the Allmans,
probably, back then barely old enough to qualify as "classic"
rock. A couple of thugs—that was Lorrie's mother's word,
"thugs"—had been casing the place for a few days, eyeing
the T-Bird he'd had up on the lift, saw that it was down now,
presumably because the work was done and its owner would

be coming for it in the morning. They just wanted the keys to
the car. He said he would get them. No funny business, they
said, and he said sure, yeah, nothing funny about any of this,
but then he reached for the big wrench on the table by the
pegboard where the keys were, or he seemed to be reaching
for it, said the shooter in his statement after they caught him,
and he—the shooter—panicked. A Saturday night special in
the pocket of his windbreaker, not that anyone would ever
need a windbreaker in this part of Florida at that time of
year. Didn't threaten, didn't pull out the gun, just had his
finger on the trigger inside his pocket and squeezed. The
bullet went through Marvin's left lung. Twenty-one years old
and gone in an instant. And the shooter, nineteen. Caught a
day later, pled guilty, given life.

Lorrie and her brother had been close. Don was Marvin's
friend, one of those guys who was around a lot. He was part
of the set dressing of her brother's life, as her brother was of
hers. Don showed up at the shiva in a shit-brown suit and a
pair of dark sneakers he hoped would pass for dress shoes.
His face was ashen, and his eyes were red. Lorrie had to
help him fix his yarmulke to his already-thinning hair with
one of those little gold pins. He didn't know how to do it.
His hands shook when he reached for the serving fork at the
buffet table. She served him cold cuts and slices of rye bread,
a smear of mustard, a stack of carrot straws, and a drizzle
of what might have been ranch dressing; the Schwartzes
weren't kosher-keeping Jews. Bitter black coffee in paper
cups. Neither of them were tasting much of what they ate.
They sat on high-backed chairs set against the walls of the
living room so the main space stayed open for the milling

mourners. The aimless shuffle and subdued din of the bereaved.

When they finished their food, Lorrie bused their plates, but he didn't want to sit there alone in his ugly suit and inappropriate shoes.

"Don't leave me here," he whispered, and followed her to the kitchen and watched her scrape the last of the carrots and dip into the trash.

When this was done, she unlocked the kitchen door and stepped outside into the humid night. She was beautiful in the glow of the security lights, where moths and other bugs were buzzing and doing loops. She passed beyond the perimeter of light and rounded the curve of the aboveground pool, disappearing into darkness, either unconcerned as to whether Don would follow her or else certain that he would. After rounding the curve himself, he found her sitting on the grass with her back against the plastic sidewall of the pool. She leaned into the hard, grooved blue.

Where was Lorrie's little sister? Lynne was fourteen, hiding out inside the house somewhere. Lorrie was seventeen and understood that her childhood was over. She had been easing toward the end of it, but now here that end was, abrupt, all at once. She had imagined herself as a taxiing plane preparing for takeoff when, in fact, she was a car going off a cliff. There was solid ground, and then there wasn't. You survived the crash or you did not. She was flicking a lighter but had nothing to light with it. Her face in shadow and then flame and then shadow again. This beautiful, brown-haired girl made somehow even more beautiful by grief, Don thought, still standing while she sat in the grass, looming over her. She was convinced of her own orphanhood despite a house full of family. He wanted to rescue her from that feeling, disprove it somehow.

"You waiting for an invitation?" she said to him.

In fact he was. Maybe this was it.

He sat down beside her, close but not touching. Close enough. He'd always liked her. Marvin had known, had vaguely condoned the crush, though he'd stopped short of giving his friend permission to ask out his little sister, which is why Don hadn't, or was one reason why. But now Marvin was gone and Lorrie seemed, maybe for the first time, to register his presence as something other than her brother's sidekick. Marvin's absence was a room, or a cave or a tunnel, where they were both trapped. It had dimensions and depth. Could they find each other there? Could they help each other find a path out?

He had the nub of a joint tucked into the plastic of his pack of Camels. He did okay fishing it out of the pack, smoothing the singed paper, but when it came time to pinch it between his fingers, his hand started shaking again. Lorrie was holding up the lighter, and his shaking hand was sort of buzzing around it like the moths around the lights outside the house.

"I don't think this is going to work," he said, and it felt like a cosmic failure. He let Lorrie take the joint from him, made his empty hands into fists, willed himself back to control. Fingernails digging into meat. When he looked at his hand later that night in his bathroom, he'd see bloody half-moons inscribed in his palm.

"Hang on," she said. "I got this." She reached over to him,

and for a moment he thought she was going to kiss him. (She didn't. That would come two weeks later, on a moonlit walk down the beach after his band's gig at Mo's. He had taken the audacious step of asking the guitar player to let him sing lead on "Layla," Marvin's favorite, and though he was too timid to dedicate it to her, he saw her sitting at her table with wide wet eyes and knew that the message was getting across.) Instead of kissing him, she reached into his hair, sort of seemed to be ruffling it—what was this?—until she found the yarmulke pin.

"Let me show you an ancient Jewish secret," she said, and popped the roach into the elbow at the top of the pin. She held the improvised clip by its bottom end, lit the joint, and took a test puff. Satisfied, she took another, then moved the smoldering nubbin toward his flushed face. She took his rough-stubbled jaw in her hot hand and guided him in for his hit.

They married a year later, over her mother's tepid objections. She was too young, it was too fast, did the boy have real prospects . . . But, of course, there was still her sister to deal with, and it wasn't the worst thing to have Lorrie out of the house. Her father said nothing. Lorrie and Don were happy. They rented an apartment, and she went to work at a department store while Don finished school. He was studying education. They both wanted out of Florida. They picked Portland, Oregon, because it seemed as un-Floridian as you could get.

Don taught eighth-grade algebra. Lorrie got pregnant. It was sooner than they'd planned on, but it seemed like a reasonable next step. If not now, when? So this would be their life. Okay. They both quit smoking dope; Don gave up cigarettes as well. Fatherhood was serious stuff, and he was determined to do it right. When they found out they were having a boy, they wanted to name him after Marvin. But the name felt unfashionable, almost antique, so Marvin David became David Marvin, and that's how I got my name.

Don was diagnosed with lymphoma when Lorrie was six months pregnant. When she gave birth, he was three floors down on the chemo ward. Her sister, my aunt, had just finished high school and delayed college a year to come out and live with them, with us, to help care for her sister, newborn nephew, and dying brother-in-law. Only Don didn't die. He beat the odds and recovered, was back at the blackboard on the first day of school. Lynne went home.

I was an outgoing kid, loud and friendly and a bit of a ham, but I had no particular aptitude for acting, no innate desire to perform. But my fifth-grade homeroom teacher, Mr. Knight, was also the drama coach, a position he had held at the school for some decades, as it was both thankless and unpaid. But it gave Mr. Knight, who had long ago harbored dreams of Broadway, a chance to express himself, and so whoever happened to be in his homeroom in a given year became the vehicle of that self-expression. The year before mine, he had presented an original adaptation of *The Tempest,* with the racism elided and a lot more focus on the magic. Really, I think, it was an excuse to buy a glitter cannon and a smoke machine. The smoke machine, unfortunately, had set off the fire alarm during the play's inaugural performance, as a result of which my year's production was a rather restrained version of *A Christmas*

Carol, in which I played the Ghost of Christmas Present. It was a small but meaty role, and though Mr. Knight never felt like I was "giving enough," a man in the audience liked my "look." He was a director of TV commercials who happened to be in town for the weekend visiting family. Our Tiny Tim was his nephew.

This is how these things happen, or one way they can. He had been looking for a look and hadn't found one in LA. He liked mine. He took my mother aside, asked if he could give her some lines to give me to memorize, asked if she had a video camera at home. We didn't, but Mr. Knight did, and so my mother asked him to borrow it, which request he refused, but counteroffered that we could come over to the house and he would make the tape himself. He may have hoped that his cinematographic prowess would draw notice from the director, or he may not have trusted my mother with his video camera. She helped me memorize the lines, and we went to Mr. Knight's house, where a framed poster for *Stage Door* hung in the foyer, and a pair of dachshunds followed us from room to room.

Mom mailed the tape, making sure to credit Mr. Knight in the note she sent along with it. A week later, the director called to offer the part. His only concern was that, for whatever reason, the producers wanted a blue-eyed boy and my eyes were green. My mother didn't know what to tell him. He quickly clarified that it was just a hitch in the logistics, easily resolved. I was taken to an ophthalmologist and fitted for nonprescription contact lenses. The doctor taught me how to pop them in and pinch them out without poking myself. It took practice. I was ten.

We went down to LA for five days. Dad came, too. Two of the days were spent shooting the commercial. The other three, they sent me on auditions that the director had helped set up. Of those, two resulted in callbacks, which would have meant either taking another trip to LA the following week, or extending our current trip, maybe doing more auditions in the meantime. Dad flew back without us, unwilling to miss any more school. I was missing school, too, but that didn't seem to matter. Mr. Knight insisted that this was a huge opportunity. We'd be fools to waste it.

The callbacks were for a fast-food chain and a drug company. The fast-food one was about how much I loved the toy that came with my kid's meal; the drug one was about how much I loved Grandpa, who could chase me around the yard again now that his knee pain was gone. I booked the drug ad, lost the kid's meal, but it was the fast-food casting director who told my mom that what she ought to do was get me an agent, come down for pilot season, give this thing a go for real. Two weeks had already stretched into three, what with the shoot for the drug commercial. We went back to Portland with a lot to think about.

My father was on the fence, but my mother was certain. This was a shot worth taking. The casting director, the commercial director, Mr. Knight—everyone said so. The two spots that I had booked (she was picking up industry lingo fast) had each paid more than she made in two weeks working at Macy's. *Imagine,* she said to my father, *if we spent time here, met people, got David some training. His entire life could be transformed.*

She wouldn't have known the word "reboot" then, except

insofar as it applied to an electronic cash register, but
something like this was on her mind: she had got married so
fast, become a mother so young, and Don had given up his
music, had his brush with death. Their lives were all about
getting by and making do. Here was something else entirely,
something unforeseen, a new frontier for discovery. And,
yes, there was the money to consider. Money meant safety. It
meant options.

We all went to Rising Star together. This was the summer
I met Shayne. Dad went back home for the new school year.
Mom and I stayed on. The first few successes had come fast,
but then there were dry spells, tough breaks, heartbreaking
losses. There were times I thought we'd give up, go home.
I didn't understand how my folks were doing it, why my
mother persisted. There were times I begged for it to be over,
but then, whenever she was on the verge of giving in to me, I
always took it back and said I wanted to stay.

Dad came down for weekends when he could.

He got sick again right after I booked *Rev Beach*. That
whole first year of fame, I mean my real and true fame, when
my face was everywhere and the money started rolling in, he
was dying. He gave up his job and moved to LA, and we were
a family for as long as we could be. We had more resources
now, better doctors, all kinds of access. Ty Travis gave us
names and numbers. But the rebooted cancer moved fast,
and nothing anyone tried worked. Don and Lorrie got, what,
four months sharing the California king in the McMansion
we were renting in the hills. Then it was the hospital, then
the hospice bed installed in the downstairs guest room. We
buried him in Portland, because we still thought of that as

home, still assumed we'd end up back there, and maybe that's why, all those years later, I did come back, because I felt guilty having left him alone in the soaked earth of that city, and if I didn't go back to be with him, who would?

Lorrie loved Don. This wasn't the reboot she'd wanted, it was just the one she was stuck with. We shot the second and third seasons of *Rev Beach* in Guiding Star. That's where she met Gerry. He had driven down from Fort Myers for the day, newly divorced, having a visitation weekend with his daughter. Kayla would at that time have been about Hank's age now. Wow. Anyway, they hit it off and started seeing each other. Mom would sometimes drive over to visit him, or he would come to see her sans Kayla. If he got on the road right after he got off work, he could be in Guiding Star by six.

Lorrie was lonely. She was a young widow with a famous son who didn't need her around. She was living in a town where she knew nobody and had nothing to do. Recaptured by the state she'd escaped from. She was within a day's drive of her own family, her sister and parents, but rarely saw them. Marvin's death had fractured something. Don's had broken it the rest of the way. Gerry was a sweet guy, good to her. She liked Kayla, liked the idea of being a mother again. It was something she knew how to be. She and Don had always planned on a family: two or even three, but after the early unplanned first one and then the psychic and financial crush of cancer, they'd been scared to try again.

When *Rev Beach* folded halfway through season 3, I went back to LA to be with Grace. My mother went back to Portland, but before long her mother got sick and Lynne called, asking for her to come to Florida. The message could not have been clearer for having gone unspoken: it was time to repay an old debt. Lynne had a husband and two kids now. She didn't have time to be a caretaker. Lorrie did. So she went back, moved into her old childhood bedroom, and helped her mother through the same illness (or nearly the same) as the one that had taken her husband. She convinced her father to move into an assisted-living place, to be paid for with the money from the sale of the house, which was now worth a small fortune. How Florida had changed!

Where would she go when the house was sold? I wondered.

Turned out she had a plan in mind, had been waiting to tell me because she'd been worried about how I'd take it. She and Gerry had kept in touch over the years, as friends, and now here they were "across the way" from each other and, well, she had been driving over to see him in Fort Myers on the weekends, just as he had done for her back in Guiding Star days. Gerry still lived in the house he had grown up in (like Lorrie was temporarily doing, like Amber with her mom and Hank) and if you think Delray was a weird place to be a Jew in the seventies, well, Gerry could tell you stories. Fort Myers was the goddamn moon.

Kayla was halfway through high school, had embraced goth culture in the way only Florida girls can, and yet she fully approved of her new would-be stepmom. Lorrie moved in. The wedding, as I believe I mentioned earlier, was in their backyard. The groom wore Tevas. I was in a four-thousand-dollar designer suit I had not paid for. My mother wore a sundress. Kayla in fishnets, combat boots, corpse makeup, a purple prom dress, and a wide-brimmed black hat. The reception was modest. The happy couple weren't rushing off to honeymoon. They said goodbye to the last of their guests around ten, bade their children good night shortly after. That left me and Kayla standing in the living room.

"Nightcap?" I asked.

"I'm health goth," she said. "Not the clove-smoking kind. And anyway I'm seventeen and aren't you supposed to be not drinking?"

"All good points," I said. "Well, it's cool that we're a family now."

"Am I ever going to even see you again?" she said. "You're, like, never around. It really breaks Lorrie's heart."

"I'll be better," I said. "I'll visit more often. And you can come visit me sometime. I've never had a sibling, so I'm excited."

"I've never had one, either," she said, perking up. "It could be—something good, I guess. I don't know."

"You'll come to Portland," I said. "On summer vacation if you want to. Stay a few weeks. Mom and Gerry can meet us. We'll go hiking. You'll need different shoes."

"I own sneakers," she said. "I run five miles every day."

"Are you serious?"

"As a heart attack. This all sounds great. I hope it happens."

"Oh, it will," I said.

And in the moment I truly meant it. The only trouble was that it hadn't. Happened, I mean. I didn't do any of the things I said I'd do. Never invited my stepsister out to visit, hadn't been back to Florida since the wedding. But I was here now, the prodigal returned, the boy with his

finger hovering over the doorbell, hesitating just as I had
over Shayne's contact icon on my phone back when I'd first
arrived in New York.

All I could do was hope that it would be enough, that it
would be something, my coming here. A down payment on
what I owed. But first I had to stop hesitating, finish arriving.
Even now it was tempting to turn tail, get back in the car,
drive the rest of the way to Guiding Star, deal with Grace's
disappointment and my own shame later. Or, more likely, not
deal with either of those things. Because that was the other
option, my perennial plan B: to stay one step ahead of myself
forever, keep running and hiding, duck and cover, for the rest
of my life.

Control, control, I thought.

I rang the bell.

Since I had last seen Kayla, she had finished high school,
dropped the goth thing, gone to college, graduated. She stood
before me wearing jeans and a Florida Gulf Coast University
T-shirt, her brown hair tied back in a loose ponytail. I opened
my arms for a hug. She let out a short laugh. I dropped my
arms. She stepped forward, embraced me.

"No, sorry, it's fine," she said. "I was just surprised." She
released me, turned, bade me to follow.

"They're not here," she said.

"Oh, that's too bad, where are they?"

"Publix," she said. "Getting groceries and stuff for dinner.
They shouldn't be long. You want a drink or something?"

I asked for ginger ale, which had always been my mother's

favorite. It arrived in a glass I recognized from her mother's house. Kayla poured water for herself from a plastic bottle. We sat in the living room. The floor was terrazzo. Native plants that I could not identify thrived in clay pots of variable size. Some were palmlike, others fern-ish. One had pink flowers.

"So shit's pretty bad, huh," Kayla said to me. It wasn't a question.

"The thing with Corey? It'll be okay. I'm gonna go see him tomorrow. He's a softie if you know how to handle him. We're old friends."

"People change," she said. "They don't stay the way you remember."

"You've certainly changed," I said.

"If you tell me how much I've grown I will throw you the fuck out of here."

"Wouldn't dream of it, but look. Some things change but not everything. Sometimes people are right where you left them. You're here, for instance. He's there. That doesn't have to be a bad thing."

"It actually sucks that I'm still here," Kayla said. "And Corey Burch is dangerous. He's dangerous because he's a fool. He thinks everyone is playing the same game of bluff and bullshit that he is, but there are people out there who are really listening. Hannah Arendt tells us that the ideology of fascism has no positive content but is rather a constant recursive motion around the void of belief. The only thing that keeps it going is inertia, so when someone pulls the emergency break, well, watch out."

"You really did go to college. I'll have to call my friend Molly to have her explain to me whatever you just said."

"Don't patronize me. Though I do think it's rad that you know Molly Webster."

"Let me get this straight—Grace Travis, Shayne Glade, this reboot project, the fact that I'm at the center of a burgeoning fandom civil war and am going to try to have a treaty session tomorrow with one of your home state's most notable MAGA chuds . . . None of this impresses you. But the fact that I know Molly Webster . . ."

"I love her stuff, been reading her for years. I wish I could be her intern."

"She's a bartender who wrote one article!"

"I'm a bartender! And she's written like a billion articles."

"No shit?"

"Yes! She spent a year on the press bus with the Bernie campaign."

"I meant, no shit you're a bartender?"

"What can I tell you? English major."

We heard a car pull into the driveway, then an engine cut followed by a trunk pop. I wanted to run to the front door but wasn't sure whether I should, so instead I got up from the couch and stood dumbly in front of it. I heard the door open and voices in the hallway. My mother appeared, saw me, did a double take. She rushed across the room and took me in her arms. We held each other for a long time. Gerry hung back, giving us our moment, like Molly had when I first saw Shayne at Driving School. I was grateful to Gerry then, for that and I guess for everything else as well. Eventually, my mother released me, stepped back to size me up.

"My sweet, sweet boy," she said, her eyes shining. "It's so good to see you. But my god, you've gotten old."

. . .

Mom and Gerry had gotten old as well. She'd been a young mother, a young widow. Even on the eve of her second marriage, she'd seemed spry. Now her hair was fully gray, her shoulders starting to slope. Gerry was almost totally bald, liver spots blooming like algae all over his scalp and the backs of his hands. He was a decade older than she was, which put him in his late sixties now, an idea I had understood abstractly but was struggling to get my head around in concrete terms. That he was a retiree drawing down a modest 401(k). That he would turn seventy the same year I turned forty. That he walked with a cane, a handsome dark red wood cane with a curved handle and a rubber tip. He didn't need it with him all the time, he said, but his knee gave him trouble, and it was helpful, maybe psychologically as much as in any other way, to have it when they were out doing errands. At the mall, for instance, or if they went to dinner somewhere and parked at the back of the lot. My mother could always drop him at the door and then go park the car, but he didn't like the thought of her walking alone at night, and usually he was the one driving. Maybe down the line he'd see about getting a handicap parking pass—Kayla, I noticed, volubly encouraged this—but he didn't think he was so far gone yet that he should take some truly suffering person's spot up at the front of the lot.

Like I said, a very sweet guy.

They'd brought home a box of fried chicken for dinner, plus sides from the deli counter: mashed potatoes, mac and cheese, steamed carrots, vinegar slaw.

"Look at us," my mother said, spooning me potatoes as I reached into the box for another drumstick. She was so happy to see me, to see me eat. "We look like the commercial."

Everyone laughed at that, and our shared pleasure brought the moment into focus. This—not just "eating dinner," but sharing a meal, being a family—was the deep meaning of this box of fried chicken and these plastic tubs of hot glop. It was a small and true contentment, evanescing even as it flowered forth into being, like the dinner scene in *To the Lighthouse*, or, if we want to go with a reference that I would actually know and Molly wouldn't, a commercial for Publix grocery stores like the one my mother had seen on TV earlier today, which had reminded her that she'd seen a coupon in the paper yesterday, which is why she and Gerry had abandoned their original plan to order a pizza, and thus why we were eating this for dinner now.

After dinner, I showed everyone photos of Henry that I had taken on our trip to the zoo, not quite a week ago, in what seemed more and more like it had been a part of somebody else's life. At the same time, this thing I was doing now, sitting with these people in this house that sat on a man-made drainage canal, thumbing through phone photos of my six-year-old while decaf coffee brewed in the kitchen—well, this didn't quite seem like my life, either. How was I to understand that the man who had signed autographs at the fan convention in LA, who'd slept with his movie-star ex, who'd nearly drowned himself in the Gowanus, who'd waited out a superstorm in sci-fi luxury, who was counting on a slice of Entenmann's marbled pound cake to be served alongside the decaf—how was I to understand that these were all the same person and that I was him? And even if I achieved that consistency of understanding, that continuity of narrative, even if I reconciled the entire timeline, what would happen when the next thing happened tomorrow, or next week, or after *Rev Beach* rebooted, or after me and Grace did? Or after we didn't? How much headcanon could be assimilated into my personal show bible? How much retcon and reboot could one life take?

"Do you mind if I step outside a sec before dessert?" I asked my mother. "I have to make a quick call."

"What," Amber said flatly when she finally picked up.

I had called four times, and she had let it go to voice mail the first three. I supposed I was lucky she hadn't blocked my number.

"I'm in Florida," I said. "And I'm sorry. I screwed up bigtime. It made your life harder, and it got Hank hurt, and neither of you deserves that."

There was a silence on her end. I held my breath and watched dead branches float in the canal.

"Thank you for saying that," she said. "But Hank is fine. He's— It wasn't. Okay, honestly? Nothing happened."

"You lied to me? About our son being hurt?" I felt rage rising up in me. I could hear a hot tremor in my voice.

"Nothing happened because I found the money in his backpack when I went to put his lunch in. But what I told you happened could have happened, very easily."

"Speculative nonfiction," I mumbled, my quick anger just as quickly crashing into something else.

"What did you say?"

"Nothing, nothing," I said. "I mean I'm not happy about this, but I guess I understand why you did it."

"I just didn't know how else to get through to you," she said.

"You got through," I said. I was crying a little. It felt good.

"Let me know when you're back, okay?" she said. "Maybe you can, I don't know, have dinner here some night."

"I'll do that," I said. "I promise."

"Great. Well, thanks for calling. And stay safe."

"Do things seem that out of hand?" I asked.

"It's Florida," she said.

"Touché," I said. "Oh, hey, before you go, is Hank around? I thought he could say hi to my mom. I think she'd really love that."

"He's in the bath," Amber said. "But we FaceTimed with her earlier."

"You did? How did that happen?"

"We FaceTime every week."

"How do you have her number?"

"She's his grandmother, David. Did you really think she was going to sit out his life because you and I, or you and her, were going through whatever? Did you think I would cut her off just because you're an erratic, self-sabotaging buffoon?"

"I have to admit that I never thought of it that way."

"No kidding. Anyway, take care of yourself. Try to come home to your son in one piece."

"Do my best," I said.

But she was already gone.

. . .

Back in the house, coffee and cake awaited. I had a cup and a slice.

"He was a sweet boy," my mother mused of Corey. "Troubled, of course, and those awful parents of his, but he was sweet. A shame they cut him out of the show when they did."

"It was my fault," I said, amazed at how easily the words had come, how after all this time I had finally told the truth.

My mother put down her coffee, caught and held my gaze.

"No, honey," she said. "I know you tried to look out for him."

I wasn't surprised by her pushback. It was her prerogative as my mother to believe the best of me, despite all evidence to the contrary, which I had given her plenty of over the years, but not about this. If I was going to tell it, I was going to have to tell it all.

"At first, yeah," I said. "But I turned on him. He was better than me, and I was jealous."

"Even if that's true, you didn't have that kind of power."

"I didn't, but Grace did. And I'm the one who convinced her to convince Ty. I knew Shayne was leaving, and Corey was popular. He was funny, people liked him. He could have carried the show, and if he'd stuck around, he probably would have. I knew that, and without Shayne there anymore I thought he'd overtake me, so I told her that it should be the two of us, that we could carry the show. I betrayed him, and in the end it was all for nothing. We couldn't do it on our own. I can't imagine what it was like, what his parents must have done to him. I feel responsible for everything he's been through since, and I guess, too, for whatever he's become. That's why I have to go see him. Also, you know, to save the reboot and my comeback. That's kind of important, too."

"I'm proud of you," Gerry said. "What you're saying sounds honorable. But take it from someone who's lived down here all his life and listens to a lot of drive-time radio. The Corey Burch you knew is gone, and there's nothing good about this new one."

"I believe you," I said. "But I have to see for myself. I'll tell you what. Let me do this tomorrow, and I'll be back tomorrow night. I'll drive back instead of staying over in Guiding Star."

"Say," Kayla said. "Where are you staying tonight?"

"Hotel, I guess," I said. "I didn't think that far ahead, but there's gotta be options around here."

"Don't be ridiculous," Gerry said. "You'll stay with us."

"I wouldn't want to put you out."

"Jesus, David," Mom said. "Imagine Henry saying that to you. How would you feel?"

"Point taken. I'll take the couch—and thank you."

"Take my room," Kayla said.

I started to protest, but they shut me down. It was settled. And it had gotten late. Once it was established that I would be there in the morning, Gerry and Mom were quick to finish dessert, load the dishwasher, and say good night. They were happy but tired. I got my bag out of the car.

And so I found myself in my stepsister's childhood bedroom, even as my son slept in a bedroom that had once been his own mother's. Everything was doubling and echoing. My life was full of motifs.

Was Corey's? And if so, what were they? I tried to imagine

what the past week must have looked like from his point of view. I didn't buy Shayne's theory that Corey was trying to leverage anything from us. After all, the *Rev Beach* reboot would be a big win for Florida, for him. We'd dump money and attention on Guiding Star, and the show itself was hardly some vanguard of wokeness. We were peddling nostalgia for a past that had never existed in the name of a future that never would come to be. Conservatives loved that! It was the basis of their entire ideology. So why provoke the fight? Why bring the Jewish stuff into it? If Molly were writing the explainer on him, on all of this, where would she look for clues?

I grabbed my phone, clicked over to Amazon, popped Corey's name into the search bar—and there it was. *The Coreyections,* his self-published memoir—long withdrawn from the market under threat of a Travis defamation claim—was suddenly back in the bookstore with new cover art and a new subtitle, e-book available for immediate download, or physical copies via print-on-demand with two-day shipping, free with Prime.

Corey was closing in on the Amazon Top 100. I wasn't sure what that translated to in sales numbers, in American cash dollars, but given the company in which he was soon to find himself—King, Koontz, and Clancy; Rowling and R. R. Martin; Child and Steel—he would be raking it in. Surely he already was.

It's hardly news that controversy moves units, but this was an order of magnitude for which I was unprepared. Another hypnotic number tumbling upward, shedding digits as it rose through the empyrean of the Everything Store to become—what? Respectable 97, awe-inspiring 43, unfathomable 18, or that holiest of holies. Could Corey hit number 1? And how long could he hold it if he did?

The old cover of *The Coreyections* was a *Rev Beach* promotional cast photo with everybody's face scratched out but his. This, he had claimed at the time, constituted protected transformative use. And that same claim, I supposed, would be made about this new image, though a smarter lawyer would argue that since he had plucked it from the internet, where it had already been reproduced hundreds of thousands of times, it wasn't "transformative use" of copyright for the purpose of satire, but rather the reproduction of something that was, de facto or in actual fact, now part of the public domain.

He had reissued his memoir with the meme'd image of me caught climbing into Grace's SUV. Author and Title in bold sans serif splashed across the Audi's grille, and where it should have said "A Memoir" it said instead, "A Novel."

And there it was. He'd shifted his claim from sordid tell-all to higher truth, and so washed his old lies and paranoia in the blood of art. This was fan fiction. It was RPF.

A lot of things clicked into place right then. I was having what Molly's writing professors would call an epiphanic moment. I suddenly got this fucker's game. I no longer pitied him. He was playing me for a fool, and he'd had help. I knew what I had to do to pay him back.

Kayla was standing in the bedroom doorway.

"Hey," she said. "I'm about to go to bed but I thought you should know that @BigDiogenesEnergy retweeted some lunatic's manifesto."

"So what?" I said. "He's some rando internet foot freak. Who cares what he thinks?"

"He has a hundred and eighty-seven thousand followers," she said. "You should see the *Shibboleth Gold* speed runs he posts on YouTube, they're really something."

"He plays my game?"

"Big, big fan of yours, actually."

"So what does this manifesto say?"

"That a small group of Jews who fled Hitler ended up in Iceland—"

"Where they eventually made their way to the Snaefellsnes peninsula and then into the hollow earth, where they rendezvoused with the lizard people, some of whom ended up converting?"

"If you already read it, why are you making me stand here and tell you what it says?"

"Jesus, Kayla, I was kidding."

"Well, he's not. The going theory now is that the Jewish lizard people have formed a secret puppet government in the Eden at the center of the earth and are coordinating with the human Jews to keep it all for themselves. It's sort of the Protocols of the Elders of Eco-Fascism."

"And how does Corey fit in?"

"Now that he's come out as Jewish, the theory is that he's the go-between for the surface Jews and the lizard Jews. Corey wanted to appeal to the crypto Koreshans, but he didn't understand that their cosmogony is totally different. They think the earth is an egg but that we're on the inside of it and they don't think there's anything outside the egg, only a void, so as far as they're concerned, if you tunnel through the eggshell you end up nowhere, and risk letting the void leak into our world. The crypto Koreshans are convinced that if the lizard and human Jews join forces, they'll try to dig deeper into what they believe is the inner earth and wind up blowing a hole in the outer wall of reality."

"If the Koreshans are crypto, how do you know about them?"

"My ex is into all this shit. It's a big part of why we broke up."

"It was part of why you broke up? What was the other part?"

"He played too many video games and watched too much Twitch. You think I became fluent in this conspiracy because it was inherently interesting to me? I'm a girl, damn it."

"Gendered stereotypes about gamers are both archaic and offensive," I said.

"Oh my god," she said, and turned on her heel and walked away.

I picked my phone back up. There was a text from Amber.

"Meant to mention this but forgot bc we got all emo— economy size box of frozen bagel bites showed up at the house, Traviscorp on return label. What's the deal?"

"Grace sends her compliments, I guess," I wrote back. "See if Hank likes them. If he does shoot a video of him eating one, ill send it to her, maybe he can be the face of the campaign."

"Absolutely not doing that," she replied. "And under no circumstance will you do it either. Our kid's not gonna have that life. Good night."

"Suit yourself," I responded, and then added a 😊 to needle her, even as a wave of relief set my heart thumping in my chest and all I could think was, *Oh thank God thank God thank God.*

Now I wanted to see what Big D's manifesto RT had manifested.

Were people calling for blood yet?

Well, yes and no.

Kayla was right about this much: the crypto Koreshans were pissed. Moreover, inspired by Corey's example, they themselves were now "coming out" as concavist-centrifugalist hollow-earthers. While the Guiding Star Chamber of Commerce wanted to bring Corey to heel so that *Rev Beach* would reboot and bring cash and notoriety to the long-suffering coastal town, the CCHE was insisting he stand firm against the show, apparently in the interest of forcing me and Sam Kirchner to finish *CM2M* so they could find out how to get to the secret Eden in inner space, which was what they called outer space, because in their understanding up was down. The CCHE furthermore claimed that shooting the *Rev Beach* reboot in Guiding Star was a desecration of their sacred ancestral land. Bear in mind that this entire movement amounted to about two dozen people on the internet and had existed for less than twenty-four hours; the last of the actual Koreshans gave their land to the state in 1961.

The emergence of the crypto Koreshans had triggered the immediate and apparently spontaneous formation of an opposing faction, its dialectical opposite I suppose Molly would say that Hegel would have said. These were the Vernians, aka classical hollow-earthers, who claimed that *CM2M* was going to be a false flag operation, its planted "secrets" intended to be revealed and disseminated to misdirect the masses, to leave the real secret Eden safe for the Jews, per the dictate of the TSJA, which you might or might not have guessed stands for Trans-Species Jewish Alliance. The only thing the CCHE and the CHE agreed on was that the TSJA had a fully operational weather machine and was responsible for what the liberals called climate change, though Molly would be quick to add here that "climate change" was outdated terminology. It was too soft. It failed to take full account. Nowadays, the preferred nomenclature was "climate collapse," and after all of eight hours back in Florida, I understood why.

I put on my socks. I had kept Kayla's door cracked, was waiting to see the hall light go off. Then I realized they must have left it on for me so I could find the bathroom. After all, I was a guest here, unfamiliar. Kayla, on the foldout couch in Gerry's home office, probably wasn't sleeping, but if I was lucky she had headphones in, was watching something on her phone. Mom and Gerry were certainly asleep. I went to the kitchen, took the notepad with the magnetic strip on the back from off the front of the fridge. I found a pen and scribbled hastily: "If you're reading this, just know I had to take care of something, will explain when I get back. I swear I'm coming back. I love you." I signed the note, left it on the table, went back to Kayla's room, changed into my Kyle Chandler outfit. The only concession I made to the heat—stifling, even at this time of night— was to opt for flip-flops instead of loafers. I turned out Kayla's light. I left the house.

. . .

I drove the Corvette to the end of the block and put it into park. Idling, I texted Grace: "Tell Corey to meet me at the old pier in an hour. He'll know where I'm talking about."

Grace replied right away: "what on EARTH would make you think i've got a number for him? or that he'd listen to me?"

"You've been funding his campaign," I wrote. "I'm turning my phone off now. Just tell him to be there. Oh PS amber says thanks for the bagel bites."

Her dot dot dots were going but I didn't wait for an answer. I didn't need Google Maps to get me to my next destination, and I didn't care what else she had to say. I powered the phone down. I drove south.

The old pier was public, but it was now behind a Margarita-ville hotel, whose lobby bar was open and fairly busy. Since I'd arrived early, I thought about having a quick fortifier before I went outside to meet my destiny.

Do you think I stopped at the bar? You think that's where this was headed all along, one last epic meltdown for Captain Screwup? The final fall off the wagon to make what happened in Brooklyn, or all my evocative flashbacks to dissipations of yore, seem like kid stuff? Refrain of my old catchphrase, "Oblivion tastes like cucumbers." Could this be the "all" that I've been building up to tell?

Nah.

I ordered a frozen virgin daiquiri, which was served in a pint glass with a bright blue plastic straw. Nobody noticed me. If my fame was borderline historical to people my stepsister's

age, it was way too newfangled for these leathery boomer
beach bums, genteel rummy swingers who'd made their fortunes in real estate and tax evasion, who valeted their Ford
F-350s. Who still used Facebook. I was safe here.

I sipped my drink, letting the crushed ice cool me, feeling
the sugar filter into my blood.

How many times had I imagined this moment? My grand
return to Guiding Star. I hadn't been back since *Rev Beach*
ended—what would have brought me?—and the main thing
I'd noticed as I wended my way from the highway to the beach
was how much it now looked like the rest of Florida. Outlet
malls and subdivisions, Starbucks and Zaxby's, Chipotle and
Dollar Tree. This Margaritaville. Maybe tomorrow I could
tour the old haunts, pose for those photos I knew that the
internet wanted. I'd selfie myself in front of the high school,
the old Jansen house, all the buildings we'd used for exteriors
and establishing shots. Assuming, of course, that they hadn't
been torn down, or renovated beyond recognition. But maybe
it would be okay if they had been. Better, in a way. If the show
was going to be authentic to the modern day, it ought to be
honest about how things had changed. I imagined making
climate collapse a central focus. Also, the real estate bubble,
assuming there was one at the moment, which I wasn't sure
about but seemed a safe bet. Florida always had some bubble
about to pop. Mostly, I was thinking about the gray in my
hair, the extra inches on my waist. I still hoped to get in shape
before we started shooting, but if I was being honest—and
wasn't that what this whole excursion was all about?—I knew
I wasn't going to. So the other option was to become okay with
being who I was.

I finished my drink. It was time to go.

I went out the back of the bar, walked past the pool, followed the path down to the beach.

I felt warm sand between my toes. It was a humid night, and without my virgin frozen daquiri to keep me cool, I was already starting to sweat. I unbuttoned my shirt cuffs, rolled my sleeves to my elbows. The hotel was a bright glow behind me. The pin lights of boats out on the gulf were not so different from the stars and satellites in the sky above the water. Assuming, of course, that one subscribes to a geospatial theory in which the classical meanings of "above" and "sky" still obtain.

I reached into my pocket for the tin of power-ups. There were three left. I ate them all, the way you do before the final boss fight. I relished the triple burst of whooshing cool neutrality. I put the box back in my pocket and walked on.

It was a public pier, but there was a usage fee. This hadn't been true twenty years ago. At some point, the city had installed a turnstile that you had to feed a dollar in order to pass through. A streetlight cast the scene in tallow. It blocked out the small lights on the water and in the sky. I could have easily ducked under or climbed over but I didn't want to. The gate felt symbolic. I was about to cross a border, the border of fate perhaps, and it was only right that I pay my way. I opened my wallet. There was the dollar bill that I'd decided not to give to Hank back in Portland. It hadn't seemed like enough to impress him, and I hadn't paid for anything with cash since then. Everything had been plastic, in-app, or charged to Grace. So here it was, my fare.

I smoothed the bill across my thigh, fed it into the cash slot. Within the guts of the turnstile something clunked like a lock tumbling and then a hidden speaker made a *ding!* sound like an incoming text message. I stepped through the turnstile. I straightened my back and made my gaze steely, hoping for a bit more Kyle Chandler–ishness, which I thought was still within my range as long as Corey didn't notice that I was wearing flip-flops. Or that I was as exhausted as Gene Hackman in *Night Moves*, which, I thought to myself in an insane and passing way, was the reboot I should have pitched to Molly and Shayne when we were high the other night. Me as Gene Hackman, Jessica Chastain as Paula, Millie Bobby Brown as Delly, Jesse Plemons as the creepy dad, maybe the British kid from *Sex Education* as the squirrely mechanic that James Woods played in the original. Assuming the British kid was capable of doing an American accent. Or maybe that didn't matter. It could be a thing like Sofia Coppola's *Marie Antoinette* where everyone just does whatever accent they want.

The pier was a straight path that led to a dead end. Waves lapped at pylons below me. Gulls huddled on the rail. I supposed that I'd spent my whole life making my way here. Every winding side road or wrong turn I'd ever taken had actually been mere mile markers on this one-way straightaway. I had perceived curves and branches, highways and byways, but there had only ever been this line. The garden of forking paths was a hall of mirrors, a trick of gravity and light, the same one, perhaps, that allowed us to believe we lived on the outer surface of a solid ball when in fact we were clinging to the inner rim of a cosmic eggshell—in which case, were we what was being hatched within that egg, or were we the unfertilized yolk? That is, were we—individually, collectively, civilization-wise—a Kubrickian space baby, or were we something only fit for being cracked open and scrambled into the breakfast that the space baby's mother was making for it? Maybe that's why it was so goddamn hot everywhere, even on the beach, even with a breeze blowing, even at night. This was us in the frying pan. Next would come the plate.

"Hi, David," a familiar voice said.

I looked. There he was, leaning on the worn rail at the end of the pier. It was Corey, at last. He'd beat me here.

"Oh hey," I said.

"Hey, old friend," he said. "Very chill and not terrifying at all, you calling this meeting like this. Are you gonna give me the Sydney Pollack billiards scene speech from *Eyes Wide Shut*?"

"Wait, are you saying you're Tom Cruise?" I said.

"It's good to see you," he said. "It really is. Long time. Really glad things have been going well for you. I mean if the internet's any way to judge."

"It's been kind of a rough week, actually," I said. "Things have gotten out of control."

"How so?" he said. "My book is back in print, and I'm up in the polls."

"Good for you," I said. "But let me tell you a story. More of a parable, really. Or maybe it's just trivia. Anyway. You know how, back in the 1950s, the CIA had this idea that the arts were an important front in the Cold War?"

"No," Corey said, and I believed him—I wouldn't have known it myself if Molly hadn't told me.

"Well it's true," I said. "Or it was for a while. Eventually the US government figured out that there were more efficient ways to enforce global cultural hegemony than by promoting abstract expressionism and literary journals, which is why nowadays they mostly team up with superhero film franchises and the NFL."

"Wait, why the superhero franchises?" he interjected. "Isn't their Übermensch ethos fundamentally libertarian and therefore at odds with all the goals of big government and the deep state?"

"That's what I thought, too!" I said. "But it turns out that all superhero narratives are meta-fascist, irrespective of their explicit politics, because they're fantasies of absolute power in a frictionless universe, where there's a perpetual state of emergency but no lasting consequences to any action, no matter how drastic or destructive. Which is what the government really wants you to believe—that their power is limitless and exists in opposition to that of an enemy with equal power and precisely opposite aims. It would almost be Daoist if it wasn't predicated on creating a permanent market for mechanized death."

"This is all fascinating," Corey said. "But what does any of it have to do with me? Or, for that matter, with you?"

"Sam Kirchner is a CIA asset," I said. "And so am I. *Shibboleth Gold* was funded as part of a joint project with the Mossad, intended to reap the absolutely lowest-hanging fruit as far as antisemites in the gaming world. We were trying to flag the Nazi wannabes and would-be lone wolves before they became homegrown terrorists, so we could try to deprogram or at least keep an eye on them. But it turns out that you really can't go broke underestimating the intelligence, or overestimating the antisemitism, of the American people. Our game got way too successful, and it's starting to produce the very thing it was designed to eradicate."

"Just like the war on terror!" Corey said.

"You know, for a far-right dogmatist you sure sound a lot like Chomsky," I said.

"Where we go one, we go all," Corey said. "And the political spectrum is a circle. Its poles touch."

"Yeah, and the center's hollow."

"Can you just tell me why we're here? I mean, you seem pretty incidental to all of this. I don't understand whatever cryptic message you're trying to deliver, but there's no question in my mind that this meeting could have been an email. I have to be up early tomorrow to go ribbon-cut a fudge shop. That is, if they haven't disinvited me yet for standing up to you Hollywood libs and your dirty money."

"You can guess who sent me," I said. "You just don't want to, because once you realize we work for the same person you know you're going to have to do what I say."

"Grace," Corey whispered. I grinned.

"Here's what's gonna happen, old friend. Upon further investigation into your family history, it turns out that your Judaic ancestry has been gravely overstated. You're going to take that back and apologize, Liz Warren style. Then you need to lose your mayoral race, and we need to reboot *Rev Beach*. After that, we don't give a shit. Claim the vote was corrupted, go launch a podcast—whatever you want."

Now Corey was grinning, and I was confused.

"What's so funny?"

"You smarmy fuck. You liar. Grace didn't send you."

"What makes you so sure?"

"Because I was always supposed to lose the mayoral race. That was our deal from the start! For all the reasons you just said: free press, build a podcast platform. Do you know how much money there is in right-wing media? Way more than this dying little beach town. We thought that my opposing the *Rev Beach* reboot was a surefire way to undercut my base enough to cost me the election, while generating tons of buzz about the show. My job was to make the reboot a cause célèbre among the ranks of liberal Gen Zers and the snowflake media. The chamber of commerce did exactly what they were supposed to do, but we weren't prepared for how aggressive these fandoms would get. Or for Molly Webster to delete her account instead of firing back or writing a follow-up. Or for how far gone so many supposedly 'normal' people in this town actually are. Now that QAnon's over, they're desperate for anything that reboots their sense of righteousness and gamifies reality. And since pizza shops keep not having basements, this seems to be what they've chosen."

"This is Florida, nothing has a basement. And you should have asked me about the fandoms, I could have told you what would happen."

"We haven't spoken in twenty years," Corey said. "You never even said goodbye when I left the show."

I had nothing to say to that, so I said nothing.

"Look," Corey said. "I'd love to weasel out of this, but I don't know how. If I drop out of the race, I've got no platform and I can't claim the vote was corrupted. If I stay in, I probably win. So I'm fucked either way."

"Drop out," I said. "Do a heel turn, like David Brooks or

Andrew Sullivan. Go full neolib. You can still be an insuffer-
able prick, and I'll get you a spot on the reboot. You can even
keep being Jewish if you want to. Do we have a deal?"

"And if I say no?"

"Then you get the other half of the Sydney Pollack speech,
the part about the girl found OD'd in the locked hotel room
and how nobody suspected a thing or gave a shit."

I paused to let that sink in. I kept my eyes on Corey, staring
him down. He wouldn't look at me. I was on the verge of victory, and we both knew it.

Then there was a strange rumbling somewhere behind
me, maybe also below us. It sounded distant at first, and then
extremely close. The pier began to shudder. I had lived in California long enough to know an earthquake when I felt one,
but this was Florida. They don't have those here. And yet I
knew what I felt. And I knew what I saw, which was Corey's
face falling. Even in the shadows I could see him going pale.
He was staring past me, mouth agape. He had his back to the
water, and I had mine to the beach. The rumble grew louder.
I turned and looked to see what he saw. I blinked and looked
again.

The hotel wasn't there.

A yawning maw had opened and was opening wider still. A
dilatory darkness come to claim the Guiding Star Margarita-
ville, its parking lot and cabana bar and swimming pool and
mini golf course and the Waffle House across the street. All
gone. Replaced by smoke and fire and an enormous debris
cloud. It looked like 9/11 or the ending of *Fight Club*. I heard
sirens in the distance already. The beach seemed to be disappearing into itself, an abyss that walked or stumbled. It was

headed our way. Below us, the gulf rushed down what was now a steep slope toward the crater opening still wider, wider and deeper, as the timber of sea surf shifted from tide rush to waterfall, wider and deeper, a cataract.

I turned my back on the disaster. I turned to Corey, my colleague or friend or enemy or antagonist or victim or whoever he was to me. This man I had thought I'd known once. His eyes were wide with horrified comprehension, mouth no longer gaping. His teeth were clenched, and his lips pulled back in a snarl.

"An inside job!" he cried. "Controlled demolition! What's that in your pocket? A chipped vaccine? Stay away from me you—you—you fucking kike! You people aren't gonna do me like you did Shayne."

"Wait, what happened to Shayne?" I asked, but rather than answer, Corey rushed me.

He punched me in the stomach hard enough to double me over. I wheezed and tried not to throw up. *Shit!* I thought. *He's really strong!* As I was thinking this, he was grabbing me by the lapels and dragging me toward the railing. He slammed my head into a pylon like we were on WWE, like this was all just kayfabe, a show. But it wasn't. I was seeing stars, might have bit my tongue. Corey had backed up a few feet. He wanted to leave but couldn't because the beach was gone. The gulf had taken it. All that was left was the pier, still standing and seemingly sturdy, but for who knew how much longer? We were stuck together. He took something from his pocket. It was the gun he'd been wearing holstered in his video. I forced myself upright despite dizziness and pain. I grabbed the rail behind me, steadied myself, and then toppled over.

Sea breeze on my cheeks and in my hair and for a moment I felt weightless, like I might take wing and disappear into the night sky, the upper registers of air. Oh, but gravity was calling. I saw in my mind the arc my body described as it plummeted through space to the roiling black water, and how I would hit that water and then be under it. One more border of fate crossed. It occurred to me that it hadn't been a gun Corey was holding, but a phone. He'd been looking for service, calling for help for us, or, more likely, trying to save himself from me. But none of that mattered now. I was knocked out on impact with the water. I was sea debris, flotsam.

I was gone in the gulf.

(And not to ruin a perfectly good cliffhanger, but come on, you know I didn't die. That's obviously not going to be the big reveal. Yes, I went ass over teakettle right off the edge of a cliff—so to speak—but I'm here to tell the tale. In the absence of any plausible life-and-death suspense, I am going instead for big hit-the-next-episode binge energy, so I'm going to tell you the rest of what happened to me before I get back to telling the inevitable, what we all know happened to Shayne.)

I awoke in a great perplexity. I was waterlogged, exhausted, in a lot of pain—but breathing. And I wasn't underwater. How long had I been out? I didn't know. The sky was lit with the light of either dawn or sunset. I wasn't sure. One way or another, it was magic hour. I could not see the sun through the unbroken blanket of gray-white cloud cover above me, lower than clouds should be, it seemed. Or maybe these weren't low clouds. Perhaps what I saw was mist or fog. *Noisome air*, I thought again, though in fact the air was clear. A slight coconut sweetness on the breeze. I was on a beach but not the same one as before. This sand was softer to the touch, and there were no signs of human life: no pail and shovel, no umbrella and chair, no litter. Wherever I was, this place was secret and pristine.

Which was beautiful *and cetera* but did not bode well for my being found alive.

It was cooler here, wherever here was, than it had been on the beach back at Guiding Star. I looked down at my feet, unsurprised to find my flip-flops gone. The emptied tin of power-ups was still in my pocket, full of wet sand now. I was going to throw it away but didn't want to disgrace the pristine beach. I put it back in my pocket next to my phone, bricked by its protracted baptism in salt water. I was lucky I hadn't been bricked as well.

I felt a flush of goose bumps on my arms as the breeze picked up. Above me, the fog or mist or cloud cover—whatever it was—undulated. Ribbons and coils, flows and eddies. The fog bank was like a babbling brook above me. I was at the water's edge, the ocean's edge, I want to say, but who says it was the ocean? Or if an ocean, which one? It had to be the gulf, but I felt certain that it wasn't, just as, looking around, I saw no sign of land to the far watery edge of the horizon, yet could not escape the uncanny sense that I was, somehow, inside. Inside of something or of somewhere. Surely, I thought, this was a mere trick of the low fog. I might have a concussion. I was certainly dehydrated from the amount of salt water I'd taken in. I could have lost an hour, or I could have lost a day, or more.

And where was Corey?

I tried to stand. A terrible pain shot through my left leg like a bolt of lightning straight from the ball of my foot to the center of my brain. My leg was broken. My vision went white, and I collapsed back onto the sand, screaming.

When I was able to sit up, I did. I propped myself on my elbows and looked at the water. It was a deep, deep blue, a deeper blue than sapphires. It was blue as night, as though this sea were nothing but its own midnight zone from bottom to surface, a surface on which countless lucifactions winked and shimmered, reflecting that sourceless and omnipresent magic-hour light that lit this world, so much gold on the face of the blue-black void.

It was a fine place to die. A lucky place, even. I thought of all the times and places I might have died, all the stupidest and most dangerous things I had ever done, of which this was possibly, but not necessarily, the most egregious. I had no food or water, no hope of rescue, and I could not walk. Here were all my motifs coming together: to die alone in paradise, this measureless cavern for my impossible tomb. In the world above, they'd never believe I was gone. They'd claim to see me at state fairs, on private islands. They'd wait for me in Dealey Plaza. People on the internet would do phrenology on screen caps to prove that some guy at a Walmart in Minneapolis, some suit at Davos, was the real me.

Others, meanwhile, would argue that Grace had me killed. Or that Corey had, assuming he was still alive. They'd get their stories straight, maybe even tell the truth, and that would only make things worse, because nothing is less plausible than the truth. If the truth were a novel you were reading, you would throw it across the room in disbelief. Or I would. But then, I'd lived the life that had led me here. No wonder I'd never been good at telling reality from dreams.

Shayne, Grace, Corey, my mother, Molly, Amber, and poor Hank—my absence would define the rest of their days. My inconclusive end would haunt them. The hordes awaiting my return and/or confirmation of my doom would harass them. My death would become their life and in this way the world would grant me an afterlife long after my bones were sunk into the sand here on the far shore of Fame Island.

Better, I thought, to disappear completely. I couldn't walk, but I didn't have to die on this beach. My power-ups were surely spent by now. All I had to do was crawl into the secret sea.

I started to nudge myself forward, kind of scooting on my butt using my elbows to propel myself, favoring my bad leg not because I thought it mattered but because I was enjoying the chill fortitude of my death-resignation and didn't want to ruin the vibe by spending my final moments in blinding pain.

My feet were in the water now, which was warmer than I'd imagined given the cool of the air. It felt like a nice bath, perfect. A couple more scoots would do it. I paused and closed my eyes and thought of my son.

I didn't think anything particular about him, just tried to summon his presence, that he would be with me in this sacred and terrible moment, and that I, if such things were possible, might somehow be with him. That he would remember, if only in his dreams, or those first few moments after waking, that once when he was a little boy, he had felt a shock of bright white love burst up from his own inner depths, sourceless and non sequitur, and knew it was his father saying goodbye.

I hoped a thing like that was possible.

I opened my eyes.

There were tentacle men emerging from the sea. Their face-tentacles were like payes and beards but, you know, squirming. They moved slowly and with great deliberation. I scrambled backward on my ass, away from the water, away from them. But I didn't get far. My leg hurt. My arms were weak. It was too hard. Let them have me, I thought. Game over.

The land was not their natural or preferred terrain, but they were capable of navigating it. One after another after another they came, three and then five and then eight and then ten. They wore tallitot and yarmulkes and came to stand around me where I lay. They prayed over me in Hebrew, chanting *Kadosh Kadosh Kadosh,* and I thought that this must be a dream not because they were, you know, tentacle men dressed as Hasidic Jews, but because I was able to understand them.

Holy, Holy, Holy, the Lord of Hosts, they prayed. *The entire world is filled with His glory.*

Then I fell back asleep—I mean that I slept within the dream—and when I rose back up through the layers of dream into true wakefulness, they were gone back to wherever they'd come from, and the sun was high in the sky, and I could feel that my skin was badly burned, and the sand was hot and I still couldn't stand. I shifted myself, and my elbow bumped something. A rock, I thought, but it was a factory-sealed twenty-four-ounce bottle of Dasani water. Maybe it had been there before and I hadn't noticed, or maybe the tentacle minyan had left it for me, but the important thing was that I wasn't dreaming it. I opened the bottle and drank half of it down in a few great gulps before realizing I ought to ration what I had left.

This wasn't the same beach as before. I was back in Florida, or, more likely, one of the many small keys just off its coast. I could see in the distance the gulf shore skyline, all those hotels and resorts and condos. The weather was back to its merciless usual. This was a worse beach to die on than the one where I'd last woken up. Assuming, that was, that I had woken up at all—then, or now.

I felt my bricked phone in my pocket. It was worthless save maybe as a beacon—which, hey, come to think of it, made it worth quite a lot. I held it up and waved it back and forth so its dead face would catch the blazing sun, send a signal to anyone who might be out there looking for me, or just out there. The pain in my leg pulsed through me in arias, in shofar blasts. Pain was the heartbeat of being itself.

Kadosh Kadosh Kadosh, I thought, or maybe said out loud. I might have screamed it. All I knew was that it sounded so much better than my old chant: *Control, control.*

I was dehydrated and delirious, drifting in and out of consciousness. I dreamed dreams that I believed were real and then I awoke believing that I continued to dream, or that there were dreams within dreams and I was several layers below the surface of them, like *Inception* or *Waking Life.*

I forgot where I was, which coast of the country I was on, or—if this was Florida—which coast of the state. I did not know which direction I faced, east or west, but also up or down. I was flat on my back and saw the sky before me, but it felt as though I were above rather than below it, like a helium balloon that floats out of a child's hand and drifts to the ceiling and then to the corner of the room and gets stuck there. From my corner, I gazed down upon the sky toward inner space.

I dreamed that the tentacle men returned at dusk. Nine of them, this time. Again, they emerged out of the sea, dressed as before in black suits with long coats, white shirts without ties, tallitot, some now in gartels and shtreimels. Their garments streaming seawater as they walked gingerly on their green webbed feet across the hot sand.

How do you swim with a shtreimel on?

"Oh, there's a little strap," one said. "You fasten it." This wasn't more dream Hebrew. He was speaking English to me. An English that was elegant, fluent, lightly accented—unplaceable. He sounded a bit like Greta Thunberg, but in a better mood.

Scartaris, I thought.

"But doesn't that make it a lot harder to move?" I asked. "Like with the resistance of the water?"

"Yes, it would be much easier not to wear it."

"Then why do you wear it?"

"Because it is hard," he said. "Because it is impossible." He paused. "Also, we don't swim much, not in the open water, not anymore. It's too polluted, and getting places takes too long. We have a submarine. I shouldn't say more than that, but just so you know, it has a Sabbath setting. And the energy it runs on is totally clean. Tech that you guys don't have yet. It cleans the ocean as it chugs along, and it's very quiet. You should see it someday."

"I wish I could."

"We wish you could, too."

He turned his gaze away from me then, looked to join his minyan. Our minyan, I should say. Only nine had come this time, which made me the tenth. I wondered if they would teach me the words to their prayers, but then leg pain swept through and broke my brain again. It was instant lights out and when I awoke it was night and they were gone. My empty water bottle had been replaced with a fresh one.

"You couldn't have left a sandwich?" I screamed into the dead black night of the gulf. "A bag of almonds? Tube of Coppertone? Bagel with lox?"

Pain blast, lights out, sunrise.

The morning of the third day dawned fair and fresh. By this point—though I didn't know it—the sinkhole disaster was under control. FEMA had swept in, secured the site, deployed teams. Search and rescue was all but finished. My absence among the survivors as well as the casualties had been noted and become a cause for concern. I finished the last of the fresh water that the tentacle men had left me. I prepared—again—to die. Every exposed inch of my flesh was burned and peeling. My broken leg ached.

I saw a boat cruise by near the horizon and with my last strength raised my phone, its dead face flashing in the sun. I saw the boat slow and turn—or thought I did. Was I dreaming this? No. It grew bigger in my swimming vision as it drew closer and within a few minutes was nosing gently into the sand. Green waves lapped at its white hull.

It was a modest pleasure craft, a twin-outboard diesel-powered Evinrude: cigarette boat, they used to call them, something you'd take out for a day of chasing redfish. But if you looked closely, you'd have noticed that it was sporting a very cutting-edge transponder and satellite rig, not the kind of thing your average angler would need. The man at the helm was no local sportsman, no tourist, either, though he'd taken care to camouflage himself head to toe in Tommy Bahama.

It was Craig Lelyveld in his trademark polarized shades.

"It's good to see you, Mr. Crader," Craig said. He stepped off the boat and onto my island. He scooped me into his arms, light as a father lifts a child.

I woke up in the hospital. Lelyveld wasn't there, but Grace was. So was my mother, my whole family. So was Molly. My leg was in a cast, and there was some kind of soothing salve all over my sunburned skin. IVs in my arms.

"Where's Shayne?" I croaked.

"Just rest," Grace said. She held my hand. I pulled it away from her, jostling some tubes in the process.

"Tell me," I said, my voice rising with anger.

Molly stepped forward. Grace touched her on the shoulder.

"You don't have to be the one," Grace said.

"Yes," she said. "I do."

Shayne typically left Midtown right after a performance, but this was the *Cosmopolis* musical's first night back. The city was still recovering, and they'd gotten a long standing ovation. It felt like there was a lot to celebrate. The cast decided as a group that they'd come out at the stage door and sign autographs, take pictures, shake hands. Do a little fan service. It was easy and it felt good. A young man in a windbreaker hovered at the back of the scrum. He had a revolver in his pocket, the same model that, in the play, Packer's barber gives him for protection, which he later casts aside. This was Daniel Madison Marchant, all-star @BigDiogenesEnergy reply guy. He was twenty-three years old.

Daniel Marchant played *Shibboleth Gold*. You can find screen caps of his best runs on his Twitter feed. He even hung around the Stay (((Gold))) Reddit a bit. So the way the story first broke was that the game had made him do it. That it had made him crazy, inspired an ardor so deep that he murdered my best friend because he thought that the reboot of our old TV show would cut into my time recording voiceovers for *CM2M*. There was a whole satanic panic–style freakout about it. *Shibboleth Gold* was pulled from every app store and shelf. So much for the sequel, the movie, the tie-ins. You wouldn't believe what the action figures go for now on eBay. If I took back all the ones I'd given my son and sold them, that'd be his college fund right there. Though they're supposed to be in mint condition with the package and everything. But surely they'd be worth more because of their provenance, i.e., because they were mine.

But I digress.

Daniel Marchant wasn't actually trying to hasten the sequel to *Shibboleth Gold*. He liked the game fine, but he played all kinds of stuff. Going by his Twitch stream (which was, like the rest of his social media accounts, taken down as soon as it was discovered, but not before an army of internet sleuths managed to find and copy it all) his top game was *Call of*

Duty, which contributed quite a bit to the narrative that gaming itself had radicalized him, those countless hours of first-person shooting. But then, how do you account for the rest of his top five: *Stardew Valley, Spells of Evermore, NBA 2K20,* and *Mario Kart 8?*

Marchant had always been a loner. He'd had a hard time in high school, dropped out at sixteen and started working retail. He got fired from a couple of restaurant jobs, managed to pass the GED, ended up as a mall kiosk cell phone guy. He talked about saving up to go away for school, but everyone knew it was never going to happen. Even his parents, crying on *Dateline,* said as much. Community college, maybe, he could have swung. But he talked a bigger game than that.

"Oh, Danny," said his mother. "His mouth was always getting him in trouble. He dreamed big, you know? But he didn't always get the difference between real life and dreams."

It was enough that he'd gotten his own apartment, or a room in an apartment, at any rate, and that he had the GED. His parents were patient, suggested trade school, even the army. Something with a little structure. A path. He said he would think about it. He said he was thinking. Mostly what he was doing, as near as the internet army can tell, is he was going from his apartment to his job and back, and not much of anywhere else, unless you count @BigDiogenesEnergy's aggregate social media presence as a space unto itself. The internet became, in effect, the third room in a life that had narrowed down to two rooms. You can see from the date stamps on his posts that he wasn't sleeping much, that he was logged in while at work. So maybe it's more right to say that the virtual world became the primary world and everything else—the job, the room, the family, the life—became smaller worlds tucked within.

The mall closed when the pandemic hit. He got laid off. His friends who worked at Fairway, at fucking Panera, were regarded as essential. But not him. He could have tried to get work at one of those places, banked the hazard pay. Instead he gave up his room in the apartment, moved home. Three rooms down to two. And then, finally, as Hal says of Hotspur in *Henry IV*, Part 1 (as if you needed another reminder that Molly's helping me here), "Now two paces of the vilest earth / Is room enough."

Henry is paying homage to Hotspur after having killed him. He gives him the eulogy befitting their rivalry, the dead man's rank, and his own dignity as heir to the throne. It's an odd choice for Molly to have made for me, quoting that speech in this context. I'm not sure what she's getting at, but she refused to cut it, so I guess it's important to her, which in turn I suppose means I ought to give it some thought, seeing as how I'd never have made it this far without her help.

I haven't read the play, and I'm not going to, but I did watch *The King* (2019), with Timothée Chalamet and Ben Mendelsohn and Lily-Rose Depp, directed by that Australian guy who made *Hesher*. And granted, I was still on a fair bit of pain meds at the time, recovering from my injuries at my mom's house, having finally made good, by virtue of my weakness, on the extended visit that I'd always promised. Anyway, if Hotspur and Henry are obvious mirror images of each other, and the action of the play traces the way their rival arcs simultaneously mirror and invert, so that when they finally meet they have each, in a sense, become the other, and so Hotspur dies the sudden and senseless death that Henry probably always assumed was his to claim because he'd courted it so relentlessly, he knows that in order to complete the process of becoming worthy of the crown, the throne, and the kingdom, he must finally make good on the long delayed promise of becoming himself. To eulogize Hotspur, therefore, is to eulogize the life he's forsaken as much as the one he took. Hotspur has led Henry across the border of fate.

That's what I think Molly meant. And I think that she wants me—and I guess also you—to consider the ways in which, while Shayne was my obvious double, at least at the beginning, and while Corey came to represent innocence deranged by time into horror, the festering past crawling zombielike out of its grave, it was Marchant who dogged all of us. A few different rolls of the dice, she thinks, and any of us could have been him: loners, losers, without purpose or options or money or any sort of safety net. Peasants instead of royals, like in that Lorde song.

@BigDiogenesEnergy's real name is Eldon Trent. He lives in Tacoma, Washington, about as far north of where I live as Guiding Star is from Delray. He never intended to be a world-class internet troll, or at least that's what he says now. He's an engineer who specializes in systems architecture, veteran of Facebook, Microsoft, and Amazon. He was working remote well before the pandemic. He and his wife (she works in finance; they're now separated) have two kids, a four-year-old boy and a girl Hank's age. By their own account they had about as easy a time during lockdown as one could: two incomes, plenty of options, no problem with childcare. It was a grind but not a struggle. It was a mess but not a wreck. They were exhausted, but they weren't crushed. And still, at the end of the day, after work was done and the kids were down and the anxiety was high and you still didn't feel like sleeping, or rather knew that you couldn't sleep and so didn't feel like trying, and your wife was in the bedroom with her eye mask on, because she'd be up first with the kids come morning, well, what else were you going to do if not log on?

Did Eldon Trent know Daniel Marchant?

Depends what you mean by "know." Knew of him, yeah. Noted his presence. Noted that he was often the first RT, the top reply. Marchant was Trent's superfan, and it felt good, amid the shit show of the everyday, to have one of those. He'd never experienced anything like it before. This fame.

So yeah, he knew him, if that's your metric. On the other hand, Marchant didn't know Trent's real name. He didn't know where he lived. They had relatively few direct interactions, all of which were on public posts: some foot-size stuff, some Mossad stuff—the usual. One time, Marchant posted something Big D felt moved to engage with. It was a version of the Black/white arm-wrestling meme mocking the *Rev Beach* fandom feud. (It's far too bespoke in its cruelty to paraphrase, and I refuse to reproduce it here, but, as always, you know where to find it if you really have to see.) Trent had happened to see it while aimlessly scrolling and it made him laugh out loud. An actual LOL. So he RT'd the post with the caption "actual LOL," and Marchant, whose avatar at that time was a close-up of Shayne Glade crying tears of blood, had replied almost instantaneously. He wrote, "thanks for the RT bro, mad respect for all u do." Trent gave this a heart but didn't respond again. This was the limit of their direct connection. They'd never exchanged so much as a DM.

And Eldon Trent didn't know much about *Rev Beach*. He hadn't watched it when it was new, wasn't interested in the reboot beyond having noticed his own ability to make himself known as a thorn in the side of its stars. His follower count was wild, his posts did insane numbers. His ad rate was rising. It wasn't a ton of money, what he was making now, and it wasn't like the family needed it, but it wasn't chump change, either. He had decided, he said later, to take whatever came in from his secret life as an online goon and do something good with it: he donated 20 percent of what he made to the Washington State Democratic Party, put the rest in a college fund for his kids.

Because Eldon Trent didn't know much about *Rev Beach,* he didn't know that the Revheaded Strangers had been a rebel faction of our fandom lo these twenty years. He read their manifesto against the reboot and thought it was the funniest, dumbest thing he'd ever seen. Mega brain-worm shit. Like @dril level, or it would have been, if they hadn't been serious. He RT'd the @Revheadedstranger post with the caption, "These guys need to touch grass before someone reboots mark david chapman, wow." It was one of five "manifestos" he'd mockingly RT'd that day.

Daniel Madison Marchant saw this and decided to make it happen. He was already thinking of killing himself, already had the gun. We know this from files found in the Notes app on his phone. He'd bought the gun the week before. He seems to have considered committing mass terror à la Christchurch or that Walmart in San Antonio, but in the end decided it was too cliché, a cheesy retro gesture, and he didn't want people getting the wrong idea about his motives. He didn't want to cause havoc, stoke fear, or purify the race. None of that mattered to him. His sole goal was to troll the losers of the Rev-headed Stranger fandom. He wanted to ruin their lives by making their dreams come true. If he could kill Shayne Glade while masquerading as one of them, he thought, it would discredit them for all time. They'd be doxed and banned, driven from the fandom, their decades-long archive sent straight to the memory hole. A false flag flying over an epic win.

As far as anyone can tell, *Shibboleth Gold* didn't cross his mind at all.

Shayne Glade was shot and killed the same night that the Guiding Star sinkhole opened. This has inevitably inspired a lot of . . . let's call it speculation. There are those who will tell you that what happened at Guiding Star was a controlled demolition, and I was its target. That the bomb planted there is what destabilized the limestone bedrock and is therefore responsible for all the subsequent sinkholes that have erupted around the state of Florida. Corey Burch, who was rescued from the pier not twenty minutes after I jumped off it, is one of these people. You can read all about it in his new book.

(He won his election, by the way. He looks miserable whenever I see him on C-SPAN, but a little less miserable every time. I think he's becoming accustomed to his office, like a hermit crab growing to fit a new shell. And let's be honest, I haven't watched C-SPAN since my leg healed and I got off

Mom's couch. I was only watching it then because Gerry put it on.)

Controlled demo is the dominant theory, but it isn't the only one. Some people will argue, and show photographic evidence purporting to prove, that the sinkholes are the inner-earthers' attempts to reach us, to escape from the effects of our climate collapse that have trickled down into their world. That when FEMA rushes in to take control of a disaster site, the first thing they do is seal up the exposed network of caves that the inner-earthers use. That all that concrete FEMA pours down there is not, as reported, an attempt to keep the next sinkhole from opening, but a plot to keep the inner-earthers in.

As to whether it's the Jews who are behind the sealing-off or the Jews who are being sealed off down there, that depends on who you ask. But Hollow Earth itself has reverted to its status as a fringe ideology. The Vernians don't squabble much with the cosmogonic-egg guys anymore. Nothing kills off a conspiracy like a good dose of validation. Now that they know they were partially right, they feel too tethered to reality for comfort, so they've gone on to think about other things—vaccine microchips and space lasers, non-fungible tokens, satanic sex islands, et cetera. I hear they're starting to get worked up about Bohemian Grove again, which if it's true just goes to show that there really is no IP in this world so thoroughly mothballed that it can't be rebooted, given world enough and time. Which is good news for the *Shibboleth Gold* IP, I hope, though world enough and time are in short supply these days. I mean they're exactly what we're running out of and can't get back.

There are people who will tell you that I planted the bomb at Guiding Star to distract from Shayne's murder, or to try to kill Corey. There are people who will tell you that I'm a Democratic operative, or Mossad, or that Marchant was. Not a lot of people say these things, but some do.

A conspiracy theory is always more tempting than the truth, not because it's a simpler story, but because it is a story. It may be convoluted, or implausible, or demand a massive suspension of disbelief, but the act of coming to terms with the convolution and contradiction—the fluency you gain in the logic of illogic—is what makes it alluring. What are any of us looking for if not a safe place to set our disbelief down? You want to believe that the Jews control the weather because it means at least somebody does. You want to believe that there are wheels within wheels, worlds within worlds, and that the sequel is going to be bigger, better, more epic than the original. Otherwise, what? Believe that even those OG conspirers, the CIA and the GOP, got in way over their heads with an internet meme? That this same fool who had been barely half a step ahead of the western fires and the northeastern floods managed to escape by the skin of his teeth one more time? And that all of this had absolutely nothing to do with the incel lunatic standing outside a Midtown theater on the first cool clear night New York City had seen in weeks? That the real villains in the story are an underfunded EPA, the taboo still felt by most men around asking for mental healthcare, and decades of institutional gridlock on gun control?

That's the story you're going with? Who could believe it?

· · ·

Cyrus Teed, founder of the Koreshan Unity, true believer in the cosmogonic egg, was a crazy person. He was a con artist. He stole land and fortunes, lured women away from their husbands, built a redoubt in the wilderness, governed by whim. Every child raised there ran away. He was ahead of his time on gender equity, but racist as hell against Asians. All his science was bullshit. He practiced surgery without license or training. His theological tracts are some of the most boring prose ever put to paper. Still, when I think about the reasoning behind his core belief, I can't help but pity him, a pity with tasting notes of affection; call it a cousin of love.

Are you ready for me to tell you why Cyrus Teed believed what he did?

The earth had to be hollow, and outer space an optical illusion, because God, he said, would never have been so cruel as to place his favored children, humanity, in a universe whose scale and complexity outstripped their ability to comprehend it. Any God that would do that, he thought, either did not love us or did not exist, and since neither of those propositions was possible, it simply had to be the case that the limits of the universe were coterminous with the ends of the earth, and mankind lived in the custody of a just and loving God. Teed's vision of a hollow earth within which all reality is contained might sound to you or me like a prison cell, but to him it was a cradle, a womb.

The hollow-earthers were more right than they knew, at least about Florida. Ocean acidification has radically accelerated the erosion of the porous limestone on which the entire southern half of the state sits. All the land south of Lake Okeechobee is getting hollowed out. Everyone down there is living on an eggshell, and whether it's the concave or the convex side turns out to be far less important than the fact that the egg is starting to crack. The Guiding Star sinkhole was the biggest in Florida's recorded history, which title it held for all of two months. The next one was twice that size, and there have been dozens of smaller ones. They're saying the next Big One could come at any time.

My mom and Gerry are at extreme risk. I'm begging them to leave, and they say they're considering it, but I don't see them making serious plans.

"Our lives are here," my mother says. "Our friends, my dentist." She gets it but she doesn't get it.

In their defense, in order to move they'd need to sell the house, which they can't do. Who would buy it? They're grandfathered into the new federal disaster insurance that's designed to keep the economy alive a little longer, but that status won't transfer to a new owner, and anyway, what good is your insurance payout if you're buried under tons of rubble?

I got Kayla out at least. She says I did her a favor but, really, she was doing one for me. I knew I needed to go back to Portland, face up to my life, run the business I owned, do sobriety for real this time, no special exceptions and loopholes, find a way to be a real part of my son's life—part of the main cast and not an occasional cameo.

I wanted someone to whom I could be accountable, with whom I could share the basic duties of dailiness. I had been a famous teenager, and I had been a world-class wreck, and I had been a monster of privilege, a hog for second chances, a reboot addict. I was determined now to figure out what it meant to be a person, a grown-up, even if it killed me. Because every other option was guaranteed to kill me, and faster than this would.

Kayla saw me through the first hard months when I was racked with grief and fear—not that the spooks or the Jews were coming for me, all that was over. As D. W. Winnicott once said, "The catastrophe you fear will happen has already happened." And maybe I picked that up at an AA meeting (yes, I've quit trying to skate by on white-knuckle YouTube) or maybe Molly remembered that Roland Barthes quotes it in *Mourning Diary*, his book about the death of his mother, which she gave me a copy of to read when I was grieving Shayne. Not to say I'm not still grieving him, or that I'll ever stop. I loved him, you know. I miss him. I miss knowing he's out there being taller and more successful than me. Without him, I don't know what to fail to live up to, how to judge my life on anything but its own terms.

That's what I was afraid of.

So my sister moved across the country for me. She camped out in my living room—a true hero—until I sold my lonely luxe enclosure and bought a house. There's a bedroom for her, as long as she wants it, though she's made some friends here and is getting on her feet financially. She manages Wing and Prayer, is doing great work. Profits are up. We're even offering insurance coverage to our staff. She brings me home fancy grilled cheese in a doggie bag, but I don't set foot on the premises myself. I will one day, but not yet. And she did meet Molly. I introduced them as promised. They had a couple of good talks, but ultimately Kayla wasn't interested in pursuing a career in cultural journalism. Thank God for that.

Grace has asked me to play myself in *Storm of the Century of the Week,* but I don't think I will. It sounds pretty stressful, and anyway, I'm not sure I'd make the best me. I asked if Paul Dano was available; he's skinnier than I am but he can always bulk up. He can come out to Portland and try the Wing and Prayer grilled cheese. Grace said I can take a little more time to think it over. Lee Pace is playing Shayne. Higley and Nichols said they're happy to play themselves. Don't know why they're there at all, since they weren't there, but I'm sure someone will figure out how to write them in.

I wondered who they were considering casting for Corey, but I didn't ask.

Eventually Kayla will get her own place. I hope I'll be ready when she does. I guess I'll have to be. The real reason I bought the house was so that Hank would have a room of his own when he comes to stay over. I had a whole playset thing built in the backyard, slide and swings, and I knew when I ordered it that he'd grow out of it sooner than later at this point, that I was probably too late, but then I thought, *Hell, it's just money. Let the kid remember that he grew up in a house with a slide and swing set in the yard.*

People say that the process of beating addiction begins when you stop running. When you turn around to face it for what it is and deal with it on its terms rather than your own. This marks the end of self-deception, the end of fantasy. I wonder if whole cultures can be psychologized this way. It's a dodgy proposition, a little new age and a little fascist, like something Corey would say. Still, if a broken clock is right twice a day, then let me just say that a trans-species alliance between us and the lizard people, if there are any listening, is exactly what we need if we're going to have a chance of crawling out of the gaping hole we've fallen into, as a planet. To inaugurate what we Jews call *tikkun olam*. I'm not counting on it, but I am hoping. AOC is old enough to run for president now. The future is unwritten, as Joe Strummer or possibly Stalin once said.

Bottom line: I walked away from my apocalypse. Or rather, Craig Lelyveld carried me. For a while I walked with a cane. Gerry's red cane, in fact, which he gave me as a gift. I bought him a new one, a nicer one, which he appreciates, just as I appreciate having this keepsake of his. A reminder of family, and of something more.

A reminder like Jacob in the Bible had. He didn't know whether he'd wrestled with the angel or if he'd only dreamed he had, but when he passed over into Penuel as the sun rose, he was halt upon his thigh.

Like Jacob, I walk with a slight limp, but at least I'm walking. I survived. A lot of other people didn't. Shayne walked right up to his apocalypse and shook its hand. It looked him in the eye and smiled and said, "Thank you," and then it put a bullet in his chest.

Where will you be when your apocalypse comes calling? Will you see it bearing down on you from a distance, filling the horizon and sky like a fire or like God? Will it rise up from beneath you like floodwater or burst forth from within like pent-up love? Will you run or bid welcome? Will you know its name and, more important, will it know yours?

These are questions for another day. I get up every morning and hope that they go unanswered. Let the day of answering be kept from coming as long as it possibly can. May it never come, though we know it must. And when I get to thinking along these lines, I can even muster a bit of pity for the Rev-headed Strangers, too.

A Friday. A perfect late-summer/early fall day in Portland, Oregon, about a year after the events that constitute the main action of this story. Molly had been in town all week, doing last interviews with me. Now she was going to take the weekend to put the finishing touches on the first draft of my memoir. I'd given her the keys to the house, told her to make herself at home. When I got back on Monday, I would read what she wrote, give her my notes. Kayla was taking the weekend off from work. She was loading the car, and then we were going to drive over to Amber's house to pick up Hank. The three of us were going to the coast for the weekend. I had rented an Airbnb in Cannon Beach, where the famous rock from *The Goonies* is. The one that you look at through the decoder and suddenly you know where the secret treasure is hidden in the ancient cave.

Hank had never seen *The Goonies,* and Amber thought he might still be a little young, but he was seven now, so she gave in without too much fuss. "It's up to you," she said. "I trust your judgment." (First time for everything!) "Just don't start texting me in the middle of the night if he's having nightmares about One-Eyed Willy and Sloth, okay?"

It was a big weekend for Amber, too. My first time taking

the kid on a trip, her first time getting to take a trip without him. She was going to the campout jamboree where we'd met, her first time back in eight years. She was excited to hear the music and see old friends, whoever was still on the scene. She went on some message board and found the Totally Sober Jammerz Alliance. They hold meetings on-site, keep each other steady. How happy does it make you that their initials are TSJA? She told me she dug her tie-dyed onesie out of the back of her closet. She'd gotten rid of most of her old clothes but had kept that one for sentimental reasons.

"Like what?" I asked, genuinely curious.

"Doofus," she said. "I was wearing it the night I met you."

We're friends now. Solid co-parents. We are two people who, in a sane world, would probably never have known each other. In some ways we still don't. But here we are with our lives bound together, doing our best.

I told her to have fun. I promised I'd take lots of pictures of our son at the beach.

It was a perfect day for driving, the sky blue and cloudless, no hint of smoke. Kayla deejayed from her phone while Hank, in the back, listened to an audiobook of *The Hobbit* on an old phone of mine. It doesn't connect to the internet, but I loaded it up with some audiobooks and some albums he likes, a few episodes of *Daniel Tiger*, which he's too old for but sometimes, when he thinks nobody's paying attention, still likes to watch. It comforts him, I think, the familiarity of it, the nostalgia, assuming "nostalgia" isn't too deranged a term to apply to a seven-year-old's memories of having been four.

We checked into the Airbnb and dropped our stuff, then

walked through the cute little downtown: a few blocks' worth
of candy stores, kite stores, real estate agencies, a couple of
Thai places, a fishmonger. It was a beach town at the end of
tourist season. We had it mostly to ourselves.

If this were a movie, or the last episode of a TV show, this
would be the scene where Hank asks if we can get ice cream,
and I say yes, the biggest sundae they've got, and you can see
from the wide smile on his face that he's not freaked out about
money anymore, that everything's better. And we ask for three
spoons this time, and me and him and Kayla go sit on a bench
by the beach, huddled around our frozen treat: a family.

And yes, all that did happen, but we don't have to dwell.

Hank wasn't worried about money anymore. He knew I was
writing a book, and for whatever reason that seemed to him to
be a real job in a way that owning a restaurant or being famous
never had. Go figure. *Rev Beach* was still off the streaming services, obviously, but *Shibboleth Gold* was soon to be quietly
restored to certain app stores, and Grace had made me a silent
partner on *Storm of the Century of the Week*. Which was either
hush money or her way of saying sorry, maybe both. I signed
all the movie money over to Amber, and soon she too will be
living a life heavily subsidized if not wholly transformed by
passive income: the real American dream. I put my ungodly,
undeserved book advance into Hank's trust, minus what I
paid Molly to write it.

And I bought him his game system. He's the envy of all his
friends.

Anyway, we ate the ice cream and then we set Hank loose
on the sand to burn off the sugar. He played chicken with the

chilly waves, asked strangers if he could pet their dogs. My sister and I followed behind him. The sun was low in the sky, and the whole coast was burnished red gold.

"So how are you?" Kayla asked. "Tell me the truth." She meant about it having been a year since my inexplicable disappearance and miraculous return. Also, of course, a year since Shayne died. A year ago last weekend. I went down to LA for the anniversary. Because he'd been estranged from his parents, there'd been no one to claim him. Grace stepped up without hesitation. He was buried on the Travis property, on the same hill as her father, but far enough away (Grace joked) that they wouldn't get on each other's nerves. Maybe it sounds grim, or cruel, an epic troll, for Shayne to have been finally reclaimed by the franchise that he spent his whole life trying to escape, and in a real sense died for. Maybe. But Grace is a practical person, and in her own way a kind one. All she wanted was to put him somewhere he'd be taken care of, and where Molly and I could visit whenever we wanted. Where he'd be safe from conspiracists and superfans, anyone who'd want to take a peace-sign selfie on his patch of earth, or dig it up to prove his casket was empty. If nothing else, she could spare him that, and so she had.

"I'm good," I said to Kayla. "I really am."

"Was it weird seeing Grace?" she asked. This trip, she knew, had been my first time seeing her since the hospital in Florida. She'd funded the rescue operation and paid all my doctor bills, but she and Lelyveld had flown out not long after I'd awoken, so we hadn't had a chance to talk. And again, there's no reason to try to figure out whether she was taking responsibility, being generous, or flexing. With Grace it's never just one thing, it's always everything at once. This was one reason why I had loved her, why I perhaps still did or could again, despite everything we'd been through. And maybe when I say "despite" what I really mean is "because."

I smiled at my sister. "You're prying," I said. "You want to know if me and Grace . . . rebooted."

"'Fucked' is the word I would have used," she said, smiling herself now. "But yeah, that was my gist."

"A gentleman never tells."

"I'll take that as a yes."

"We're figuring it out. Just don't tell the tabloids, okay?"

"You can afford the catch and kill."

"I can't, but she can."

We bantered on. The rest hardly bears transcribing. We kept an eye on Hank. We watched the day wane. We started to think about walking back to the rental, what we'd eat for dinner, all the humdrum stuff that makes a life. Kayla ran over to catch up with Hank, to give him his five-minute warning, and I watched them from a distance, took a moment to myself by the water's edge. I gazed out over the ocean and thought of Shayne.

He was at peace, I hoped. I conjured his perfect smile and bright eyes in my mind, and tried to feel his phantom presence in the sunset glow, like he was standing right beside or just behind me, and all I had to do was turn around to see. As long as I didn't try to do it, maybe it could still be true.

And if things had gone the other way, if I'd died in the gulf and he'd survived his attack, I liked to think he would have done the same for me. He would have stood here—or, at any rate, stood somewhere—and dreamed me back to life.

Then he would have walked away before any tentacle men had a chance to pop out of the water. He would have known it was time to let this episode, this whole season, draw to a close. We were coming up fast on curtain and *fin.*

My sister and my son came back to meet me. "Kid wants French fries," she said. "I tried to explain that's not dinner."

"Not fries on their own," I said. "But we can do fish and chips, if you promise to eat all your cod."

"Will I like cod?" Hank asked.

"I think you will," I said.

We walked back the way we'd come along the beach, then along the access road toward the modest main drag, toward the promise of fresh-caught local seafood embalmed in batter and drowned in burning grease. Cue the crane shot here, the wide pull back. Or pan away from the three of us entirely, swing toward the water. Long shot of the setting sun and lapping waves while credits roll. Or cut to black first. Soundtrack kicks on. What should play over the credits? Some touching but vaguely ironic cover, like Bon Iver doing "Ooh La La" by Faces, or Cat Power's "Reelin' in the Years." I'd have liked to get Taylor Swift's take on "Shelter from the Storm," but Grace has already claimed it for her movie, and we can't afford those rights anyway.

We could try for Phoebe Bridgers doing "Silver Threads and Golden Needles."

Japanese Breakfast, "After the Gold Rush."

Guided by Voices, "Let It Be."

Or forgo irony and just pick something sweet and true, sad but not too sad, maybe something you could tap a toe to. If it were Molly behind the bar calling closing time, she'd play us out with Jerry Garcia's "Goodnight, Irene."

I'm stalling. This is over, and I'm not sure I'm ready. I'm worried you won't be satisfied, that I left too many loose ends hanging, like where things stand with me and Grace's romantic reboot. Or Corey's status as a bona fide rising star in the Republican Party, the stress of trying to be both a DeSantis apparatchik and a Trump loyalist; wishing he could know which creep to simp for long-term with the same certainty that he knows secret lizard people control the weather. Or what about the fact that Florida's collapsing into the ocean and the whole world is burning? Or the still-thriving-online conspiracy that figures me for part of the deep state, that I'm a CIA agent and Daniel Marchant was my asset? That I sent him on his suicide mission in the service of some inscrutable aim of the TSJA?

What about poor Eldon Trent, aka @BigDiogenesEnergy, cleared of criminal wrongdoing but facing massive civil litigation brought by Daniel Marchant's parents, in a case that experts are saying will hinge largely on the question of whether RTs constitute endorsements.

(If I had made a donation to his defense fund, I certainly would have done so anonymously and wouldn't reveal it here.)

What if I don't know whether or not I dreamed the creatures who saved me, the place they took me, the world I saw? What if I told you that I kept the power-up tin full of sand, that it is tucked away safe on a high shelf in my bedroom closet? That I consider it proof even though I don't know what it proves. What would it mean to be sure I had seen what I saw, to know that they were out there somewhere, cruising the deep in their eco-friendly super sub with its Sabbath setting, praising the lord of creation in their dutiful Hebrew with its beguiling Nordic lilt?

Molly says a good ending should raise at least as many questions as it answers, that what you walk away with, what you keep turning over in your mind, becomes the true meaning of the work. I don't know if she's right about that. Personally, I like endings that feel like endings. But I've knocked around showbiz long enough to know that you always save something for next season, for the sequel. Plant the seeds of the spin-off and the reboot in the original. It gives the fans Easter eggs to hunt for and saves you the headache of having to retcon it later. Sow the IP and reap the expanded universe. World without end, Amen.

CREDITS

THANK YOU

LISA LUCAS, ZACH PHILLIPS, AND EVERYONE AT PANTHEON BOOKS
FOR GIVING THIS BOOK A HOME.

AMANDA BULLOCK, FOR BEING MY PARTNER, READER, CHAMPION,
AND (WHEN NEEDED) VOICE OF REASON.

MOM, MELANIE, MARK, LISA, ROYCE, RACHEL, CARYN, ANDREW,
AVA, AND LILY.

ADAM WILSON, FOR THE TRIP TO PITTSFIELD AND THE CATS UNDER
THE STARS HAT. AMONG OTHER THINGS.

SUSAN GOLOMB AND EVERYONE AT WRITERS HOUSE.

EMILY ADRIAN, RYAN CHAPMAN, JOSHUA COHEN, NICK DOUGLAS,
ALEX HIGLEY, DANIEL HORNSBY, ANIKA JADE LEVY, ALEC
NIEDENTHAL, TRACY O'NEILL, MIRANDA POPKEY, KAREN RUSSELL,
AND NELL ZINK FOR READING, CRITIQUING, AND ENCOURAGING
REBOOT WHILE IT WAS IN MANUSCRIPT AND ITS AUTHOR NOT
INFREQUENTLY AT WIT'S END. I AM GRATEFUL FOR YOUR
ATTENTION AND YOUR FRIENDSHIP.

MELISSA VANDEBURGT AND BAILEY RODGERS AT THE FLORIDA GULF COAST UNIVERSITY LIBRARY, FOR ARRANGING MY VISIT TO THE KORESHAN UNITY ARCHIVES AND FOR GUIDANCE THROUGH THE COLLECTION. PLEASE FORGIVE MY DELIBERATE DISTORTIONS OF THE HISTORY AS WELL AS ANY INADVERTENT ERRORS.

APRIL ALVAREZ, ALL MY COLLEAGUES AT SEWANEE, AND THE STUDENTS AND FACULTY OF THE SEWANEE SCHOOL OF LETTERS.

L'ANCIENNE AUBERGE, MACDOWELL, THE OREGON LITERARY FELLOWSHIP, THE VERMONT STUDIO CENTER, THE SOU'WESTER AIRSTREAM FELLOWSHIP, AND THE BROWN FOUNDATION FELLOWSHIP AT SEWANEE.

THE CHAT, SHAKESPEARE CLUB, THE MOTHER FOUCAULT'S CREW, AND THE "GOOD FOR THE JEWS?" WORKING GROUP; KATHLEEN ALCOTT, STEPHEN ALVAREZ, NOAH BALLARD, HILARY BELL, DAVID BENHAIM, ISAAC BUTLER, CAROLINE CASEY, MADELINE CASH, ALEXANDER CHEE, PATRICK COTTRELL, ELLIOTT DAVID, MARK DOTEN, DEBRA MAGPIE EARLING, RACHEL FERSHLEISER, CRAIG FLORENCE, SARAH GERARD, GABE HABASH, CHESTON KNAPP, TAYLOR LEWANDOWSKI, PETER MASIAK, MICHAEL MILLER, SCOTT NADELSON, SAMUEL NICHOLSON, BENJAMIN NUGENT, ELENA PASSARELLO, TONY PEREZ, AMANDA PETERS, KAREN PROCTOR, MINNA PROCTOR, JAMIE QUATRO, ALICIA JO RABINS, JON RAYMOND, ADAM ROSS, ED SKOOG, ERIC SMITH, DAVID TURKEL, CECILY WONG, AND CARLOS ZAYAS-PONS.
BARRY HANNAH HAD IT RIGHT—*HEAVEN IS PALS.*

END TAG

It's a Sunday afternoon, say seven weeks after our trip to the
beach, so two months after my visit to LA. I'm parking my car at
Amber's house. Kayla's with me. Amber and her mother smile
and wave from the front door, waiting to receive us. There's
a rental car behind us; Mom and Gerry are in it. Hank's with
them. We're all coming over for dinner.

My phone buzzes in my pocket.

"I'll be right behind you," I say to Kayla.

She gets out of the car, joins the rest of the family as they
make their way toward the house and file inside. I take my
buzzing phone out, check it.

A text from Grace.

"I'm late," she says.

"For what?" I reply, then realize what she meant as soon as
I hit send. "Sorry, duh, I get it."

😏, she replies.

"How late?" I ask.

"Late enough," she says.

I look away from my phone and toward Amber's house.
They've left the front door cracked for me.

"It's great news," I type. Hit send. Then: "It's great news,
right?"

"If we want it to be," she says. Dot dot dots appearing and disappearing. Finally: "Do we?"

"We do," I reply. "Can I call you?"

"Later," she says. "I've got an Insta Live thing I gotta do in five and then I'm meeting with my vintners about the upcoming harvest."

"Ok call me when you can," I write. "XO until."

"XO to you too."

I put the phone down on the dash, lean my head back, close my eyes. My mind is a cool neutral whoosh. But no, not quite neutral. I'm happy. Sequel, not reboot, something to infuse the venerable if admittedly uneven David Crader franchise with fresh life and a heightened sense of stakes.

I open my eyes to see my son standing in the doorway of his mother's house.

"Dad," he's hollering. "Dinner's almost ready. Mom said to get you. I need to help set the table! Are you coming?"

I stick my head out my rolled-down car window.

Big smile on his face, big smile on mine.

"I'll be right there, Hank. Tell everyone I'll be right there."

Justin Taylor is the author of the novel *The Gospel of Anarchy* and the story collections *Everything Here Is the Best Thing Ever* and *Flings*. His memoir, *Riding with the Ghost,* was published by Random House in 2020. His work has appeared in *The New Yorker, Harper's Magazine, Bookforum,* and *The Oxford American.* He is a contributing writer to the *Washington Post's Book World* and the director of the Sewanee School of Letters. He lives in Portland, Oregon.

A NOTE ON THE TYPE

The text in this book was set in Miller, a transitional-style typeface designed by Matthew Carter (b. 1937) with assistance from Tobias Frere-Jones and Cyrus Highsmith of the Font Bureau. Modeled on the roman family of fonts popularized by Scottish type foundries in the nineteenth century, Miller is named for William Miller, founder of the Miller & Richard foundry of Edinburgh.

Composed by North Market Street Graphics
Lancaster, Pennsylvania

Printed and bound by Berryville Graphics
Berryville, Virginia

Book design by Pei Loi Koay